The Pursuit

LORI WICK

DOUBLEDAY LARGE PRINT HOME LIBRARY EDITION

HARVEST HOUSE™ PUBLISHERS
EUGENE, OREGON

Scripture quotations are taken from the King James Version of the Bible.
Cover by Terry Dugan Design, Minneapolis, Minnesota
Cover photo © Clay Perry/Corbis

THE PURSUIT
Copyright © 2003 by Lori Wick
Published by Harvest House Publishers
Eugene, Oregon 97402

ISBN 0-7394-4006-3

Printed in the United States of America

This Large Print Book carries the
Seal of Approval of N.A.V.H.

For Larry

Acknowledgments

The fourth book is done! I'm so excited. I can't tell you how much I enjoyed this book and series, but sometimes finishing a series is like taking a much-needed breath of air.

I've learned many things in the last months—mostly that God is unendingly patient. And that He always puts people in my life who make a difference. A big thanks to . . .

—*Mary Vesperman.* A thanks to you, Mary, is nothing new, but since this book took a little longer, I need you to know how much I appreciate your patience and your listening ear. As always, you are invaluable as a friend, a sister in Christ, and a coworker.

—*The staff at Harvest House.* What a fabulous job you did putting this book on the market. Thank you for all your hard work and marvelous support of this project. I love and appreciate each one of you.

—*Matthew.* I found you this year in a way I never had before. You became the big brother—working to sail over the bar with amazing ability. I'm proud of you—more than I can say. You make my world a wonderful place.

—*Bob.* The man who dishes the ball never gets credit for the shot, but the assist is what you're best at. You're so willing to sit quietly and cheer from the back of the room, not needing everyone to know that you were a huge help. I guess the ones who know are the ones who need to know. I love you.

The English Garden
Collingbourne Families

~Frank and Lydia Palmer
Children: Frank, Walt, Emma, Lizzy, and Oliver
Home: Tipton

~William and Marianne Jennings (William Jennings is brother to Lydia Palmer)
Children: Thomas, James, Penny, Catherine, and William
Home: Thornton Hall

~Robert and Anne Weston
Children: Sarah
Home: Brown Manor

~Pastor Frederick and Judith Hurst
Children: Jeffrey, Jane, Margaret, John, and Robert
Home: the manse

~James and Mary Walker (Marianne Jennings' parents)
Home: Blackburn Manor

~Henry and Edward Steele
Home: Newcomb Park

~Thomas and Elizabeth Morland (Elizabeth is sister to Henry, Edward, and Cassandra)
Home: Ludlow

~Alexander and Cassandra Tate (Cassandra is sister to Henry, Edward, and Elizabeth)
Home: Pembroke

Prologue

Africa
November 1812

Edward Steele sat comfortably in the warm morning sun, writing a letter to his brother, Henry. Henry had been with him on the trip but had already headed home to England. Feeling a bit bereft without him, Edward's quill moved as he shared his heart.

The ship leaves 5 December. I almost wish I'd gone home with you, Henry. I'm weary of travel and long for Collingbourne. I should be home in plenty of time for Christmas, and then it's home I will stay. I've enjoyed this year on the move, but I long for Newcomb Park and the family.

There is so much that I miss. I miss you. I miss my sisters and their husbands. I miss home and Pastor Hurst's way with the Word. I miss England and Collingbourne. In truth, I can't think of something I don't miss. I had a yearning to go with you when you left. I can't think right now why I didn't.

I've rambled long enough. I shall get this in the post and send myself directly after. See you soon.

Warmest regards,
Edward

Edward studied the letter he'd just written and then added at the bottom, *Please give my love to the girls.* This done, he folded the missive and readied it for mailing. It was impossible to say what delays he might encounter once his own journey began, but he wanted Henry to know he would be on his way in two weeks' time.

"Edward?" a child's voice called just then from inside the house, causing the youngest Steele male to hide behind a large chair. He peeked out as Victoria Middleton came to the veranda, clearly looking for him.

"Edward?" she tried again. "Are you out here?"

"I might be," he said in a low voice, causing Victoria to giggle with delight and run in his direction. Her brother, Walter, was swift on her heels. Both found Edward and threw their small arms around him. He pretended to be frightened and allowed them to tumble him to the floor.

"Were you scared?" Walter asked, panting a little.

"Terribly. I thought you might be wild beasts."

Victoria, a rather serious child, took his hand.

"It's just us, Edward. We'll protect you."

"You are very brave, Victoria. Thank you."

The smile Edward gave her was invitation enough. Even though he was still sitting on the floor, she climbed into his lap.

"I'll get our book!" Walter volunteered, quickly dashed for the door, and soon returned with the volume. The day was warming swiftly as Edward made himself comfortable. His back against the side of the house, all settled in, he began to read. The session lasted for a solid 20 minutes before the children's father, Lucas Middleton, came looking for them.

"This looks fun, but it's getting warm out here."

Edward smiled a little. The children were snuggled against him as though the day were freezing.

"Why don't we take this inside, children," their father suggested, and both willingly obeyed.

"Why is it that children don't seem to notice the heat?" Edward asked his friend as the two men brought up the rear.

"I don't know, but whenever they share the bed with us, they're happy to be smashed against us all night."

"Something you could bear in England, but a little tougher here."

"Indeed."

With that word the men went inside. Edward had been honest in his letter to Henry: He wanted to go home. But if anything could make him hesitate, it would be how much he enjoyed the Middletons and their children. Nevertheless, he would soon be England bound.

Chapter One

Edward Steele loved sea travel. He knew of people who became dreadfully ill when the waters were rough—Henry had experienced a bit of trouble—but Edward weathered it like a Viking. Indeed, as he boarded the ship dressed for cooler temperatures in an overcoat and top hat, traveling bag in hand, he breathed deeply, letting his lungs fill with sea air. Some of the odors on deck were not so pleasing, but that didn't hinder Edward's pleasure in his surroundings.

Traveling alone, no servant in attendance, Edward gained directions to his cabin on the *Red Dragon* and settled in, knowing the ship would be docking briefly in Lisbon, Portugal. In a cabin with two bunks but no roommate, he stowed his bag and then went out on deck to watch the activities before getting underway.

Captain Spencer, an Englishman and a man Edward had met on one other voyage, joined him at the railing where Edward watched the loading of cargo.

"Headed home, Mr Steele?"

"Yes, Captain Spencer. It's time."

The captain smiled. Having spent most of his life on the sea, he knew that feeling well.

"Were you told we'll be stopping briefly in Portugal?"

"Yes, sir. Thank you."

"If you need anything, Mr Steele, you need only ask."

"Thank you, sir. Is some of this cargo intended for Lisbon?"

"That is the plan, yes."

"What are you carrying this voyage?"

The captain explained some of the shipment, pointing to certain bales and crates as they swung on board with the aid of hooks and ropes. Edward could have listened to him for the next hour, but the captain was needed just a short time later and moved on his way.

Edward strolled about, not wanting to miss anything. The ship rocked gently under his feet, and for a moment his mind moved to his brother. Edward wondered if Henry had enjoyed his voyage home. He knew he'd arrived safely back in England, but not if he'd been ill or uncomfortable during the journey.

Edward chose another place at the railing to lean against, his head tipping back as he took in the mast high over his head. The whole concept of sailing was a fascination to him, and he enjoyed thinking about those sails at full mast, billowed with the wind.

In the midst of all of this Edward suddenly realized he was in the way. Sailors were moving past him, having to skirt his body to do their job. Not wanting to make more work, he moved back to his cabin. The moment he entered he knew something had changed.

Glancing around, he found that his own gear was just as he left it, but someone had taken the top bunk. He hadn't expected a roommate, but that wasn't what confused him. What surprised him was that he hadn't noticed a single man come on board. He'd seen a family—father, mother, and two children—and two women traveling together, but no man who appeared to be alone.

With a mental shrug, he dismissed his poor observation skills and moved toward his large satchel. He'd sent most of his things separately so he could travel light.

He opened the catch and reached for his book and Bible. When he had his Bible in hand, a paper fell out.

Edward smiled as he picked it up and saw that Walter and Victoria had drawn a picture. Edward studied the childish drawings and words, remembering their last night together in Africa.

"Will the ship be large?" Walter wanted to know. That little boy had sailed many times in his life, and the larger ships were always his favorites.

"I'm not sure. What do you think?"

"I think I should go with you," Victoria interjected.

"Why is that, Victoria?"

"You might be lonely and sad."

Edward leaned to kiss her small, smooth brow.

"That's very sweet of you, dear, but I have a book to read, and the journey doesn't take that long. I shall be home in no time at all."

"Will you visit again soon?" Walter asked.

"Not for a time, old chap. I shall never forget the fun we've had and all the adventures we've shared, but I'm going to stay home in England for a time."

"Our vacation is over, and we'll be going

after Christmas," Carolyn Middleton reminded her son. "So it won't be many
weeks before we follow Edward home to
England."

"Will we see you in England?" Victoria
asked next.

"I think you shall. I'm not exactly sure
when, but I'm sure we will see each other."

Victoria, always warmed by his smile,
climbed into his lap.

"Is it story time?" Edward asked, knowing
their father held the book.

"I think it is," Lucas answered, opening
the book to read.

The children stayed close to Edward—he
was always such fun—and listened to the
story until their lids began to droop. Edward
kept his place as Lucas and Carolyn
scooped their children up to take them to
bed. He wouldn't see them in the morning
as he was leaving very early, but he hoped
they would remember this last night as long
as he would.

The door opened suddenly, bringing Edward back to the present.

"Excuse me, sir." A gentleman's gentleman bowed as he shut the door. "I won't be
a moment."

"That's fine. I'm Edward Steele, by the way."

The servant bowed again. "Denley, sir."

"Are you traveling alone, Denley?" Edward asked as the man went to his bag, opened it, and fetched a small case.

"I am not, sir. I am in the employ of Mr Osborne in the next cabin. If you'll excuse me, sir."

"Of course."

Denley, who reminded Edward a little bit of Jasper at home, exited just a moment later. Edward spoke to the empty room. "Well, Edward, not only did one man come aboard, but two. You missed them both."

Deciding not to worry about it, Edward removed and hung his coat and jacket and stretched out on his bunk, his book and Bible near at hand. He picked up his Bible first, thinking he would read until the ship was underway, completely unaware of the fact that he was the main topic of conversation in the cabin next door.

❧ ❧

"Did I hear voices?" Mr Osborne asked his man, his voice naturally soft.

"Yes. I have a roommate, a Mr Steele."

"An Englishman?"

"Yes."

"Did he say how far he was going?"

"No. I didn't ask any questions."

Mr Osborne looked at Denley in thoughtful silence. He was a man Osborne trusted with every fiber of his being. The servant was privy to his every plan and action, nearly to his every thought.

"How old is Mr Steele?"

"I would guess mid-twenties."

"This might be helpful."

"How is that, sir?"

"We've been traveling as a duo for a very long time. A threesome would certainly throw people off our path."

Denley nodded. "A fine point, sir. I'll see what I can find out."

"Go ahead now and make sure we haven't been followed on board. Let me know when we're underway, and I'll go on deck for a time."

Denley obeyed without further comment or question. He was tempted to check on his roommate, just to gain another glimpse of him, but was afraid that would look odd. Working not to be in the way and scanning everything with the most surreptitious of movements, Denley went about his job. When the boat was finally out to sea, he returned to Osborne's cabin to tell him all was in order.

ॐ ॐ

"Excuse us, sir," a female voice spoke from behind Edward, who had been watching the swiftly receding shoreline of Africa. He turned to find he was being addressed and bowed after removing his hat.

"Did you need something?" he asked good-naturedly, not missing the way both women smiled and relaxed a little under his kind gaze.

"We were wondering," the shorter of the two offered, "if you've been to Lisbon before. We have not and would like to know what to expect. Oh, I should have told you, I'm Berneen Ryan, and this is my sister, Maura."

"It's nice to meet you, ladies. I'm Edward Steele, and I must tell you that I've only been to Lisbon one time, but I do remember a little about it."

The three of them standing near the railing, Edward gave as much detail as he could recall. He'd been to one inn and one tavern, both respectable but probably not suitable for women traveling alone. Edward remembered a statue in the square—not who it was, but where—and had only just finished describing it when Captain Spencer joined them.

"How are you ladies faring?" he asked solicitously. With their pretty faces peeking out of bonnets and their fine cloaks, they had caused something of a stir among his men. He wanted to make sure they felt safe.

"We're very well, Captain," replied Berneen, taking the lead. "Mr Steele was telling us about Lisbon. He said that we should probably stay on board when you dock."

"I think that's wise counsel, ladies. We have no plans to be overly long, and you will be able to see something of Lisbon from the railing."

"Thank you, Captain. Thank you, Mr Steele." This said, the women smiled at both men and moved on their way.

"I was hoping Mr Steele would offer to take us ashore," Maura admitted when they were safely out of earshot.

"So was I."

They laughed a little and talked about going into Lisbon on their own but decided against it. Talking their father into allowing this trip had been difficult enough. If something were to happen, they would never be allowed to set foot out of Ireland again.

≈ ≈

Overcoat and top hat in place, Osborne made his way along the deck, his eyes missing nothing. Denley had told him that things were secure, but the life Osborne had chosen to live never allowed him to get too comfortable.

He passed the Ryan sisters, giving them a small smile that did not invite interaction. Up ahead, he could see the captain and the man he assumed was rooming with Denley. He knew there was also a family on board, but he had yet to see them.

Reaching Edward and the captain, Osborne would have nodded and kept moving, but the captain stopped him.

"Are you settled in, Mr Osborne?"

"Yes, thank you."

The softness of his voice was nearly lost

on the wind, but the captain didn't seem to notice.

"Have you met Mr Steele?"

"I have not, sir."

The two men were introduced and bowed in polite fashion. Osborne bowed again, and as soon as he could manage it, moved on his way.

"Royalty?" Edward questioned the captain.

"He doesn't have an entourage, so I can't attest to that, but I'd be willing to guess he's an aristocrat at the very least," Captain Spencer answered. "I've not sailed with him before, but he carries a certain air, does he not?"

"Indeed."

"And so young," the older man observed.

Edward smiled, thinking, *You don't learn to carry yourself like that in an afternoon. This one surely carries a title of some sort.*

And for Edward that was the end of it. He found it a bit curious but knew it wasn't his business and could find no reason to pry. He found out in a hurry, however, that not everyone had that frame of mind. When he regained his cabin, his roommate was there, and he was in a very talkative mood.

"Are we off?" Denley asked, as if he didn't know.

"Yes. I was just speaking to Captain Spencer. He said we left ahead of time."

Denley began to dig in his bag. He seemed to be searching for something when he asked, "Do you suffer from sea-sickness, sir?"

"Not usually," Edward told him. "Do you, Denley?"

"Not unless the waters are very rough. I have a vial of something if I feel it coming on. You're welcome to use it as well, Mr Steele."

"Thank you."

"I understand that we're bound for Lisbon?"

"Yes, I'd heard that as well."

"I've never been," Denley told him. He'd gone to work on more things in his case, finding a coat brush and such, but he seemed in no hurry to stop talking.

"You'll have to come again when we're going to be docked longer."

"Is it to be swift?" Denley asked.

"That's my understanding."

"Well, maybe there will be time to see a few things."

"That's possible."

Edward watched Denley place a coat on a hanger. He held it to the lamp light in several directions, brushing at it and fussing over a few areas.

"I need to take this next door," he said absently as he started toward the door. His hand was on the handle when he stopped. "Is that your coat, sir?" He indicated the coat Edward had hung on a hook. "If you'd like, I could give it a brushup when I come back."

"Thank you, Denley. I would appreciate that."

Without further ado, Denley slipped out the door and knocked on Osborne's door. Osborne answered and shut the door behind him.

"You did say you'd met him?" Denley clarified as he hung the coat.

"Yes, on deck with the captain."

Denley shook his head a little. "He didn't ask a single question. Not one."

"Did he speak at all?"

"Nothing worth mentioning. He said we'd only be in Lisbon for a very short time, not even time to go ashore."

Osborne fell silent—he was thinking

again. Denley went about putting a suit of clothes together in case Osborne wanted to change, but no words were spoken. Not until it was time for supper that evening did the two discuss any sort of plan. Osborne confessed that he wanted to relax but knew he mustn't. The ship seemed safe. The ship made him feel as though he was out of reach, but he knew better. He knew anyone could be watching.

ल्व ल्र

Dinner was served in shifts. The dining area was small, and although some meals might be delivered to cabins, this ship was a working vessel, and passengers were expected to remember that.

Captain Spencer, however, was not without compassion. The Waldengrave family with small children and the Ryan sisters were invited to eat a little earlier. The girls would have enjoyed the company of one of the single men on board but understood the need to keep silent about this.

As it was, Mr Waldengrave did not actually eat with his family. He helped his wife see food into their young children and assisted her with their bedtimes, but when Edward, Osborne, and Denley arrived for their meal, he was also in attendance.

"Waldengrave," he said as he stood and gave his name, bowing to each man, even Denley.

"Edward Steele," that man volunteered, and Osborne and Denley did the same. Denley became instantly invisible at one corner of the table, his manner doing nothing to attract attention as he waited. He didn't have long. Bowls of food began to appear and the men, more than ready for food, began to eat.

"To where are you traveling?" Waldengrave asked Edward.

"England. And yourself, Mr Waldengrave?" he asked out of courtesy. He wasn't certain he was comfortable with this man. He knew he was traveling with his family and couldn't understand why he would leave his wife and children alone on this ship.

"I'm headed to London. How about you, Osborne?"

"London also," he said calmly, using his fork with quiet efficiency and reflecting an unconscious air of royalty.

"Have you lived there long?" Waldengrave wished to know, actually wondering
what palace he might be headed to.

"All my life. How about yourself?"

This was all the invitation Waldengrave
needed. He began to speak about his life
and family. Edward and Osborne were very
good listeners, nodding in all the right
places and seemingly filled with interest.

"What took you to Africa?" Waldengrave
asked Osborne when he finally stopped for
air.

"Travel as well. I'd never been."

"How about you, Steele?"

"Just travel. I have a few friends there."

Waldengrave was off again after this,
telling the men why he'd been in Africa. Edward did his best to attend, but the man
changed subjects very swiftly.

"I thought you said you'd been in Africa
for four months," Osborne suddenly interjected, not having raised his voice in the
least.

"We have."

"But you just now said you were in Italy in
September."

Waldengrave looked confused.

"What month is this?"

"December."

With little more than a shrug and a grunt, Waldengrave went back to his supper. Osborne's and Edward's gaze met for just a moment before they returned to their own plates. Denley, of course, said nothing, but he hadn't missed a thing.

❧ ❧

Edward was alone in the cabin as he woke the third morning of the voyage. He washed and shaved, an interesting feat with the wind having picked up a bit. He'd only just finished dressing when Denley returned.

Edward watched as that man sat on the room's one chair, his eyes on nothing. The lighting wasn't the best, but Edward could tell he was unwell.

"Do you want your bag, Denley?" Edward asked kindly. It never once occurred to him not to help. "Shall I find that vial for you?"

"I don't believe I'm seasick, Mr Steele, but thank you."

"Should I tell the captain that you're unwell, or Osborne?"

"No, but thank you. I believe I'll just sit for a time."

Edward took him at his word but still went next door and knocked.

"Denley?" Osborne asked from within.

"No, it's Edward Steele."

The door opened.

"I wanted to make sure you knew that Denley wasn't feeling his best."

"Thank you."

"Let me know if there's something I can do."

"Yes, I'll do that."

Edward walked away thinking that if he hadn't watched Osborne in action the night before at the supper table, he'd think him a complete snob. Osborne could do things with his voice that only his friend, Bathurst, could pull off. And he was the son of a baron.

Putting both Osborne and Denley from his mind, Edward went in search of breakfast. He wasn't at his best with an empty stomach and thought his feelings might be more charitable if he had a little food.

ᔕ ᔕ

"How are you?" Osborne had gone next door to check on his man. Denley had climbed into his bunk, and Osborne's height gave him a perfect view of the man's face. There was no mistaking the misery in Denley's eyes.

"I have the most dreadful headache, sir. I can't think what's brought it on."

"I'll order some breakfast for you and have it sent."

"Thank you."

Osborne placed his hand against the man's brow. It was hot to the touch. He didn't linger but went directly for the captain. The boat might only be docking briefly at Lisbon the next day, but Osborne thought he and Denley might be forced to disembark.

❧ ❧

"Good morning, ladies," Edward greeted the Ryan sisters as he took a seat at the small dining table. "I trust you slept well."

"It was rough last night," Maura answered, her eyes a bit large.

"Yes, I believe the wind has picked up. Eating might help."

Both women had cups of tea in front of them but nothing on their plates. Edward had no desire to make anyone feel worse, but he had to have food. He began to serve himself eggs and bacon, aware that the ladies had turned slightly away from him.

He was in the midst of his meal when the captain arrived. He greeted the three at the table but went directly to the ship's cook. He wasn't with the cook very long before coming and sitting close to Edward. He spoke, keeping his voice low.

"Denley, your cabin mate, is quite unwell, Mr Steele. Would you like me to move him down with the men?"

"No," Edward told him without hesitation, thinking that would be most uncomfortable for the man. "I don't mind, Captain, and I can tell Mr Osborne if Denley needs something."

"Very well. If you have any concerns, please come to me."

The moment Edward finished eating, he returned to his cabin. Osborne was on hand, helping Denley eat. Edward did not linger.

"Let me know if I can assist with anything."

"Thank you," Osborne said, turning to

see him at the door. "Is it going to bother you if he stays in here?"

"No. We'll get along just fine."

"Thank you," Osborne said again, his voice even lower.

Edward didn't know what he would do for the next few hours. He took himself on deck and stared at the miles of ocean around him, never tiring of the sight. Finding his mind strongly on Denley and Osborne, he prayed for both men.

Chapter Two

"Hello."

Edward stopped his slow promenade along the deck and turned to the owner of the young voice. He smiled when their eyes met.

"Hello. How are you?"

Ralph Waldengrave, the youngest member of his family, looked back at him.

"I'm fine" were the young man's words, but Edward wasn't certain they were true. For three days Edward had seen him on deck and greeted him, but the boy of approximately eight years had said nothing. Now on this day, when Edward hadn't even noticed him, he spoke.

"It's a rough sea today," Edward commented, thinking the child looked rather forlorn—not seasick, but lonely.

"Yes. My family isn't well."

"Do they know you're out here?"

"I don't know."

Edward debated what to do.

"Would you like to walk with me awhile?"

"All right."

They had no more begun to stroll slowly along when Ralph's father appeared at a distance. That he was not at his best was very obvious. When Edward raised his hand in acknowledgment, the older Waldengrave raised his in thanks and turned back in the direction of the cabins.

Edward wondered if he might have misjudged the man. He wasn't the most likeable fellow, but even amid his seasickness, he'd come to check on his son.

"Was that my father?" Ralph stopped and asked, having only just noticed.

"Yes."

"Did he want me?"

"I believe he was just checking on you, and I would feel better if you were with me or in your cabin. Do you think you can do that?"

"Yes."

The wind snatched all words away for a time, but the two stalwart strollers did not appear to notice. When Edward saw something of interest, he pointed it out to young Ralph, but for the most part, the two just walked. Not until he noticed that his small companion was shivering did he suggest they head to the dining room and ask for a cup of tea.

Ralph needed no encouragement, and just minutes later the ship's cook was eyeing Ralph from across the table.

"I just made up a tray for your family, young Master Waldengrave. Are you not feeling sick today?"

"No, sir."

"A sailor you must be."

Ralph smiled a little, the first Edward had seen.

"May we trouble you for a pot of tea?" Edward asked, his manner as engaging as ever. For some passengers the cook would decline, saying he was too busy, but not Mr Steele. He wasn't uppity like that Osborne chap with his sick servant.

"Sit yourself down," he said rather gruffly. "I'll see what I can do."

"Do you want your coat off, Ralph?" Edward asked as he removed his.

"No, I'm still cold."

"Well, this tea will take care of that. Do you drink much tea?"

"A little."

"I like mine strong. How about you?"

"My grandmother likes it strong," Ralph volunteered. "She says she likes it strong enough for a mouse to trot across."

Edward threw back his head and laughed. He'd never heard it put that way, and while the image was slightly revolting, it was nevertheless amusing. Ralph smiled at Edward's laughter and began to feel a bit warmer.

It was onto this scene that Osborne suddenly appeared. Looking as regal as ever and entering quietly, he removed only his hat before sitting at the end of the table.

"How is Denley?" Edward asked.

"Just now he's sleeping."

"Any improvement?"

"I don't believe so."

Cook didn't look overly pleased to see Osborne, but he still produced a third mug and delivered the tea to the center of the table. Edward took pains to make Ralph's tea palatable, adding great amounts of milk and sugar, and then watched him drink.

"How is it?"

"It's good. Thank you."

"You're welcome."

A plate of biscuits appeared a short time later, and Ralph took three.

"How old are you?" Osborne suddenly asked.

"Almost nine."

"You're very grown-up."

"My sister is 11," Ralph told Osborne, not seeming put off by his superior demeanor.

"Is she ill today?"

Ralph nodded around a full mouth. Osborne's eyes studied the lad as his own cup went to his mouth. He liked children very much, and if Denley had not been so ill, he thought he could remain in the company of this young lad all day. It might help pass the time.

The ship rocked almost violently for the next few minutes. Everyone was aware that Lisbon was the goal for the next afternoon, but going inland and docking in such weather could be tricky.

Edward might have commented on this fact if Ralph had not been in attendance. He had no desire to worry the boy. As it was,

Osborne finished his tea—never having touched the biscuits—and exited before Edward could say another word.

❧ ☙

A thump in the night woke Edward. He lay for a moment, working to orient himself, and then heard a groan. Rising swiftly out of his bunk and lighting the lamp, Edward found Denley leaning weakly against the wall, a cup of water dangling from his fingers.

"Let me help you." Edward went to him and, taking the cup with one hand, supported him with his free arm.

"Did you get some?" Edward asked.

"So thirsty," Denley managed.

Edward held the cup while the man drank. Edward filled it again, and Denley downed that as well. The moment he was done, Edward helped him back into his bunk. The gentleman stood watching him a moment and even in the dim light could see that his eyes were still open.

"Do you need something?" Edward asked.

"Only to get off this ship."

"I can imagine. Maybe you should go ashore at Lisbon and take a later one."

"Maybe."

"Do you want me to get Osborne for you?"

"No, but thank you."

Edward turned down the lantern, plunging the room into darkness again. He climbed back into bed, thinking the wind might have calmed some. He enjoyed the rocking of the ship—it was soothing to him—and he didn't think many minutes would pass before he would be sleeping again.

"Mr Steele?"

"Yes, Denley?"

"Did I wake you?"

"No, I wasn't back to sleep yet."

It was quiet for a moment. Edward nearly questioned the man, but Denley began.

"At this moment in time I fear I won't live through this."

"It might help to get you off the ship."

"That's true, but if I die, I—" Denley hesitated, and Edward gave him time. "I think, Mr Steele, that you might be a very fine man." Denley's voice was weak, and again Edward just waited. "I don't wish to overstep myself, but please look after Mr Osborne. He has needs. He's strong, smart, and capable, but he has needs. Please, Mr Steele."

A note of pleading had entered the man's voice, and Edward would never have ignored it.

"Of course, Denley. Don't give it another thought."

"He's never dealt with things like burying a servant." Pain in the man's voice was all too clear. "I don't know what he'll do."

"It's all right, Denley. Don't worry at all."

"Thank you," he said, his voice growing even quieter. "If only I could get off this ship. If only the rocking would stop."

Denley uttered his last coherent word, mumbling a bit after, and then fell asleep. Waiting a moment, Edward got out of bed, his heart pounding, to see if the man had died. His own heart thundered with relief to find him still breathing. He climbed back into his bunk, feeling like he'd run a marathon. Once on his back, he prayed.

You have a plan here, Lord. I'm sure of it. Please help me to know how I fit in. Please touch this faithful servant and heal his body. If that is not Your will, Lord, help me to know how to help Osborne. I can't see him wanting my help. I'm not sure I would know how to go about it.

Edward prayed for quite some time. He thought sleep would come quickly, but it didn't. He took time in the darkness of the cabin, with only the ship's faint noises around him, to commit this entire situation to God and ask for His help in the hours that lay ahead.

ဢ ဢ

"It's Edward Steele." Edward stood in front of Osborne's door for the second day in a row.

"Just a moment" were the words that came from within, and Edward waited until the portal opened.

"How is he?" Osborne asked the moment he saw Edward.

"Very ill but still with us. I don't wish to overstep here, but we should be docking in Lisbon in several hours. I think we'd better get him off this ship."

Osborne nodded.

"What will that do to your travel plans?" Edward asked.

"It doesn't matter. I'll take him ashore as soon as we dock."

"I'll go with you. I know of an inn where he'll be comfortable."

"Thank you," Osborne said, adding, "for everything."

"You're welcome. I'll make sure he's still resting and then go to breakfast. Feel free to check on him whenever you wish."

Osborne nodded and shut the door. Turning his back on the portal, he leaned against it, his head tipped back as he stared unseeingly at a spot on the wall.

This had never happened before. In all these months and years of travel and being on the move, they had never been forced to contend with an illness.

Osborne thought about Edward Steele. It might have helped their cover to look like the three were traveling together, but not like this, not with Denley unwell.

And then there was the matter of their plans. Steele had asked about those. It wasn't strictly true that their travel plans didn't matter. As a matter of fact, Osborne's plans were very important. It was crucial to be back in England by Christmas, but he could never follow a direct path to his destination. However, there was nothing he could do about that right now.

Realizing he'd been standing there speculating for far too long, Osborne finished dressing—pulling his shoes on and buttoning his vest. After reaching for his coat for warmth, he moved to the cabin next door.

☙ ☙

"Good morning, Mr Steele," Berneen and Maura Ryan greeted him the moment he set foot in the dining room.

"Good morning, ladies. Was last night a little more comfortable?"

"Yes," they answered, looking very relieved. The seas had calmed in the night.

"I'm glad to hear it," he said kindly, thinking they both looked better.

Edward sat down and began to work on breakfast. A single page of news print had been left on the table, so after Edward had fixed his plate and tea, he began to read. It was a few weeks old and not about England, but he still enjoyed it. He was almost done when he realized the Ryan sisters were watching him. Edward briefly wondered what he had missed but went back to his reading. A moment later, however, he glanced up and found their scrutiny still in place.

"Is everything all right, ladies?"

"We want to be terribly bold," Maura admitted, "but we're afraid."

"Of what exactly?"

"Of asking you to escort us into Lisbon. We know it's presumptuous and rude, but we would so like to see it."

Edward smiled his kind smile, the one that usually put hearts at rest.

"As a matter of fact, ladies, I would have no objection to escorting you, but Mr Osborne's man, Denley, is quite ill. I'll be going with Osborne when he takes Denley to town."

"How awful," Berneen said sincerely. "Do you think you'll be able to locate a doctor?"

"I think so. It will help to get the poor chap off this rocking boat. I'm certain of that."

As disappointed as the women were, they truly understood. They didn't question Edward further, allowing him to go back to the newspaper as he finished his meal and enjoyed one more cup of tea.

The Waldengrave family came for their

breakfast as he was leaving, all seeming to be in better shape, but Edward didn't tarry. He thought Denley or Osborne might need him and headed that way.

ᘏᘓ ᘏᘓ

"Denley," Osborne tried again, working not to panic. "Please wake up, Denley. Please."

Osborne stopped speaking when he heard the door behind him, but he didn't turn away from the top bunk and the pale face that concerned him.

"When was the last time he spoke to you?" Osborne wished to know.

"Just before I came to see you."

Osborne nodded, relief filling him. Edward stepped up and took the ailing man's wrist. His pulse was strong, but his skin was still hot to the touch.

"I'm going to find the captain," Edward said. "I'll tell him of our plans to head into Lisbon. Once there, I'll go ahead and secure some type of carriage or other conveyance to transport him."

Edward half expected this specimen of apparent royalty to object or take umbrage, but he only looked tired and relieved. It made Edward want to ask who he was and what he was about, but that was not important at the moment.

Denley feared he might not make it. Edward thought that if they didn't find a doctor, the servant's fears might prove to be correct.

ɤ ɤ

Lisbon

The soft moans that came from Denley as he was transported off the ship were nothing short of pathetic. Edward's heart twisted a little as he watched the pair of them: Osborne as erect and proper as always, but his eyes glued to his man's miserable face, and Denley, so ill he was unaware of where he was or who was taking care of him. The ride was short, but when one was in pain, time always seemed to stand still.

The name of the inn was the Silver Cup. Edward had not actually stayed there, but on his previous visit he'd taken a meal in their great room and been treated with respect. When he'd gone ahead of Osborne and Denley to secure a cart, he'd also spoken for two rooms and was treated well.

"It's just up ahead," he told Osborne, who nodded.

"Easy," Edward said to the driver, who took a hole in the road rather fast and elicited another moan from Denley.

"Sorry, sir," the driver said, trying to sound as though he meant it. He wasn't overly fond of waiting on royalty—they tended to tip as though they couldn't afford it—but the man next to him seemed of a different caliber.

"Here we go." Edward didn't speak again until they were in front of the inn. Two servants came to their aid, and with a minimum of jostling, they transported Denley upstairs to a bed.

"Fetch a doctor," Osborne commanded, speaking some of his first words since disembarking. He'd completely packed all of Denley's and his own bags, clearly willing to wait for a ship after his man was back on his feet.

Edward noticed that he missed little. His eyes had scanned the men helping him and even checked to make sure all bags were in place. Denley's words from the night about

Osborne's needing special care came rushing back. Edward could not figure out what
the man might require. He seemed capable
and quite aware of his needs. And he certainly wasn't afraid to tell someone what he
wanted.

"We need some towels," Osborne said,
as though he'd read Edward's mind.

"Very well, sir," the innkeeper, now on
hand, replied. "My wife can find a nurse if
you need one."

"The doctor and some towels will do for
now."

Someone was already arriving with the
towels. The innkeeper handed them off to
Osborne, not looking put out in the least
over Osborne's tone, before taking himself
back out the door.

Edward stood back while Osborne dis-
carded his coat and went to work. He
opened Denley's shirt, and using water from
the basin, sat on the edge of the bed and
began to bathe the servant's face and neck.

"How old is Denley?" Edward asked.

"He's 31."

"Have you known him long?"

"Yes."

"Has he been ill like this before?"

Osborne turned to look at him, his eyes a bit hostile.

"If you were a doctor, it would have helped to know that on the ship."

"I'm not." With that Edward became silent. Osborne went back to his ministrations.

"Mr Osborne," Denley said weakly, finally coherent.

"It's all right, Denley. I'm right here."

"You mustn't do that."

"The doctor is on his way."

Osborne stood and went back to the basin. He soaked the towel again and returned to the bed. Denley was now wide awake.

"We're off the ship," the servant said with wonder.

"Yes, we're in Lisbon."

"I didn't pack our bags."

"I took care of it."

Osborne stopped for a moment, his hand going to Denley's brow. The servant's eyes closed—Edward couldn't tell if it was in pain or with relief. Osborne went back to his gentle bathing and was still at it when there was a knock on the door. Edward answered it.

"I'm Dr Mora," a man said in thickly accented English.

"Please come in," Edward invited, standing back.

Osborne had also come away from the bed, his eyes watchful and guarded as the man approached. He introduced himself again and went directly to the patient.

He asked Osborne some of the very questions that Edward had wanted to ask. He listened to Denley's breathing and said they might need to bleed him if the fever didn't break.

Osborne said nothing to this, and Denley was sleeping again.

"Are you from the ship just into harbor?" the doctor asked as he repacked his bag.

"Yes."

"Well, it will be leaving without this man." He closed his bag with a snap. "Keep him comfortable. Try to get fluids into him. Call me if he's worse before dark."

"Thank you," Osborne said shortly, not moving as the doctor saw himself to the door.

Denley chose that moment to groan. Osborne went to him, the cool cloth in hand once again.

Edward made his first move since entering the room. He walked to the other side of the bed where he could see Osborne's face.

"You did get all of your belongings from the ship?"

"Yes," Osborne answered without looking at him.

"I think you may be here for a time," Edward commented, waiting. Osborne finally looked up at him. "Clearly Denley is very ill and needs time to recuperate. I don't know what your time schedule is, but I will inform you that he's afraid he's going to die and leave you alone."

Osborne's eyes were glued to Edward's, but he said not a word.

"He asked that I keep an eye on you if something should happen to him. He said you have special needs. I'm not going to pepper you with questions at this moment, but I think there's one thing you should tell me."

"What is that?" Osborne asked, his voice guarded.

"Why are you dressed as a man?"

Chapter Three

Osborne stood slowly and stared across the bed at Edward. Neither moved for a full minute. Finally, Osborne spoke.

"How did you know?"

"I have three sisters," Edward said simply, his voice a bit dry.

Osborne's hand came to her face. Who was this man? Could he be trusted? It was almost more than she could take in. Denley had never spoken to anyone in such a personal manner; she was sure of that. Why this man? Did he really feel that he was going to die?

Her eyes suddenly swept to the prone man on the bed. He was her friend and often her protector. The thought of him dying was almost more than she could bear.

"Are you going to tell me?" Edward pressed her.

"It's complicated," she said shortly, her

eyes still on Denley even as the air of royalty fell away.

"I assumed as much," Edward said, his voice not divulging any of his feelings.

Osborne looked at him. "It's not fair of me to ask your discretion when I'm willing to say so little, but there is no point in my telling you anything."

"I see."

The room was silent for a moment, Edward seeing that he would get no more at the moment and Osborne still trying to recover from her surprise.

"Well, I'd best get back to the ship and gather my things."

Osborne, whose mind had been casting about for something to say, turned swiftly in surprise.

"You're staying here in Lisbon?"

"Not just in Lisbon, but right here in this inn. Denley asked me to look after you. I told him I would."

Osborne was still framing a reply when Edward went for his hat and coat. "I'll be back," he said quietly before slipping out the door.

Osborne didn't move from her spot for a long time. She had dealt with many unpleasant situations, but never something like this. Her eyes went to Denley again. He was out cold. If he wasn't, she thought she might be tempted to cry on his shoulder.

༆ ༆

"What made you decide to stay?" Captain Spencer asked before Edward could disembark.

"Denley might not make it. He's very ill. I'm not sure that Osborne has dealt with burial details and such. I still think I'll be home before Christmas so it won't hurt to alter my plans a bit."

"Well, the *St James* should pass this way in another week or so. Maybe you can find passage with her."

"Thank you, sir."

Edward didn't waste any time. Needing the walk, his bag in hand, he set out for the inn. He didn't know when he'd ever had an experience quite like this. It was only natural for him to wonder what was going on, but he couldn't exactly force it out of Osborne.

Edward's swift pace slowed to a crawl. He had absolutely no reason to believe her name was Osborne. If she could travel as a man, she could easily change her name. But none of that answered why. Was she guilty of something, or was she the victim?

Edward's thoughts had been so active that he was back at the inn almost before he was ready. He entered, gave a small nod of his head to the proprietor, and then took the stairs that led to the rooms. He knocked quietly on the door and waited for Osborne to answer it.

She did so without comment or ceremony, stepping back to let him in and then shutting the door behind her.

"I don't know if you should do this," Osborne began.

Edward set his bag down and looked at her.

"I mean," she tried again, "I don't know what motive Denley had for asking you such a thing. You don't need to take care of me."

"When Denley is well enough to assure me that he can be the escort he's been to you in the past, I shall go on my way."

It was not what she wanted to hear, but she didn't argue. On ship she had thought it might help to have a third member in their party, but she had not counted on this.

"Has he stirred?"

"Yes." Her voice sounded relieved for the first time. "While you were gone he drank a bit of water."

"Good. Do you want me to sit with him for a time?"

Osborne hesitated. She had just been thinking that she needed to take care of a few things but hadn't been willing to leave Denley alone.

"Are you certain?" she asked, unaccustomed as she was to help from anyone aside from Denley.

"Yes, very."

Edward was headed to the chair by the bed when he noticed Osborne moving directly for the door.

"Wear your coat," Edward commanded quietly.

Osborne looked down at the front of herself, checking to see if her vest still lay flat against her. When she found all in order, she looked back to Edward.

"You don't look like a man from the back."

She didn't blush, at least not where Edward could notice, but her face told of her embarrassment. In truth, she rarely went out without some sort of long coat, but her distraction over Denley's illness was very real.

Wishing she didn't even have to turn her back to the room in order to retrieve the coat, she went for the garment and slipped into it the moment it was in her hands. She left the room without further word.

Edward looked down at Denley, his mind running in many directions. He simply couldn't leave these two on their own; it went against every part of him. But with whom was he aligning himself? And how would he explain to his family if he landed himself in trouble with the law because his actions might be seen as aiding a criminal?

❧ ❧

Playing the part of a young gentleman, when you were, in fact, a young gentlewoman, was something that took constant work, Osborne decided. Her guard had been down since arriving in Lisbon, and she knew she could not afford to relax. It was too easy to make mistakes.

Some would call her paranoid, but then they might not understand what was at stake. She didn't expect others to agree with her. She was doing what she felt she had to do. Her mind swept into the past for a moment, a past filled with loss, betrayal, and pain. Some things she had no control over; others were within her power to change. To that end, she was drawn into desperate circumstances.

"Did you wish to see me, Mr Osborne?" the innkeeper suddenly broke in, bringing Osborne back to the present.

"Yes." The haughty air was back, hanging on Osborne like a cloak. "I need a servant girl, someone clean and responsible. I will need her to sit with my man morning and evening while we take our meals," Osborne said quietly, only just remembering to include Edward Steele. "After today we will take our lunch in our rooms, but then we will want the girl to sit for a time while we take a bit of exercise. I am willing to pay well if the job is done as I desire. Are you able to find someone?"

"My daughter would be only too happy."

"Very well. I will expect her in two hours, so we may come downstairs to dine."

"As you wish, sir. Are you in need of anything just now?"

"No. I shall be out for a time, but my companion is in the room. Please check on him shortly in case he has a need."

"Yes, sir," the man said, his English very good.

Osborne did not so much as nod in his direction as she headed for the door. She wasn't overly pleased to be out on her own but remembered how blind people could be. Remembering that Edward Steele was the first to ever confront her, she kept her head up, every move aristocratic, and kept moving.

"*Banco?*" she questioned a man who passed her. He stopped and pointed.

Osborne kept on. She didn't need a bank, but if she found one, she was certain that a post office or mailing facility would be in the vicinity.

A few questions later, she found herself close to the bank, her eyes scanning for signs of a post office. It took the better part of the block, but she eventually spotted a nondescript door and went toward it.

"*Fala inglês?*" Osborne asked the woman inside, who said no.

Osborne reached into her vest and brought out the letter she'd written while Edward had been gone from the inn. Seeing it, the woman nodded and began to speak. Osborne caught little of it, but she pulled forth a few coins. The woman took two of them, and Osborne understood that her letter would be sent.

Feeling tired, her feet hurting, she started back toward the door that led to the street. She remembered who she was supposed to be for her walk back through town, and even as she entered the inn and went upstairs. Not until she was safely inside the room with Denley and Edward did she let down a bit.

"Any change?"

"No," Edward told her.

Osborne nodded.

"A servant will be here in a little more than an hour to sit with Denley while we go down for lunch."

"All right."

"I'm not sure if I need to explain this to you, but Denley ill or not, I need to keep a normal profile."

Edward nodded, but she hadn't looked at

him yet. She did so when he remained quiet.

"Is there a problem?"

"No. I nodded, but you didn't see me. Who is coming to stay?"

"The innkeeper's daughter."

"Rosario?"

"I'm not sure."

"Well, if it's her, we've met. She appears kind and competent."

Edward watched her shoulders sag a little. Not for the first time, he wondered what drove her. He looked to Denley, his heart aching with prayers for this man. Edward so wanted to trust God for the outcome, but he was tempted to beg his heavenly Father to heal Denley . . . not just for the servant's sake, but so as not to leave Osborne on her own.

"I'll sit with him for a time," Osborne said to Edward, who was still in the chair.

"All right. It's warm in here. Shall I open a window?"

"Maybe a little."

Edward noticed that she did not remove her coat. He wanted to tell her she was safe with him but didn't know how to go about it. He went to the window and opened it some. They were on the second floor, and for a moment he looked out. The docks were not far off, and he knew that the town stretched off to his left. The fresh air felt invigorating—he could smell the ocean. It wasn't overly warm; just pleasant. It would have been a fine day to walk about Lisbon, but he knew he couldn't leave just then.

A soft moan from the bed brought Edward's mind back to the room. He turned from the window and approached the bed. Denley had begun to slide down in the bed again. Edward had noticed it before and shifted him so his head was back on the pillow. This time he bent over the man and gently removed the pillow.

"He doesn't seem to want it under his head," Edward said when he found Osborne's eyes on him.

Osborne was utterly silent with mental castigations. She knew very well that Denley preferred a very flat pillow or none at all, but she hadn't even noticed.

"Are you all right?" Edward suddenly asked.

Osborne's eyes flew to him. She had been completely unaware he'd been watching her so closely. Was she that comfortable in this man's presence or just that upset over Denley's condition?

"Yes," she answered shortly, forcing her eyes from his probing gaze. She went back to bathing Denley's flushed face and head, giving her an excuse not to look at him.

Edward could see her need for privacy and turned away, going toward his bag.

"I'm going to settle in my room. I'll check on you shortly."

"Shall I knock on your door when Rose gets here?"

"Rosario," Edward corrected. "If I don't come back first, that will be fine."

Not until he exited did Osborne realize she wasn't certain which room was Edward's. She nearly came to her feet and went after him but changed her mind. Even if they were late to lunch, Osborne decided that she'd rather Edward came to her.

∾ ∾

"Did Rosario meet with your approval?" Edward asked the moment the *gentlemen* took a seat at one of the tables downstairs. There were other diners in the large room, but their place by the window gave them a modicum of privacy.

"Yes. She seemed capable and kind."

Edward nodded, but Osborne didn't notice.

"Had Denley roused at all?"

"He took another drink of water, but I don't believe he was very aware."

Both of his questions had been answered absently. Edward had never taken his eyes from his companion, slightly amazed at how good her disguise was but also waiting to see if she would look at him. Not until he asked his next question did her eyes turn in his direction.

"I think you should tell me your name—your real name."

The eyes that looked at him were guarded and keen. They were eyes that had been forced to weigh every circumstance, person, and event. Edward knew he was being evaluated.

"Why do you wish to know?"

"I just think it wise. I'm not asking that you trust me—you have no reason to—but I would like to know your name."

When she didn't speak right away, Edward said, "I'm not like Waldengrave."

"Why did you mention him?"

"I got the impression you didn't trust him."

"I didn't at first, but then I realized he just liked to talk."

The table was silent again for several moments. The room around them hummed with low voices and the sound of cups and plates moving. Edward waited this time, his eyes ever watchful.

"Niki," she began softly but stopped and took a small breath. "Nicola Bettencourt."

"Bettencourt," Edward tested the name, having caught the perfect pronunciation. "You don't look French."

"I'm not."

Edward stared at her a moment before saying, "But Nicola is French also, is it not?"

"That is true."

This said, Edward's companion turned her eyes to the window, clearly indicating the conversation to be over. Nevertheless, Edward waited. She volunteered no other information. Not that he was surprised. This woman had secrets to keep and no reason to share them with him, but her name made him more curious than ever. Was she running from her husband? That might explain the French name for a woman who was not French. Or had she been telling him the truth about that name?

"Niki," Edward said softly, only to have her instantly turn.

"Why did you do that?" Her voice had turned sharp.

"To see if it was truly your name."

Niki sighed, her eyes lowering.

"I know this must seem very curious and odd to you, Mr Steele, but I beg your indulgence in this matter. I ask that you not give me away. I promise you that all I hold dear depends on it."

Edward continued to watch her. She was either the finest actor in the world or speaking the truth. Edward could not find it in his heart to deny her.

"Unless I am asked to do something that goes against my beliefs, I shall go along with this and help where I am able."

Relief was written all over her when she said, "Thank you," and turned to the window again.

Their food arrived shortly after. Both were hungry and enjoyed the meal, but each was busy with myriad thoughts: Edward speculating on the whole affair and Niki asking herself what she would do if she did not reach her destination before Christmas.

✇ ✇

"Over there is a small bakery." Edward pointed. "They make marvelous breads and pastries."

"You talk as though you've been here often," Niki commented, carrying herself through the streets of Lisbon as though she owned the city. She had gone upstairs to check on Rosario and Denley before leaving, but now she was on a walk with Edward, strolling as though she had nothing the least bit troublesome on her mind.

"Just one other time," Edward told her and then fell silent, not because he was out of things to say but because he rather hoped she would talk a little.

Edward remained quiet for the next 20 minutes, but Niki said nothing more. Some of Lisbon's architecture was lovely, and Edward watched her take notice, but she didn't comment or even look in his direction as they walked.

She also seemed content to let him lead

the way. He took them in a circle that allowed them to enjoy many of the sights but still managed to land them back at the inn.

Once inside, Edward followed Niki back to the room. He listened while she asked about Denley and then dismissed Rosario. When he glanced over to find Denley's eyes open, he went to him.

"How are you, Denley?"

"A woman was here," he managed quietly.

"The innkeeper's daughter. A good woman."

"Osborne?"

"Right behind me."

Edward watched the man's eyes go to Niki.

"Are you all right, sir?"

"Yes," Niki said quietly, and added, "worried about you."

"I'm so thirsty."

Edward didn't move out of the way so Niki could reach him but went ahead and gave Denley something to drink. The ill man lay back, his eyes on the two of them, and knew that something had gone on. Alarm rose within him, but he had no strength to act.

For as long as he could keep his eyes open, the servant watched Edward's face, silently begging him to be a man of honor. His thoughts were still tormenting him when he fell back to sleep.

≈ ≈

Niki surrendered her vigilance and went to sleep in the chair by the bed. Edward had gone across the hall and returned with his Bible, only to find no answer to his knock. When he quietly entered, he found both Denley and Niki asleep. Something told him this was highly unusual for this woman and that he would startle her if he woke her suddenly. Moving as quietly as he could manage, Edward took the other chair and opened his Bible. He'd been reading for 20 minutes when he heard Niki stir.

"What are you reading?" she asked, coming instantly awake and seemingly aware of everything around her.

"My Bible."

In an unconscious move, Niki sat up a little straighter.

"Which book?"

"Isaiah."

"What does it say?"

This surprised Edward, but he answered.

"I'm in chapter 66. Some of the word pictures are incredible."

"What, for instance?"

"The first verse says that heaven is God's home and the earth is His footstool."

"Do you think that's meant to be literal?"

"No, I don't. The picture just helps us to understand how huge and powerful God is. The verses go on to say that no house could contain Him and that He made everything."

Niki nodded but said nothing more.

"Have you spent much time studying the Bible?" Edward asked.

"Not as much as I'd like."

"You're welcome to borrow mine."

Niki stared at him.

"Do you doubt my sincerity?"

Niki looked slightly embarrassed before admitting, "No, I'm just unaccustomed to trusting so quickly. I've had to be cautious, and that makes me wonder why you would be so kind to complete strangers."

Edward smiled. "At times I've wondered myself."

It was meant to be a joke, but Niki didn't

laugh or even smile. She looked at Edward a moment longer and then turned to Denley, touching his brow and reaching for the cloth.

Edward did not interrupt her. He'd been completely honest with her. Indeed he'd been utterly candid with her since they'd met. But he would have to let her figure that out for herself.

Bending his head again, he went back to studying his Bible. He sensed that Niki looked at him from time to time, but he didn't look up. There was no precedent in his life by which he could judge this situation. He read on, deciding to take things one moment at a time.

Chapter Four

"He knows," Niki said quietly.

She and Edward had just finished dinner. Edward had retired to his room, and she'd gone back to the room she shared with Denley. After thanking Rosario and paying her for the day's work, Niki saw her to the door. She found Denley awake and asking questions.

"How do you know he does?"

"He asked me to tell him why I'm dressed like a man."

Denley's eyes closed in pain—emotional pain. *I know I talked on the ship. I don't remember what I said, but I must have given her away.*

"Are you all right?"

"Is that why he's hanging about?" Denley asked, ignoring the question. "Is he hoping to hold it over you?"

"No. He said you told him that I had

needs and that until you were back on your feet to look after me, he was going to stay."

"This is all my fault."

"No, it's not," Niki said, her heart turning with tenderness for this dear man. "You were only doing what you've always done: taking care of me."

"What if he gives you away?"

"I don't think he will. I don't know why I trust him right now, but I do."

"Have you explained?"

"No, and I don't plan to."

Denley nodded, still so weak he wanted to die. He was not convinced that the blame for this did not lie at his door, but the job was done. Much as he wished it, he could not turn back the hours on the clock.

"What day is it?"

"Still Tuesday. We left the ship this morning."

Denley became restless, his head tossing in torment. "I've got to get out of this bed. I've got to get you back."

Niki said nothing. She laid her hand on his shoulder and waited. It was not an issue that needed to be debated. Yes, she needed to be somewhere—she needed it desperately—but she was no longer in control and neither was Denley.

When Denley's thrashing subsided into sleep, Niki wasn't certain. Her mind was hundreds of miles away, her heart as well. Trying not to panic over being on her own, she rose slowly and forced herself to think only of the moment, and that meant readying herself for bed.

$$\infty \quad \infty$$

When Edward woke the next morning, the inn was quiet, telling him it was still early. He thought that if he let himself, he could fall back to sleep, but his mind began to move in several directions, causing all remnants of fatigue to fall away. Would his brother ever believe this situation when he told him? Did Edward believe it himself? Barely. Niki Bettencourt, alias Osborne, was utterly fascinating. One moment she was telling the owner of the inn what she wanted and how swiftly it needed to arrive, and later—with great interest—she was quietly asking him about the Bible.

Edward could feel his head starting to pound. If he gave too much thought to this, he would become distracted and be of no use to anyone.

Reaching for his Bible, he settled in to read for a time. He knew he could take it to the other room, but reading next to Denley's bed might not prove very effective. For now he needed quiet to study and pray, and ask God for more wisdom than he'd ever called for in his life.

∂ ∂

"What kind of a night did Denley have?" Edward asked from across the table a few hours later.

"Not bad," Niki answered briefly. "Awake some."

The breakfast tray had been delivered, and the two were seated at the room's small table. Throughout the meal Edward took surreptitious glances at Niki, but she didn't seem to notice. He thought she looked tired.

"I was wondering whether you want me to move in here so you could take my room."

Niki stopped eating. She looked up from her plate and studied Edward.

"Why?"

Edward shrugged a little, still working on his food. "You didn't share a cabin on the ship, so I assumed this was unusual."

Niki told herself to calm down. It was a reasonable request. Returning her concentration to her food, she answered him.

"My privacy is not an issue with Denley being so ill, and once he's feeling better, we'll be on our way."

Edward gave a nod and kept eating. He would have liked to ask what *on our way* meant but knew better.

The meal continued in silence. Edward didn't try to engage her in any type of conversation but forced his mind to relax. He'd set his Bible on the window ledge when he'd come in and glancing at it helped to calm him. He might feel out of control, but Someone else certainly wasn't.

A knock at the door sounded just as Edward put his napkin down. Niki rose to answer it, and Edward watched as the door opened for one of the young men who worked around the inn.

"The broth you asked for, Mr Osborne."

"Thank you," Niki said softly, slipping the lad a coin and shutting the door.

Not wasting any time, Niki went to the
bed. She put the tray with its bowl and
spoon on the side table and tried to rouse
Denley.

"Come along, Denley," Edward heard her
say. "You need to drink a bit."

"Are we leaving?" Denley mumbled as his
eyes opened slightly.

Edward watched Niki try to raise him up
and went to help. When Denley's eyes fully
opened, Edward spoke to him.

"I'm going to roll this pillow under your
head, Denley. We'll go easy."

"All right."

"There's some broth you need to drink."

"I need . . ." Denley began and then
stopped, his eyes pleading with Edward.

Niki rose swiftly and moved toward the
door.

Without even glancing at her, Edward
said, "Your coat."

Niki changed directions long enough to
grab this garment and fled. The moment
she was gone, Edward took over.

He'd never assisted someone with such a
personal need before, but the compassion
he felt for this helpless, dignified man com-
pelled him to action and little thought. He

settled Denley back against the pillow as soon as he could and then began to spoon small sips of broth into his mouth.

Tears came to the prone man's eyes, but Edward didn't comment or appear to notice. Weakness was an awful thing for someone capable and usually strong. Edward knew that anything he might say would only sound hollow to the sick man.

The door opened slowly a short time later, and Niki peeked her face in. She came to Denley's other side, sitting close, her face showing every bit of concern she felt. It had been embarrassing earlier, and not for the first time was she thankful that her face never blushed. Seeing Denley make an effort to drink and keep his head up, Niki put her own feelings aside and stayed close.

Without warning Denley's eyes closed, and he went limp. Niki paled with fright until Edward spoke.

"He's just worn out and has taken all he can."

Niki nodded, unable to speak.

"Would you like me to sit with him?"

"No, I'll do it."

"I'm going out for a little while."

"All right.

Edward left without further word, unaware of the way Niki sat and thought about him for a long time. She then remembered his Bible on the ledge. Hoping he'd meant what he said before, she went for it and returned to the bedside.

ॐ ॐ

I've been delayed but still plan to be with you before Christmas. Don't worry after me, but please pray for wisdom as I make final plans to come home. If I don't make it by Christmas Day, I shall be with you shortly thereafter or send word to the contrary.

Edward hated how cryptic his note sounded, but he was not willing to be more informative at this point. Had a few more answers come to the surface, that might have been possible, but right now he felt it best to be as secretive as his traveling companions.

Having written and posted the letter to Henry, Edward made his way slowly back to the inn. He passed the bakery and purchased a few sweets, enough to share with Niki, but then moved directly on. He wondered whether his absence might be taken as suspect, but he knew better. He also knew that if Niki asked him, he would tell her the truth: He'd sent a letter home, telling his family he'd been detained.

❧ ❧

"Your eyes have darted behind me to one corner of the room the entire meal," Edward commented during supper that evening. "What is going on?"

Niki looked at him in surprise. The day had been quiet. Lunch and their walk after had been uneventful, and Edward had said little even when Denley had managed more broth and remained awake a bit longer. The servant even had some color in his face.

"I think I've been spotted."

"By whom?"

"Someone I wish to avoid."

Thinking, *What a horrible way to live,* Edward asked, "What will you do?"

"I'll wait until morning and see if I'm right."

"And if you are?"

"We'll have to move."

"Move where?"

Niki's eyes were suddenly full of suspicion.

"What did you do this morning when you left for a time?"

"I wrote my family a letter to say I'd been delayed in my return."

Niki watched him carefully.

"If you're thinking that I've betrayed you in some way," Edward went on quietly, as though they were discussing the weather, "I haven't. I have no reason to do such a thing. I've tried to assure you of my honesty, but I realize you're going to have to learn that on your own. As for my involvement with you and Denley, I only hope I don't land myself in trouble because of it. If I do, you'll have to live with the way you betrayed me."

Niki couldn't hide her surprise. While brief, it nonetheless showed in her eyes just long enough for Edward to be convinced that he'd figured her out.

"So I'll ask you again," he started quietly. "Move where?"

"From here."

"The inn or Lisbon?"

"Lisbon."

"With or without Denley?"

"I would never leave Denley behind. Surely you've assumed that much."

"True, I have, but since I don't know how desperate you are, from whom you're hiding, or why, I naturally have questions."

Niki nodded in understanding even as her eyes darted across the room again.

"I'm quite finished," Edward said. "Shall we go up?"

Niki met his eyes, questions filling her. Why was he helping? Why did he care? And how did he seem to know her needs before she could even voice them?

With only a nod of agreement, Niki rose to her feet. Not for the first time Edward reminded himself to treat her as he would another man. He was at the stairway ahead of her and started up. It went against everything he'd been taught, but he did it. Not even at the bedroom door did he stand on propriety. He went in ahead of Niki, nodded to Rosario, and checked on Denley.

Niki paid the young woman and joined Edward across the bed. Denley opened his eyes.

"I think we've been discovered," Niki wasted no time in saying, seeing no need to be clandestine.

Denley tried to sit up.

"We've got to go."

"I'll check again in the morning and hire a coach if we need to."

Denley nodded, lying back in exhaustion. "I should be doing this."

Niki ignored him because Edward was asking a question.

"Do you plan to slip away while I'm still in my room?"

Niki looked across at him.

"No." Her voice was flat and resigned. "Much as I hate to admit it, I need you."

"So what is the plan?"

"We'll eat downstairs in the morning, and I'll ask a few questions. If we need to leave, we'll go directly after breakfast."

"And what of this coach you need? You've never been in Lisbon. How will you arrange that?"

"Money talks, Mr Steele, or haven't you figured that out yet?"

Edward watched her for a moment.

"And what of tonight? Are you not worried that someone will come here to your room?"

"No, that's not the concern. That's never been the concern."

Edward had all he could do not to shake his head. He didn't know when he'd ever been so confused or in the dark on an issue. His temple throbbed a bit, and he knew he was going to have to let this go and take Niki at her word.

"Well, I'll retire," he said, turning to the door. "I shall assume you'll come for me if there's a need. If not, I'll be ready for breakfast a bit early."

"Thank you. Good night."

Niki stood still even after he exited. She looked down at Denley and was surprised to find him still awake.

"Do you feel better?"

"A little. You still trust him, don't you?"

"Yes, but I'm not sure why. Why did you trust him?"

Denley managed a small smile. "He's more than a gentleman. I don't meet men like him very often."

Niki didn't reply. Her eyes swung to the doorway as though she were still seeing Edward Steele. *More than a gentleman.* She'd never heard the phrase before but somehow knew that Denley had hit the matter squarely on the nose. She looked back to Denley to ask one more question,

but his eyes were closed, his features relaxed.

It wasn't overly late, but Niki still readied
for bed. Unless she missed her guess, they
would leave Lisbon in the morning. For that
reason alone she needed her sleep.

❧ ❧

The coach was more than adequate. It
wasn't fancy or huge, but it was comfortable, and Edward settled back, Niki beside
him, and looked across at Denley, who was
already lying on the seat, sound asleep.
Just getting dressed and exiting the inn had
exhausted the man. The color had receded
from his face, and he'd panted with the la-
bor of it all. It was no surprise that he was
out cold.

Edward's attention suddenly swung to
Niki. She had been looking at Denley also,
her expression as closed off as ever.

"Where are we going?" Edward asked of
Niki's ear, as she'd yet to look at him.

"Coimbra."

"Will we stay there?"

"If it's safe."

Edward wasn't sure just how many miles

that would be, but he had a notion the ride would be long. He'd slept well in the night and was wide awake. The hours suddenly loomed ahead of him. He looked back to Niki, still getting her profile.

"So," Edward began, "how shall we pass the time?"

Niki turned slowly to look at him, her eyes giving nothing away. She stared at him for several seconds before her gaze returned to Denley.

"I know!" Edward was not put off. "I'll try to guess why you're dressed as you are."

This time Niki didn't even bother to look at him.

"You have found some sort of hidden treasure, and even the map leading you to the treasure is hidden."

Niki didn't comment or turn.

"No? All right then, you've stumbled across a plot to assassinate the king, and you must keep moving until you can return home and tell the royal family what you've learned."

Niki didn't so much as blink.

"No, wait!" Edward sat up in excitement. "You're an international jewel thief."

This statement managed to bring Niki's eyes to his.

"Do I look like an international jewel thief?"

"I can't actually say. I've never known one."

His disappointed tone and the perplexed look on his face were too much for Niki. She had to turn away or laugh.

Edward kept guessing, but Niki did not look at him. Dismissing Edward, her thoughts remained far away. She could hear him speaking but didn't pay him any mind. They would stop in Coimbra for the night. They would find a doctor to check on Denley. She hoped they would not be followed and he could rest a bit more. They must continue their journey. It was so very important to keep moving.

Suddenly so tired that she wanted to sleep, Niki let her head fall back against the seat. For the moment she could do nothing. She was in the coach and the decision was made. Willing her mind to slow down, she let her eyes shut. She wouldn't sleep, but for the moment it felt good to sit still and relax.

❧ ❧

Niki woke slowly, her neck feeling cramped. She felt the fabric of the seat under her cheek and pushed away from it, only to find she'd been lying against Edward's sleeve. Her gaze going up, she saw that he was watching her, and for the first time he saw irritation on her face.

"Why didn't you wake me?" she asked crossly, sitting up, her hand going to her hair.

"I've only just awakened myself."

Looking into his bright eyes, Niki wasn't convinced.

Edward read the look but didn't comment. He thought again that it would do no good to tell her she was safe with him. He would have to prove it, not to mention that if he were to speak of it, he'd have to be downright insulting. His taste did not run to women who looked like men. His sisters, all three very feminine, were curvy in all the right places. He wasn't so shallow as to believe that only looks mattered, but he'd be lying not to admit that women who looked very different from Nicola Bettencourt attracted him.

"How long did I sleep?"

"I'm not certain."

Niki looked at him. "So you were asleep?"

"For a time, yes."

Niki's eyes went to Denley.

"Has he been awake at all?"

"No."

Niki moved across and touched Denley's cheek. He didn't feel overly warm, but she wondered if she should try and get some water into him.

"Do you want the water?"

"Yes," she answered without turning around. "Denley?" She touched the man's shoulder and gave him a small shake. "Can you wake up?"

Edward had a cup ready long before Niki had Denley awake. It took some coaxing to rouse the man, which concerned her even more.

"What is it?" he finally asked through dry lips. "Are we there?"

"No, but it's been some hours, and I think you need something to drink."

Without being asked, Edward moved and helped Denley with the cup. The servant drank gratefully, and Edward filled the cup again. The water revived the weak man. Sitting up, Denley's eyes opened wide, and he looked around the carriage.

"Where are we?" he asked of Niki.

"Somewhere between Lisbon and Coimbra."

"Will we stay there?"

"That's the plan. How do you feel?"

"Tired, but not as ill."

"I hated to wake you."

"It's all right."

Edward was opening his mouth to ask whether Denley wanted anything to eat but hesitated. All three occupants of the carriage felt it at the same time. The coach was stopping. The horses were being drawn back, and the coach was coming to a slow halt.

From his side Edward moved the curtain.

"We have company," he said even as Niki looked around his shoulder and also saw the two men on horseback.

Niki looked to Denley. "Stay in here. I'll handle this."

Edward looked to see if she was serious and realized she'd been speaking to Denley. He didn't think Denley would obey, but a moment later, when a man opened the door of the carriage and ordered all of them out, Niki was the first to emerge, moving like a man in control. His heart beating painfully against his ribs, Edward followed her. And to his utter surprise, Denley kept his seat inside.

Edward felt the ground beneath his feet, but not even the firmness of the earth could give him a sense of reality. It would seem they were being held up, something he'd never experienced in his life. He would have wished for several different companions in this situation, his brother or one of his brothers-in-law to name a few, but that was not to be.

Accompanied by a woman and an ill servant, Edward Steele was in Portugal, out on a road that was miles from anywhere, and about to be robbed of his possessions. He wondered if his family would ever believe this story. He then had the sober thought of wondering whether he'd be alive to tell them.

Chapter Five

"Out!" the man who opened the door ordered Denley.

"That's my servant," Niki said in a cold tone. "He's ill."

The man by the door sent another look toward Denley before directing his gaze to the one man still on horseback. Niki didn't see the exact communication, but the man on foot suddenly backed away from the coach. It took Niki no time to figure out who was in charge.

"What do you want?" she asked of the man still on horseback, her tone commanding his attention.

The man who had opened the door had moved to a safe distance; he did not appear to be armed. The other man, larger than the first, had come off of his horse to approach.

"What do you think we want?" he asked.

Niki took in his dirty red vest as she answered.

"I'm in no mood to play games," Niki said, her voice low and deep. "State your business!"

The man smiled an ugly smile, full of malice and greed.

"My business is your money, sir. I will wait patiently while you hand it over."

With a long-suffering look, Niki reached for her pocket. Edward did the same, but before he could lay his hand on his wallet, a short sword appeared in Niki's hand. Where it had come from he hadn't seen, but it was now up against the neck of the man with the red vest, pressing hard enough to draw blood.

The first man, now standing next to his horse, had drawn a pistol. This did not escape Niki's notice, but she spoke calmly.

"He might shoot me, but you'll still die. The choice is yours."

"What do you want?" red vest asked, visibly sweating.

"Throw the gun down."

Niki heard more than saw it hit the ground.

"Now," she spoke to red vest again. "I

want you to get on your horses and ride away from here very fast. Do not bother us again."

Anger filled the man's eyes, but he stepped back. His head jerked and the other man climbed into his saddle. Niki followed red vest for several steps, her sword still out, waiting for him to dive for the pistol, but it didn't happen. Some words were spoken that she did not understand, but just a few moments later the men wheeled their horses about and took off. Niki watched until they were a good distance away and then rounded on the two coachmen.

"Who told you to stop this coach?"

"We thought they wanted a ride," the one explained in poor English.

"I hired this coach. It is not your place to offer anyone else a ride! If you stop this coach again before I tell you, I'll drive it myself, and you can walk back to Lisbon."

They nodded, fear apparent on each of their faces. Edward was a little afraid himself but followed when she climbed back inside. Her fist hit the roof, and the coach set off.

His back against the seat, and his heart

still pounding, Edward could not stop look-ing at Niki. He turned a few times to look out the window, but his eyes came back to her after only a moment.

"Where did that come from?" he finally voiced.

"The sword?"

"Yes."

"I keep it in my coat."

"And would you have actually used it?"

"I've never killed a man if that's what you're asking me, but, yes, I would have protected myself."

Not until that moment did Edward notice the way she trembled and the small quiver in her voice. Compassion filled him, and he looked across at Denley.

"Are you all right?"

"Yes, Mr Steele," he answered quietly. "Thank you."

"Niki?" Edward asked, turning back to her.

"I'll be fine," she answered without look-ing at him. In truth she wasn't sure. She had pulled her sword out before but never used it. Her eyes closed to try and dispel the im-age of the drops of blood on that man's neck, but she could still see it.

Edward looked across at Denley, whose eyes were riveted on Niki. He looked shaken and weary, and Edward tried to shake off the shock that had come over him.

"Lie back down, Denley," he ordered. "Rest as much as you can."

Denley did lie down, but his eyes were still on his employer.

Edward then took one of Denley's blankets, and without permission, put it over Niki. She only looked at him.

"Lay your head back and try to rest."

She still stared at him.

"I may not be good with a sword or marauders, but I know what to do when someone is upset. Here." He held out a cup of water. "Take a drink."

Niki did as she was told, the feelings of unreality still stealing over her. She couldn't remember the last time someone had taken care of her, not in this way. Denley was ever faithful, seeing to each need, but he was not the idea man. He didn't tell her what to do or demand that she take care of herself. Edward Steele had no such inhibitions. Right now he was the one giving the orders, and he obviously expected to be obeyed.

"Close your eyes," Edward commanded, taking the cup from her grasp.

"Every time I do that, I see that man's bleeding neck."

Edward took a breath. It had been awful.

"He would have robbed you," he said at last. "And he might have killed you. You did what you had to do. I, for one, am very thankful that I didn't lose my wallet. Thank you for what you did."

Niki nodded, suddenly very ready to close her eyes. Where the tears had come from she didn't know, but they were rushing in, and that was something she couldn't let anyone see.

Though not actually sleeping, Niki lay still for a long time. She pushed the robbers from her mind time and again and then realized someone was reading a book near her. She heard the pages turning. She peeked over at Edward and found him bending over his Bible.

"Does something in there comfort you?"

"Yes," he answered softly.

"What is it?"

"I'm reading in Genesis—the first few chapters about creation."

"And this brings comfort to you?"

Edward looked over at her. "After an incident like that, I need to be reminded of the orderly God who loves me and who would never let me out of His sight."

Niki sat up a little. "And you get that in Genesis?"

"Yes. You see, God's design and plan are perfect. He doesn't let things happen without a reason. I may never know why we were stopped today, but God had a plan, and I can rest in that."

Niki had to think on this one. Edward stayed silent. Aware that Denley was asleep again, she realized they were basically alone.

"But there are verses that speak of comfort?" Niki asked, leaning toward him a little.

"Yes, many of them, especially in Psalms. Would you like me to find some?"

"You don't have to." Niki caught herself and pulled back, emotionally and physically.

Edward ignored her and turned to that book. He began in chapter 119, reading several verses.

" 'This is my comfort in my affliction; for thy word hath quickened me.' That was verse 50. Then verse 76 says, 'Let, I pray thee, thy merciful kindness be for my comfort, according to thy word unto thy servant.' A verse from chapter 86 doesn't use the word comfort, but the message is still there. 'For thou, Lord, art good, and ready to forgive, and plenteous in mercy unto all those who call upon thee.' Another one like that is in chapter 91, verse 2, 'I will say of the Lord, He is my refuge and my fortress, my God; in him will I trust.' "

"How do you know of those verses?"

"I have them marked in my Bible."

"So you've studied it quite a bit."

"Off and on for many years," he answered honestly.

"What's been most significant to you?"

Edward cocked his head to think.

"It's probably the fact that salvation is only the beginning. Once we trust Christ for our eternal destination, we still have a life to live on this earth. I spent too many years living for myself and not really seeking what God would have of me."

"So eternal life might have been lost to you?" Niki asked.

"No, my salvation, the trust I put in Christ to save me, was real, but I was ignorant and blinded by my own desires about living for

Him. I would not have been lost, but neither would I have been able to stand before God and say that I'd chosen to devote my life in order to live as His child. By that I mean making Him my God in every sense."

Niki looked as confused as she felt. Edward read it on her face and searched for a way to explain.

"Let me put it in earthly terms. Maybe you had done something wrong, a crime of some type, and you were going to be put to death. But then the king comes forward and pardons you. He saves you.

"Clearly you would owe him, but you could choose not to live a life of obeisance to him; you could choose to live your life your way. You might think of him as your savior, even your friend, but not your king, because a king has rule and authority.

"I can think of God as my savior and even my friend, but I must never forget that He is God, and after He saves me, I must put myself in subjection to Him and His will."

"How long did it take you to learn all of this?"

Edward smiled a little. "Quite a while, but He's a most patient God, ready to forgive me of my foolish pursuits."

"So you believe forgiveness continues?"

"What do you mean?"

"You believe you can be forgiven even after salvation?"

"Absolutely. All sin can be repented of and forgiven."

Niki opened her mouth with another question, but the coach rocked, and Edward swiftly reached to steady Denley. He had looked to be on the verge of rolling off the seat. Edward laid a hand on his brow.

"He's warm."

Niki's fist went to the roof. The coach came to a stop, and she got out.

"How much further to Coimbra?"

The coachman began to give the answer in miles. Niki cut him off.

"How much time?"

"Less than two hours."

Niki nodded.

"We'll stop here for a few minutes and then be off. I need that box," she ordered, and pointed to a small hamper atop the coach.

One of the men retrieved the hamper with their food and put it inside. While the coach was stopped, Niki prepared the meal, but just as soon as she had given some to Edward and Denley and taken some for herself, she signaled the driver to leave again.

"The coachman said less than two hours, Denley," she told him.

That man nodded, a piece of bread that he hoped to swallow in his mouth. He didn't know that time could move so slowly. It felt as if they'd been in the coach for days. He ate everything that was handed to him and drank more water, but it did nothing to revive him. The moment he lay back down, he slept again, hoping that when he woke the jostling would all be over.

ஒ ஐ

Coimbra, Portugal

"Did you locate a doctor?" Edward asked when Niki entered the room, this one much smaller than the last.

"Yes, he's on his way."

Niki went to the bed, much as she had in Lisbon, to check on Denley. He was sleeping hard and very warm to the touch.

Regret filled her. She was certain that if they could have stayed in Lisbon, he would have gotten back on his feet and they could have taken a ship to Portsmouth, England.

Moving by way of coach had probably been the worst thing they could have done.

"Are you going to let the police know about the robbery attempt?" Edward was suddenly standing across the bed from Niki, looking for an answer.

"I can't exactly do that," she said, meeting his look squarely.

"Why is that?"

"They'll naturally wish to know why we weren't robbed, and I'd rather not go into it."

Edward nodded, but he wished there was some way to report it.

"Why is it important to you?"

"We didn't do anything with the pistol that was left on the ground. The men are free to stop the next coach. I'd hate to see someone else go through that."

Niki nodded. She'd had some of the same thoughts, but no solution on how to go about bringing the men to justice presented itself. At this point she didn't feel she had a choice.

"I would be sorry for anyone put in such a position, but right now I have to think of Denley's and my safety. All else comes second."

Not for the first time Edward found himself asking, *What is it that drives you, Niki Bettencourt? At what price have you chosen this life?* He had never known anyone like her. The desperation she felt was almost tangible.

An uncomfortable silence fell between them, lasting until the doctor arrived. His command of English was poor, but the innkeeper's young son stood by and did his best to translate. Niki found out what she'd known all along: Denley needed rest and fluids.

Paying the doctor, she took up a seat by the bed, seeming to forget that Edward was present.

"I'm going to head out and look for a room."

Niki's head sprang up.

"There's nothing here?"

"No. Did you not hear him tell you this is the last room?"

Niki shook her head no, guilt swamping her for having given so little thought to this man who had helped them.

"Will you be leaving from here?" Niki suddenly asked, assuming he'd had enough of the whole situation.

"Whenever you go."

"I won't be out much," Niki told him when he started toward the door. "I'll have my meals here and keep Denley as quiet as possible. When he can rouse a bit, we'll try to make Porto and find a ship."

"I believe that's the most information you've given me. Why the sudden trust? I could be hunting you myself."

"You're not," Niki said, her head dipping as she broke eye contact.

Edward studied her bent head for a moment, the perfectly cut dark, straight hair. He thought it must be very nice when it was long.

"I shall probably be across the street. Send word if you need me."

Niki watched him leave. He did not look back. She sat for a long time and worked to figure him out. It would have been easier if Denley had been awake and had needs that could distract her, but he was very still, leaving Niki alone with only her thoughts for company.

∾ ∾

Edward gave Niki and Denley the rest of the day on their own. He wasn't trying to distance himself, but she was tense with him, and the room was a little too small for comfort. Indeed there had been only one chair. They could have requested a second, but there was barely room.

Edward dined alone that evening and retired late. For that reason he slept later than he planned. After a quick shave and a bath, he made his way down to the common room but stopped short of sitting down at one of the long tables.

Standing just outside the building, a man, his clothing and looks very English, was watching the inn where Denley and Niki had their room. Edward studied him, thinking that traveling with Niki was making him paranoid, but the man never moved or altered his gaze.

Edward went ahead and sat down. He was offered strong coffee and breakfast, which he accepted. Doing nothing to hurry his meal, he took note of the fact that the man never moved from his place.

"Is there a back door?" Edward asked the woman who came to refill his cup.

She didn't understand at first but eventually smiled knowingly and showed Edward the way.

Walking ever so nonchalantly, Edward skirted the buildings around him until he'd landed himself at the rear of Niki's inn. He wasn't certain he would find a rear door to the lobby, and he was right—there was none. However, on the far side, away from his lodging, he found a portal. Opening it, he realized it led to the kitchen area.

Making his way quietly through those rooms, he found the back stairs as swiftly as possible and hunted down Niki's door. No one had questioned him. He knocked and waited.

"You're still here," Niki said the moment she saw him in the hall.

Edward stepped inside, shut the door, and leaned on it.

"This building is being watched."

"Are you certain?"

"Fairly so, yes. A British-looking chap is stationed outside my inn."

"And you sauntered across the street to tell me." Niki's voice was dry with chagrin.

"Not at all!" Edward looked excited. "I exited out the back of my building and found my way to the rear of this inn. I'd wager he never saw me."

"You're enjoying this!" she accused him, her mouth open in surprise.

"No," Edward denied and then hesitated. "Maybe a little."

Niki turned away, knowing she would laugh otherwise. His eyes had a way of speaking volumes, and she often wanted to laugh at the child she saw there.

"How is Denley?" Edward remembered to ask.

"Resting easy. His fever is down."

"What will you do about the man across the street?"

Niki went to the window to spot him. Standing in the shadows, she stood for a moment in thought.

"If he's there all day, we'll assume you're right. We'll leave before morning and probably not be spotted."

"Until we get to the next inn."

"What do you mean?" Niki finally turned back to him.

"I mean, you can't keep on as you are. We have to find you a new set of clothes."

"What will that accomplish?"

Edward looked patient.

"You act and dress like royalty, making you far too noticeable. You're remembered

everywhere you go. We'll find you something more suitable to the look of a servant.
Something like Denley wears."

"What good will that do?"

"Well, it's not at all unusual for a man of
my station to travel with several servants."

Niki's mouth gaped open. "And you
would do that—pose with us?"

Edward nodded calmly. "Until Denley is
on his feet, yes."

Watching him, Niki felt breathless with
fear and excitement. She wanted to trust,
but there had been no room for such luxury
for a very long time. Yesterday she had felt
so sure; now the doubts were flooding in.

"I'll head out," Edward said, not having
caught her tortured thoughts. "I'll find some
clothes and come back."

"How will they fit?" Niki asked the inane
thought, the only one to come to mind.

"They might not, but we'll keep at it until
we find something. If we're not leaving here
until daybreak tomorrow, we have all day."

This said, he turned for the door. Niki's
voice stopped him.

"Edward."

He looked back.

"Thank you."

Edward smiled the warm smile that came so easily to him, briefly held her eyes, and went on his way.

On legs that would barely support her, Niki went back to the side of Denley's bed and the room's only chair. She was nearly sick with fatigue and worry, and very real tears came to her eyes.

Please God, her heart whispered, *I've never understood the part about making You more than just my Savior, but I don't have anywhere else to turn. Please help me. Please help me to get home, and I'll learn. I'll do anything I can to make You my God.*

Wishing desperately for the luxury of a good cry, Niki knew it would be a waste. Instead she checked on Denley one more time before laying her head near the end of the bed. It wasn't comfortable, but her body was too weary to notice. Wondering where Edward would find suitable clothing in this unfamiliar Portuguese town, she fell asleep.

ৰে ৶৶

"Let me see that shirt," Edward requested, charming as ever, as several shop employees rushed to serve him and be understood. Taking his time, Edward examined the cut and then asked for a smaller size.

Nearly an hour passed before he exited the store, a young man carrying his bags. He returned to his own room, compacted the things he bought into one bag, making everything as small as possible, checked on the man who was still out front, and used the back exit.

Once he was safely at the back of the inn across the street but before he entered, he stopped to think. She had accused him of enjoying this escapade, and to an extent he was, but just now the gravity of the situation hit him.

Denley was ill. Niki was running, quite possibly for her life. Edward had made something of a game out of finding her clothing, but there were still so many unanswered questions. If she was in trouble with the law, he would never be able to explain his innocence.

Please, Lord, let me be wise, he prayed as he made his way inside. *I don't want to leave them alone. I want to help and be a light. Help me to find out a little more. Help me to aid them without jeopardizing myself.*

Even to Edward's own ears the request seemed outrageous, but in his mind it was too late now. He had said he would help, and he would stand by his word. So far he'd not been asked to deny his principles. He prayed it wouldn't come to that, for in that moment, he would leave Niki and Denley, helpless or not.

Chapter Six

"Here you go." Once in the room, Edward handed Niki the bag. "Go over there and try these on," he commanded.

Niki looked in the bag and saw shoes, pants, shirt, jacket, and a vest. She looked from the bag back to Edward.

"Are you leaving the room?" she asked him.

"No, I'll just sit here."

Without hesitation Niki shook her head.

"You'll have to leave."

Edward frowned. "Don't be silly. I'll sit here with Denley, my back to the room, and you'll change. I can't go out again until we see how these fit."

"You can wait in the hall."

"To anyone who cares to notice," he replied, his voice holding the patience of Job as he attempted to explain how odd this would appear, "there are two men staying in this room. Why would I need to exit while you change?"

Edward held her eyes for just a moment. He then repositioned the chair and sat down, his broad back toward her.

Niki stared at the width of his shoulders, just five feet away. She might not look like a woman, but she was one. If he ever decided to do something against her will, she would have only her sword as a defense, and at the moment it wasn't close by.

"Are you done?" Edward asked, his back still to her, fairly certain she hadn't made a move.

"No."

"Well, get going."

Niki saw no help for it. Rushing so that she nearly tore her fancy clothing, her eyes on Edward at all times, she changed as swiftly as she could. The pants were a good fit, as was the shirt, but the vest was on the large side, and she suspected the jacket was too short.

"All set?" Edward asked when she stopped moving.

"Yes."

Edward stood and faced her.

"Not bad," he commented, his voice detached. "Turn around."

Niki's look was long-suffering and a bit mutinous.

"Go ahead," Edward commanded, making a circular movement in the air with his finger.

"No," he said when she spun for him, still sounding like a man on a mission with little emotional attachment. "That jacket won't do at all, much too short."

Niki stood mute.

"Take it off so I can see how we did with the vest."

Niki obeyed, a sense of unreality stealing over her.

"Perfect," Edward declared.

"It's huge."

"Not for a servant's servant."

"Is that what I'll be?" Niki sounded slightly horrified.

"Of course. You'd be a lousy gentleman's gentleman. You're too used to being waited on. You'll answer to Denley and he'll answer to me."

"Denley is sick," she reminded him patiently.

"We'll give the *appearance* of your answering to Denley. In truth, you'll probably be doing all the work."

"I can hardly wait."

Edward ignored the comment and put the coat back in the bag. He started for the door and then stopped.

"Once I leave, change back to your gentleman's clothing. You shouldn't be seen like that until we're headed out of town."

"Then you'll probably have to hire the coach."

"I'll take care of it. What time do you wish to leave?"

For a moment Niki didn't know. Edward had taken over in the last few hours, and she'd let her guard down.

"Five o'clock and with as little fuss as possible."

"I'll arrange it."

The door had closed, but Niki had still heard the words. *I'll arrange it* was something Denley would say. Niki never doubted the job would get done. Edward had proved to be good at his word.

Her heart heavy inside of her, Niki went to the chair by the bed. She didn't change as she should have but sat close to Denley, aching for some sign that would comfort her heart and assure her that everything was going to be all right.

❧ ❧

Denley felt himself wake up but didn't open his eyes. He lay still, feeling some relief, as though he'd just awakened from a long, restful nap. A few more minutes passed, and then without stirring he opened his eyes and had all he could do not to jerk with a start.

Sitting by his bed was Nicola Bettencourt as he had never seen her. The clothing was clean and new, but the gentleman was gone. An ill-fitting vest in colors that were all wrong for her hung on her frame, changing her looks entirely. While Denley still studied her, she turned.

"You're awake."

"And you're not a gentleman anymore."

Niki looked down at herself.

"Mr Steele's idea. What do you think?"

"I think you'll throw them off."

"I hope so. We leave at dawn. I'll be a servant's servant now."

It was too much for Denley. His eyes closed in pain.

"It's the only way, Denley. I keep getting spotted, and we have to get back."

Denley nodded and sighed deeply. There was no help for it.

"How are you feeling?" Niki asked.

"Better," he answered, looking into her eyes. "I'm actually hungry."

"That's a good sign. I'll change and order food."

Denley nodded, even as he closed his eyes again. Niki changed without a thought, forcing her mind back into the role of being in charge. Edward might be outfitting her as a servant and taking care of their transportation, but Denley's needs and their destination were ultimately her responsibility.

ॐ ॐ

"Here," Edward said in the quiet of Niki's room the next morning, handing her a cap. "I picked this up after I dropped off your coat yesterday."

Niki placed the gray cap on her head. Edward reached to adjust it a bit.

"What do you think, Denley?"

"The change is amazing," Denley commented, unable to take his eyes from Niki.

"Shall we be off?" Edward asked.

Niki nodded and started toward the door. Edward caught her arm and bent a little to catch her eyes under the brim of the hat.

"You have to carry the bags."

"Oh, right," Niki said, giving her head a little shake.

"Also, sit in the seat with Denley until we leave. Once we get underway, we'll move around so Denley can rest."

Once the plans were in place, they exited. On his feet but still weak, Denley took the lighter load. Edward acted very much himself. Having been waited on all his life, he took it all in stride, even as his eyes darted for signs of the mystery man.

He was careful to give no deference to Niki, expecting his needs to be met and seeing to his own comfort with apparently no thought for anyone else. Once the carriage set off, he felt as though he could breathe again and moved over so Niki could join him.

"Did you see him?" she asked, settling on the seat. It was very dark inside the coach.

"No. All was very quiet."

"Last night I paid the innkeeper for tonight and asked that we not be disturbed today. If someone asks after us, he'll be mute."

"That was good thinking. By the way, did you know the man watching the inn?"

"Not personally, but they all look alike."

"How's that?"

"They're either French or British, and they don't blend in very well. Added to that, each one thinks I'm a fool."

"So they know you travel as a man?"

"They think I *am* a man. Osborne has been acting as Nicola's solicitor, so they think that by following him they can get to her."

Edward thought the whole plan rather clever but didn't comment.

Alone with her thoughts, Niki remembered the price she paid for her deception. She made up her mind. This was the end. She would get home and not do this again. It was too taxing; the cost was too high. It might seem sudden to some, but she had been coming to this point for a very long time.

"Are you all right, Denley?" Edward asked.

There was no answer.

Niki moved to check on him.

"I think he's asleep."

"That sounds like a good idea."

Edward settled back and got comfortable. He never minded the rocking of a carriage; he found it relaxing. Niki wasn't in the same state. Until it grew light, they wouldn't know if they'd been followed. Wishing there was some way to know so she could turn her brain off, she laid her head back and tried not to think.

ॐ ॐ

It had happened again, only this time Edward had decided to use Niki as a pillow. She woke up to find the carriage well lit with daylight, Edward's head heavy against her shoulder. She shifted a little, but he didn't move.

When she looked across at Denley, she found him sitting up and awake.

"Are you all right?" he asked.

"Yes. You sound as though you feel better."

"I do, thank you."

Their conversation did not reach Edward. Niki gave him a little push, but that was just as ineffective.

"Shall I wake him?" Denley offered.

"I'll do it. Edward," Niki tried, but he only moved to make himself more comfortable, even going so far as to slip an arm around her waist.

"Wake up, Edward Steele!" Niki commanded, but her voice was never very loud, and Edward was quite sleepy.

Seeing no help for it, Niki pinched the skin on the back of his hand. Edward started a bit and opened his eyes.

"I'm sorry." He was instantly contrite as he sat up. "Did I smash you?"

"No, I'm all right. I couldn't wake you."

"What did you do?" Edward asked as he worked to orient himself, vaguely aware that he'd been hurt.

"I pinched your hand."

"Were we followed?" he asked, his eyes already bright.

"It doesn't appear so, but we won't actually know until we arrive."

Edward consulted his watch and saw that they'd been on the road for several hours. The warm darkness of the coach had served to make them quite comfortable.

"I think a stop is in order," Edward commented, his fist going into the roof without waiting for permission.

It felt good to stretch their legs. Once in the nearby woods, Edward and Denley headed one direction and Niki another. When they met back at the carriage, Edward told Denley he wanted something to eat. That man was swift to obey and turned to Niki.

Denley gave quiet orders to Niki, and Edward glanced from time to time to see if the coachmen had taken any interest. They checked their horses and the bags loaded at the rear, not appearing to pay any attention to the travelers.

When the carriage was back on the road, the three ate without conversation. Denley slept again, this time sitting up with his head against the seat. As the coach continued toward the port city of Porto, Edward found that his mind had done some traveling of its own. He suddenly spoke to Niki.

"I have it figured out."

"What's that?"

"You have an overbearing father who's forcing you to marry a man twice your age, a business partner of his. The arrangement is intended to keep the money in the family."

Niki's brows rose. "Has anyone ever told you that you have an overactive imagination?"

Edward looked back at her and smiled a little. "Has anyone ever told you that you look good as a servant? You should take it up."

"You told me I wouldn't be any good," she reminded him.

"That's true; I'm probably right. We'll have to work on that."

Niki shook her head a little. "Did you say you have sisters?"

"Yes, why?"

"It's beginning to make sense."

"What is?"

"You must be the youngest in the family; you're something of a pest."

"I'll have you know I am *not* the youngest in the family," he took pleasure in informing her.

"Then you must be the youngest male."

That she had guessed accurately made him smile.

"I thought so."

"What gave me away?"

"Your unruly nature. As a child you would have been called incorrigible."

She had pegged the situation again, and Edward shifted in the seat so he could stare at her.

"And what of you? I would have to guess you to be a bossy older sister. How close am I?"

"I'm an only child."

"Ah," Edward sounded triumphant. "That makes my overprotective-father-with-the-forced-marriage theory look better all the time."

Niki had all she could do not to laugh. Instead, she changed the subject.

"When are we supposed to arrive?"

"Probably another hour at least."

Niki nodded. "I want to find lodgings near the docks so we can get underway as swiftly as possible."

"Have you been to Porto?"

"No."

"Neither have I. It's hard to say how busy it is. There are no guarantees that a ship will be leaving tomorrow."

Niki had no answer to Edward's warning, but she didn't want to hang around Porto any longer than she had to. She wanted to find a ship headed for England, board it, and be left alone. Laying her head back, she closed her eyes and tried not to worry.

           ഌ ഌ

Porto, Portugal

Porto, on the banks of the River Douro, was an active destination for the three weary travelers, but at least part of Niki's wish came true. They found an inn, a clean one, near the docks. Two rooms were available, and they settled Denley inside one of them before walking toward the ship that was in the harbor. They were told that the vessel was headed in the wrong direction but also informed that the *Henderson* was due in the next day. It was headed for England.

"Which means it might not be leaving until Sunday," Edward told Niki as they walked back to the inn. "You'll be stuck in the role of my servant until we leave here."

Niki idly wondered if Edward might think of sparing her by taking all his meals in his room but didn't voice this.

Edward glanced at Niki's enigmatic little face under the flat gray cap and wondered what she was thinking. Taking a second look, he decided not to ask. At any rate, it was more interesting to watch the people who walked past and around them. To a person, no one gave Niki a second glance. She looked like a male servant walking with his employer, and they took that at face value.

Back at the inn, Edward almost stopped and let her precede him inside but remembered just in time and went ahead. In the common room the innkeeper was on hand, and he asked after their accommodations. Edward stopped to speak to him.

"Ready my clothing for dinner," Edward ordered Niki casually and then turned away as she went silently up the stairs.

He didn't linger over his conversation with the innkeeper, telling him that for the moment all was in order. He did ask about the regularity of passenger ships headed for England and learned a little more. He then took the stairs two at a time and went to the room where he'd last seen Denley. He entered without knocking.

Standing in the middle of the room, Niki rounded on him and glared. Edward just held his laughter as he commented, "I take it my clothing isn't ready."

"You know it's not." Her voice was cold.

He smiled then, his sense of humor still in place.

"You look the part, but I was right, you make a dreadful servant."

Not waiting for her to reply, even though her mouth opened in outrage, Edward walked to the bed and put his hand on Denley's brow. The servant was cool to the touch, his breathing easy.

"It looks as though he's out of the worst of it. You'd better order him some food before we go down for supper."

When there was no answer, Edward looked at Niki. She was in the same place, looking none too happy with him, her mouth set in a grim line. It looked as though she might be ready to give him a full view of her anger, but Edward spoke first.

"I don't know exactly what you have at stake," Edward shocked her by saying, his voice compassionate. "If Osborne has been followed, you'll never be spotted. The change is that drastic. If you want me to go below and dine on my own, I can do that, but I dare say you're better at spotting these chaps than I am, and as I said, you certainly must have more at stake than I."

Niki's shoulders slumped with the truth of it all.

"Do you really need me to see to your clothing?" she asked.

"Not at all. I'll take my time changing, so you can see to Denley. We'll go down when you're ready."

Niki only nodded, unbelievably relieved that he wasn't going to be impossible after all.

ⓡⓢ

"My tea is cold. See the kitchen about a fresh pot," Edward ordered Niki an hour later, nearly unrecognizable with his bored looks and condescending air.

Niki lifted the cool pot but did not immediately move from the table near the window where he was the lone occupant. Her eyes spoke volumes, and seeing them, Edward's voice dropped.

"If you dump that over my head, you're sure to be noticed."

"You're enjoying this way too much," she hissed at him.

"Do you think?" he asked, his eyes grow-ing so large with feigned innocence that she had to turn away or laugh out loud.

She moved to the kitchen—her third trip—and returned with the hot tea. She no-ticed for the first time that he was nearly done and hoped that meant she could eat next. The incongruity of it all suddenly hit her, and she had all she could do not to howl with emotion.

Edward, a near stranger, ate in comfort while she waited on him. Her servant ate in the privacy of their room, with no need to take care of anyone but himself. Niki thought she might last another few minutes but no longer.

"I'll order a tray for you," Edward said quietly, not even looking at her.

"Thank you," she said softly, her shoul-ders slumping again and thinking he was the better actor. The thought sent her eyes to him. She looked at him a moment too long and was caught.

Edward's eyes twinkled with amusement, as though he could read her mind, before he shifted to greater comfort in his chair and reached for his tea, seeming for all the world like a man with nothing on his mind.

❧ ❧

Denley stood by the side of the bed to stretch his legs. He didn't think he would ever be well again, but there was no denying that his body was finally on the mend. Those hours in the carriage and sleeping in beds he couldn't even remember were blurry just now, but they still managed to bring a vague, unsettling memory.

And now Mr Steele was helping them. Or had he been helping them all along? Denley shook his head. There were a few things missing in his mind. Still testing his legs some, he was moving to the basin to wash his face when the door opened. Edward walked in, Niki behind him.

"How are you?" Niki asked immediately.

"I was wondering that about you. Have you eaten? I can order a tray for you."

"Mr Steele has done that," Niki answered. She thought Denley looked pale. She could also see he needed a wash.

"I'll take my tray in Mr Steele's room if he has no objection, and that will give you time to clean up."

"Thank you."

"Will you be all right alone for that time?"

"Yes."

Edward had stood back and remained quiet for this exchange. When Niki looked at him, he moved to the door. She followed, her stomach growling a bit. Not until they were across the hall in Edward's room did Niki wonder what had possessed her to suggest such a thing.

Chapter Seven

"I could just go below and eat," Niki said in her quiet, deep voice.

The door was shut, and Edward, who had strolled into his room and lit the lantern without a thought, turned to look at her.

"Why would you do that?"

"I just thought of it. There's really no need to trouble you."

Edward watched her.

"Where did this come from?"

Niki turned away. "I don't know what you mean."

"I mean you're suddenly nervous and shy with me. I can't think what I've done to cause that."

Niki's chin lifted a bit and she faced him. Wishing she'd kept her mouth shut, she still said, "Maybe I'm afraid you'll want your shoes polished."

"Actually it's my boots that need a good rub. You don't want to see to it?"

Niki's gaze became stern, and for the first time Edward realized it was what she did when she wanted to avoid a smile or possibly even outright laughter. He took pity on her, turned away, and placed his hat out of the way. He didn't know who would be delivering the food, but he slipped out of his coat because the room was warm.

"I've a letter to write. Feel free to make yourself comfortable and take as long as you like to eat your food."

Niki didn't answer.

"I forgot to ask you if there was anyone suspicious downstairs."

"No, I didn't see anyone."

Edward walked to the window. It was dark, but he still looked out and scanned the docks.

"The innkeeper pointed out that my window gives me a fine view of the harbor. I'll keep an eye out for that ship tomorrow."

When Niki didn't answer, Edward looked to her.

"If you recall, the *Red Dragon* pulled into Lisbon only long enough to unload cargo. Maybe tomorrow's ship will dock and be off all on the same day, and we can be on board when she sails."

"Maybe," Niki said, her mind on a thousand different things.

"What happens if someone tracks you aboard? What do you do then?"

"Get off at the next port and keep moving."

With that type of schedule, no wonder Denley became ill. I'm surprised you're not both sick.

A knock on the door caused them both to turn. Niki answered it and found Denley there with the tray that had been delivered to his room.

"Where would you like this?" he asked softly.

Niki could see that he'd had time to wash and change.

"Across the hall." She turned back to Edward. "Thank you for your hospitality. I'll see you in the morning."

Edward nodded and watched them leave. He stood for a moment and thought about the last few hours. Finally, he moved to the room's table. He had been quite honest with Niki: He had a letter to write.

న్ స్న

Edward lingered over breakfast the next morning. Denley had come to the dining area to check on him, almost feeling himself again. Edward did not ask about Niki. He knew these two were more than capable of taking care of themselves. He wanted to worry and step in even more than Denley did but this time refrained.

Dismissing Denley and forcing his mind to relax, he spotted a newspaper written in English and settled in to read. An hour passed before he thought he might be needed. He checked first at the window in his room to verify whether a ship had docked. Seeing no vessel, he ventured across the hall.

"Is there a ship?" were the first words from Niki's mouth.

"No, but I have to mail a letter," Edward told her, stepping into the room. "Do you want to stretch your legs?"

Feeling more than a little restless, she said, "Yes, I believe I will go with you."

"I'll meet you downstairs."

The two set off a short time later. Niki was tall, just a few inches shorter than Edward's six-foot frame, and had no trouble matching him stride for stride. As they walked, something came to Edward, causing him to move slower and slower. By the time they reached a nearly empty street, he was at a crawl.

"What's the matter?" Niki stopped, realizing he had been darting glances at her for some time.

"Did you wash your hair?" he asked suddenly.

"Yes." Niki's voice was cautious.

Edward's brows rose.

"Why? What does it matter?"

"You smell a little too good for a man in your position."

To his surprise, Niki frowned at him.

"I don't care! I couldn't stand it any longer. All those coaches and this moving about. It was too much!"

Edward smiled. *It would seem that there might be a woman in there after all.*

"What is so amusing?"

"You are."

"I'm so glad to oblige." She was becoming ill-humored. "Are you going to post that letter or not?"

"Yes, and then we'll head to the dock."

"I thought you said there was no ship."

Edward nodded, his gaze going behind her. Niki turned. Over the top of the building in front of them, the masts of a tall ship could just be spotted coming up the river.

"It might be the *Henderson,*" Edward stated calmly before starting off again. Niki worked to remain calm. She had never depended on anyone but Denley, and now with Edward involved she was letting her guard down continually. She should have been the one to spot that ship. There was no excuse for such a blunder.

Still castigating herself but back in control, she followed Edward into the post office and then over to the bank. She stood quietly nearby while he took care of his business, but her eyes took in every person and detail. She would not let her guard down again.

❧ ❧

"What will be the plan aboard ship?" Edward asked of Niki an hour later. The *Henderson* was in port and leaving Porto for Brest, France, and then on to England in just two hours' time. The three travelers had passage. "Will you travel as Osborne or as you are?"

"I'll remain like this."

"Traveling alone or as my servants?"

Niki thought about it. In the quiet of the room Denley cleared his throat.

"What is it?" Niki turned to question him.

"If we separate from Mr Steele, and they run short of rooms on the ship, one or both of us might be asked to bunk in with the crew."

Niki's eyes closed on the memory. It had almost happened one time and been nothing short of a disaster. As Osborne, Denley had to be her buffer. If he'd been separated from her, her disguise might have been ruined.

"If you have no objections, we'll leave things as they are," Niki told Edward.

"I have no objections, but it might not be very fun for you."

"In other words," Niki stated baldly, "you plan to be a dictator."

"Not at all. I just like my tea hot."

Her frown made his eyes dance.

"And of course," he went on, his voice a little too caring, "Denley should reserve some of his strength—he's been very ill, you know—so you'll have to do the lion's share."

Denley turned his laughter into a cough and suddenly became involved with the buttons on his vest.

Edward was still smiling when he said, "It's time to go." He stood to his feet. "Don't forget to carry my bags."

Niki had a frown for Edward and then one for Denley. Both men were wise enough to remain silent.

ℛ ℛ

"Does anyone on board make you nervous?" Edward asked when they'd been to sea for several hours. Edward was sitting on the deck, and Niki had just brought him a blanket.

"No. All seems to be clear."

"And what will you do when we make port before England?"

"Just keep my eyes open."

Niki left him without waiting for permission, and Edward was reminded of how hard it would be to take on such a role.

A few minutes later two rather elderly

women strolled by, both very friendly and ready to talk. They stopped and conversed with Edward for quite some time. He dozed when they went on their way, but the blanket wasn't warm enough, and he kept waking with a chill. He was about to give up and return to his cabin when he saw Niki headed his way. She came and stood next to him but didn't speak.

"Did you have a question?"

"No." She sounded completely put out, her voice still managing to be soft and deep. "Denley reminded me that you had to be checked on often."

Edward chuckled softly.

"As a matter of fact, I'm cold. I'd like another blanket and some hot tea or coffee."

Niki opened her mouth to retort, but someone wandered by just then, and she managed a "Yes, sir," through gritted teeth.

Edward nodded at the folks walking past and then smiled at Niki's swiftly retreating back.

It's most unfortunate that she never had a brother. She's missed so much.

❦ ❦

"Now he wants his notebook!" Niki informed Denley an hour later, her face red with emotion. "I've just taken him another blanket and some tea. Now he wants to do some writing!"

"Why don't I take it?" Denley offered.

Niki looked at him and calmed. "Edward is right. You're supposed to be resting. He won't leave us until he knows you can do your job again."

"And would it be so bad if he sees you all the way there?"

"I'd like to trust—truly I would—but I can't. Not yet."

Denley stood up.

"I need a bit of air. I'll take the notebook."

"You're sure you're up to it?"

"Very sure."

"All right. Thank you, Denley."

Denley found the notebook Edward wanted and walked sedately onto the deck. He did feel better, but he could tell that his illness had been of a nasty variety.

"Well, Denley," Edward greeted him. "Are you feeling better?"

"Yes, sir," he answered quietly. Edward studied him.

"Is Niki all right?"

"Not at the moment," Denley told him, managing to keep a serious face.

Edward had no such qualms. His smile went into full bloom.

"I'll go and see her in a bit. Don't bother to check on me again."

"Very well, sir."

Relaxed, now that he'd been understood, Denley handed off the notebook and went on his way. Edward sat for a long time and thought about the way he'd teased her. It wasn't anything he planned to do, but when he saw her dressed as she was, the scamp in him came out.

Settling down to write a letter to the Middletons, Edward realized there were several things he couldn't communicate. There was no easy way to explain Niki and Denley, and he wasn't even home yet, something they would expect.

After setting the notebook aside and gathering his things to go in, Edward walked slowly along, never tiring of the sea air and the wind on his face. He was at the cabin before he was ready but still stepped in to see if Niki was around.

Still not overly happy, she was alone in the cabin and appeared to be waiting for him. Without warning, she came to her feet and verbally pounced.

"When do I get to tell you how I feel about this whole thing?"

"That depends."

"On what?"

"On where your sword is?"

Without warning a small laugh escaped her. Edward looked taken aback and then pleased.

"You laughed, Niki Bettencourt. There's hope for you yet."

The amazement in his voice took all the spunk out of her. It was all so wretched. She sat on the bunk, her eyes downcast.

"Go ahead," Edward prompted, taking the other bunk. "Tell me how you feel about this whole thing."

"I'm heartily sick to death of being a servant and waiting on you." Niki answered quietly, her eyes still staring at the floor. "I don't know how Denley stands it."

"But aren't you glad he does?"

Niki sighed. "I am glad. You're certainly right about that."

"We've made good speed today. We'll probably be in England in no time."

"Where we part company."

When Edward didn't reply, Niki looked up at him.

"Where we part company," she repeated, her voice telling of her want.

"As soon as Denley tells me he's ready to take care of you, I'll go."

Niki shook her head in amazement.

"What is it that compels you, Edward Steele?"

"I could ask you the same thing."

Niki's eyes cast about, her head shaking in self-derision. "It's all so complicated."

"I imagine it is. I only hope for your sake that it's worth it."

This time Niki looked him square in the eye.

"The prize is beyond value. I would give my life for this cause."

Edward ached for the desperation he saw in her eyes. What a horrible spot to find oneself in. He wondered if it was of her choosing or completely out of her hands.

"Have you thought any more about the verses we talked about?" Edward asked suddenly.

"The ones on comfort?"

"Yes, and the way the Bible tells us that God has a plan. Do you believe any of that, Niki?"

"I believe all of it, but I don't think it would change my course of action."

And unless you can explain it to me, I won't be able to help. Edward felt defenseless in light of this fact and said only, "I hope it's all right that I pray for you and Denley."

Coming from this man, Niki felt shaken by the words but didn't comment. She stood, quietly thanked Edward, and exited the small cabin. She knew Denley was in the other cabin and that he would leave her in peace. But for the moment she desperately wanted to be alone. Wishing she'd grabbed her long coat, even though it was too elegant for a servant, she began a slow walk along the deck, hoping the sea air would clear the emotions away. Emotions could cause her to make a mistake, something she couldn't afford right now.

∾ ∾

"Well, now," Edward said to the little girl at the table when he arrived for dinner in the small dining area of the ship. "Are you eating alone?"

The little girl only looked at him and didn't answer. Edward tried again in French and watched her light up with delight.

"I'm dreadfully slow," she explained. "Mother had to take Annette back to our cabin but left me to finish."

"Is the food good?"

"Not like home, but it's fine."

"Do you think I shall like it?"

"If you're hungry enough."

Edward laughed at her deduction and took a seat across the table from her.

"Is Annette your sister?"

"Yes. She's older and eats faster."

"Maybe you'll eat faster when you grow older."

She looked doubtful, and Edward smiled at her.

"You haven't told me your name."

"I'm Karoline."

"It's nice to meet you, Karoline. I'm Edward."

"Just Edward?" She looked surprised. "Not Mr Edward?"

"Edward is my first name. Shall we be on a first-name basis?"

"Mother would never approve."

She was petite and young-looking, but her vocabulary spoke of someone older. The two continued to visit for the next 30 minutes until Karoline's mother arrived, looking more than a little unhappy that her daughter was still eating.

"It's my fault," Edward explained in very good French. "We've been talking."

"You are too kind, sir." She smiled at Edward, but it was strained. "Karoline," her mother said in a no-nonsense tone, "I want you to finish right now."

"Yes, Mother."

Karoline's mother went on her way, and Edward watched the little girl obey. He ate his own food at a leisurely pace, not talking to his dining companion but noticing that she did take an inordinate amount of time with each bite. Edward found himself wanting to laugh.

At last he saw that she was done. He was getting ready to walk her back to her cabin when her sister arrived, an older version of Karoline but looking as impatient as their mother. On her heels was Denley, who took a seat as soon as the girls exited.

"Did you both eat?" Edward asked.

"Yes, thank you, sir. Mr Steele," Denley continued, his voice and expression respectful, "I wish to express my thanks for all your help."

"Not at all, Denley. I'm only glad you're back on your feet."

"It's good to be well again, sir."

"I can imagine."

Denley did not hang about but returned to Niki. They shared a cabin this time, since Niki's clothing had changed her role. Edward didn't see them until the next day when the charade continued. He could tell that the whole ordeal was starting to wear on Niki. She looked tired, and there was little of the spunk she'd shown the day before.

"I think I could tell you to polish my boots today, and you would actually do it," Edward said to Niki when she joined him at the railing.

"Why is that?"

"There's no fight left in you today." Edward watched her face as he said this. "You must be missing your sword."

He had done it again. Niki had all she

could do not to laugh. Instead, she continued to gaze out to sea.

"Does everyone at home get teased like
this?"

"I'm a perfect dear, if that's what you're
asking. They all adore me."

Niki kept her eyes on the sea. If she saw
his mischievous expression, she would be
lost. The thought disquieted her. When was
the last time she had felt like laughing?
When had she met someone who was so
good-natured and willing to help?

"I think you have much on your mind,"
Edward commented, interrupting her
thoughts.

"You're right. I do."

"How long after we arrive in England will
you be at your destination?"

"If all is clear, only a few days. How about
yourself?"

"About the same."

"No doubt your family will be missing
you, dear soul that you are."

This said, Niki tossed him a challenging
glance and moved on her way. Edward
watched her for a time. She was careful to
keep her head down and play the part, but
to someone who knew her even a little,

there was a regal air about her that could not be disguised.

Edward decided it wouldn't be a surprise to learn she was royalty after all and then realized he would probably never know. The thought left his heart in a quandary.

∾ ∿

Brest, France

Once in port Denley never left the deck. The *Henderson* did not waste time at the dock. There was cargo to unload and passengers to disembark, but both Denley and Edward knew that the ship planned to be back underway long before evening.

To anyone else's eye, Denley's actions would not be suspect, but Edward knew what he was about. Edward did some looking himself but saw nothing alarming. He reminded himself that he could have been fooled but was fairly certain that no one who would be cause for alarm lurked about or boarded the ship before it left for English shores.

Indeed, in very short order they were back out to sea. And this was the last leg of the voyage. Edward didn't see a lot of

Niki—Denley was on hand to play the part—but he thought that might be for the best. Even with Denley available to see to her needs, Edward knew he was going to worry when they said goodbye.

Chapter Eight

Portsmouth, England

"Are you all set?" Edward asked, having slipped into the cabin next door. Passengers leaving the ship could disembark at any time.

"Yes," Niki said, working hard to hide her feelings and almost wishing Denley were present.

"Good. Take care of yourself."

"You do the same."

Edward hesitated and then threw caution to the wind.

"I hope you won't find me presumptuous," he ventured, aware of the way she tensed, "but I wrote some verses down. You don't have to take them if you don't want to."

"I would like to see them," Niki said with relief, unaware of the yearning Edward could see in her eyes.

Edward pulled a paper from his coat pocket.

"I wrote many of them out, and when I ran out of room, I just put the references. Maybe you'll have a chance to look them up."

"I'll do that. Thank you, Edward."

She was too vulnerable for him just then. With a brief nod, Edward slipped out the door. Denley was just coming back. The two stopped in the passageway.

"Take care of her, Denley. And yourself."

"I'll do my best, sir. I wish you well."

The men parted, Edward making his way toward the gangplank and Denley into the cabin, where he found Niki sitting on a bunk studying a piece of paper. She didn't even look up when he entered.

"Everything is ready."

Niki looked up, her face thoughtful.

"Are you all right?"

"Yes." She gave herself a mental shake, folded the paper, and placed it in her pocket. "What do I carry?"

Denley had lightweight cases for her, and, though it was against his grain, led the way from the cabin, appearing to all as the older, superior servant. Niki knew her part by heart, and no one gave them a single glance as they left the ship, walked toward town, and rented the first available coach.

"Did Mr Steele say where he was headed?" Niki asked when they were underway.

"Not to me he didn't."

"How far is this driver willing to take us?"

"London."

Niki sat doing sums in her head, figuring out when they would get in and whether they would continue on from London that night or wait until morning. She was anxious—there was no getting around it—but she didn't want to arrive exhausted.

ဢ ဢ

Kendal-in-the-Forest

Niki and Denley arrived at the home of Edgar and Juliana Lawton in the late evening. Niki had not wanted to stop over in Bath but had forced herself to do so, so as not to arrive at Kendal in the middle of the night.

The forest was dense and heavy around them, but as soon as they drew near the house, light could be seen. The coachman,

familiar with the area, made his way compe-
tently up the lane and to the front door. Niki
was emerging from the coach's interior when
the front door opened. She slipped inside,
nodded to the butler, and immediately made
for the stairs. The rustle of fabric sounded
behind her, but she didn't look around.

At the top of the stairs she turned right
and went to the bedroom she'd claimed as
her own. Once inside she turned to see a
longtime friend enter, lantern in hand.

"Heavens, Niki!" Juliana wasted no time.
"Why in the world are you dressed as a servant?"

"It's a long story," she said as they em-
braced. "Help me with my hair, will you,
Jules?"

"You're late, you know," Juliana scolded.
"Gar and I have been worried for days."

"I've been a little worried myself."

"Which dress?" Juliana asked, getting
down to business.

"Anything will do."

Ten minutes later, feeling thrown together
and not caring, Niki made her way down the
stairs. She stopped at the door of the large
drawing room where Gar met her. She
sighed over his tender embrace.

"Hello, Gar."

"Hello, Niki. Are you all right?"

"I am now. How are they?"

"Wonderful, as always."

Niki took a huge breath, suddenly overcome with emotion.

"Don't fall apart now," he encouraged.

Niki nodded. "I'll go in."

Edgar opened the door and let her enter alone. As the door shut, she stood still for a moment and only looked at the little boys inside. Still in the shadows, they did not notice her entrance. Knowing her voice was going to shake, she called to them.

"Christopher. Richard."

Hearing her sent them into immediate motion. The blocks on the floor forgotten, they sprang up.

"Mama!"

Niki began to run, meeting her five-year-old twin boys in the middle of the room and going to her knees to hold them. She tried to touch every part of them, kiss them, and talk to them all at one time, and all while crying.

They tried to talk as well, and after a few moments of damp mayhem, Niki fell silent.

"We missed you," Christopher admitted, his eyes on her face.

"And it's almost Christmas!" Richard put in.

"I made it just in time, didn't I? And I missed you too."

"Where did you go this time?" Christopher asked.

"You'll never guess," Niki teased them.

"France?"

"No."

"Italy?"

"No, much farther."

The boys looked at each other, and Niki took pity on them.

"I was in Africa."

Their little mouths rounded with surprise, and Niki laughed. At the same time she heard the door open.

"It's Denley!" the boys cried, scrambling from their mother's arms to greet him.

"Hello, Master Christopher; hello, Master Richard."

"Denley," they told him, very serious, "Mama's home, and she's been to Africa!"

"Africa?" He appeared to be amazed. "How splendid. Did she see elephants?"

The boys looked to her, and Niki laughed.

They ran back, headed for her lap, but she had come to her feet, knowing Denley needed her.

"Yes, Denley," she prompted kindly.

"If I may, Mrs Bettencourt, I think I might retire for the evening."

"Of course, Denley. Thank you."

He nodded, weary but at peace, and slipped back out the door. The boys already had their mother's hands, taking her to see their blocks and the small town they were building. Niki went back to the floor and listened to their chatter, a mixture of French and English.

"Were you good boys while I was away?" she asked them, watching as they grew quiet. Niki looked between them, surprised by this reaction.

"Does someone want to tell me something?"

"We fought today," Richard admitted. "I punched and Chris kicked."

"What was this about?"

"We both wanted the special ball."

"And who got it?"

"No one. Uncle Gar took it, and we had to sit in chairs."

"Did you apologize to each other?"

Their heads bobbed, their looks contrite.

"Did you apologize to Uncle Gar?"

This one stumped them, and looking at their adorable faces, fair hair falling on their brows, Niki had all she could do not to laugh.

"Shall we go and find him?" their mother suggested, her eyes soft with tenderness toward them.

The little boys agreed, and since it was growing a bit late, they found Gar and Juliana in their room.

"May we disturb you?" Niki asked even as the boys climbed on their bed, clearly having been there before.

"Of course," Juliana replied as she stopped brushing her hair and Gar set his book aside.

"The boys have something to tell you."

In another mix of French and English, the boys reminded Gar that they had fought and were sorry. Gar held them close, and told them all was well. They kissed him soundly and returned to their mother.

"Go to your room now, and ready yourselves for bed," she ordered. "I'll be right along."

Niki watched them head out and then turned back to her friends.

"Where did the French come from?"

"That's my fault," Juliana admitted. "I thought I would teach them a little, completely forgetting the years they'd been around it, and with a few lessons, it came pouring out of them. Now every sentence is a mixture of both languages. It's so amusing, I can't stand to correct them."

Niki laughed. "I can't believe how big they are. Have you ever seen anything so precious?"

"Never," Gar agreed.

"I'm going to sleep in with them tonight. I'll see you in the morning."

"Be ready to talk," Gar ordered, and Niki said that she would be.

Once Niki had gone to her own room to change into her nightgown and robe, she slipped down the hall and found the twins making little progress with their bedclothes. They were looking at a picture book and not moving very fast. Niki didn't lecture them but worked on small buttons and shoes, content just to be near them.

When the boys were finally ready, Niki climbed into the middle of the bed they shared, and smiled as the two of them moved to either side of her.

"Are you going away again?"

"No," Niki said, begging God to let it be so. "We're going to be together now."

"Here at Kendal?"

"Yes. Won't that be fun?"

Without warning the boys agreed, both speaking at once and in the hysterical mix of a dual language.

"Can you do something for me?" Niki cut in gently after letting them ramble for a time. "I would like you to speak only French until you go to sleep."

Thinking this a great game, Christopher and Richard giggled and concentrated, saying things just to try them out.

Niki corrected them a number of times and worked on their pronunciations until all three were spent. The small group fell asleep as they were, snuggled close without moving.

❧ ❧

Several hours later, Juliana found she couldn't sleep. Taking the lantern, she went to check on Niki and the boys. Holding the light high, she studied the three fair heads, looking even younger in sleep. They belonged together as they were right now.

Her heart ached for their dilemma. The thought of losing the boys was almost more than she could bear, but Niki's separating from them again was worse.

Wondering if she would sleep at all, Juliana went back to her bed. She had things to say, and in the morning she would say them. She finally fell asleep with a plan, completely unaware that Gar would beat her to it.

಄ ಄

"You can't do this any longer," Gar came right out and said at the breakfast table just hours after his wife had been in the boys' room. "You're thin and pale, Niki, and you can't go on this way."

"I won't be doing it any longer," she said quietly, still in her robe and sipping tea from a perfect China cup. "I decided on this trip: I won't be separated from the boys again. It was too much this time."

"What happened, Niki?" Juliana wanted to know. "Where were you?"

"Denley became ill. I've never seen him like that."

"How ill?"

"Very. He slept all the time and had a high fever. One doctor even spoke of bleeding him."

"Where was all this?"

"We were on a ship out of Africa. It was to make a swift stop in Lisbon and go on, but Denley was too ill to continue. We disembarked and stayed at an inn."

"And you handled all of this on your own?" Juliana sounded as horrified as she felt.

"As a matter of fact, I didn't. There was a gentleman who stepped in."

The Lawtons stared at her.

"Who was it?"

"His name is Edward Steele."

"Was he one of Pomeroy's men?"

"No, nothing like that. He and Denley ended up in the same cabin together on board ship. Denley was so ill that he asked Edward to look after me. Edward agreed and would not be parted from us until Denley was back on his feet. It took several days, but it felt like weeks."

"Well, there's no harm done in that," Gar

spoke with relief. "We're just thankful you had someone."

"He figured it out," Niki added and waited. As she expected, her hosts were stunned.

"Is that why you arrived here last night looking like a servant?"

Gar had not been aware of this, and Niki sat quietly as Juliana explained. "You can't believe how different she looked. I would have passed her on the street and never known her."

Gar looked back to Niki. "All right, Nicola, all of it. I want the whole story—every word."

Niki began. It was early, and the boys would not be awake for some time, so the three were not interrupted. The Lawtons had occasional questions, but for the most part they sat in silence and listened to Niki's unbelievable tale.

"You were actually held up?"

"Yes. They didn't take anything, thanks to that sword we worked into my coat."

"So that was before your servant act?"

"Yes, I didn't become a servant until the very end."

"And did you actually work as a servant to this man?"

To their surprise, she smiled and laughed a little.

"He was without mercy," she told them, still chuckling. "He wanted his tea hot and his boots shined."

"And all this time he knew you were a woman?"

"Yes. He has three sisters, and I get the impression that he teases them nonstop."

The Lawtons were utterly silent. This had not been a part of the plan, and Niki's looking back on it with laughter threw them off completely.

"I almost forgot," Juliana suddenly said, going to the sideboard and coming toward Niki with a stack of letters. "Some mail caught up with you."

Niki looked through the letters and even read one of them. She looked thoughtful, and Gar would have questioned her, but the boys came tumbling in.

"Good morning, my darlings," Niki greeted them, bringing them close for warm hugs and kisses.

Declaring themselves to be starving, they sat at the table and waited patiently for food to arrive. It didn't take long.

While they ate, Niki talked with them. She

learned more about the things they had done in the weeks she'd been away. She had only been gone six weeks this time, but it seemed much longer. The boys were taller, and she thought their vocabulary had improved.

An ache filled her over missing these developments, causing her to be more determined than ever to miss nothing more. She didn't know what the days would bring in the near or far future, but whatever it was, the three of them would go through it together.

❧ ❧

Her excitement at seeing the boys notwithstanding, trooping through the woods with them for more than three hours exhausted Niki. Her feet hurt from the shoes she wore, and she'd scratched the back of her hand on a branch. When Gar, who had led this little expedition, said he was going on to the creek to fish for a time, Niki waved the white flag.

"I'm headed back to the house. I'll see you when you return."

Not willing to miss an opportunity to fish,

even for their mother, the boys blew kisses to her and merrily chased after Gar. Niki would have liked someone to carry her back but forced herself to keep moving, even going so far as to search for Denley when she returned.

She found him sitting quietly in the side yard, a book open on his lap.

"How are you?" Niki asked, waving him down when he started to stand. She took a chair nearby. "Please tell me you're getting lots of rest," she begged.

"I am, thank you. Are you well?"

"Yes, just concerned about you."

"I'm fine. I'll take today and tomorrow off, and then I'll be ready whenever you are."

"You're a gem, Denley. Have I told you?"

He smiled a little and inclined his head modestly. Niki left him to his book, circling around the house and going in the front door. She had no more stepped inside then Juliana snagged her.

A hand to her arm, Juliana said, "We'll just head into this small, sunlit parlor right here and have a little talk."

"All right," Niki agreed with a laugh, wondering at her hostess' singsong voice.

"Sit down," Juliana commanded after she'd shut them inside.

Niki did so and noticed that her friend took a chair that put them very close together. Juliana leaned toward her in a conspiratorial manner.

"All right, it's just the two of us now. Tell me about this man."

Juliana felt an alarm when Niki didn't laugh, make light of it, or try to change the subject.

"What do you want to know?"

"Tell me his name again."

"Edward Steele."

"And where is he from?"

"You mean specifically where in England? I don't know. I was willing to say so little that I never felt I could ask."

"But he did stay here in England? He disembarked from the ship and remained here?"

"Yes, he's English."

"How old is he?"

"I would guess mid to late twenties."

"Good-looking?"

"Very."

"Dark or light?"

"Medium brown hair, and very tan."

"Why had he been in Africa?"

"I don't know."

"Why did he help you?"

"I think because he told Denley he would."

This gave Juliana pause. It was almost impossible to get a clear picture when Niki knew so little, but this man could not be ignored. Niki's entire face changed when she spoke of him. She simply must know more.

"What if he's married?" Juliana questioned, asking the next thing that came to mind.

"Well, he did nothing improper, so he has nothing to be ashamed of."

"But that doesn't help you."

Niki smiled at her in understanding.

"I know little beyond his name, Jules, and I certainly told him next to nothing about myself. I highly doubt I will ever see him again."

"But you'd like to, wouldn't you?"

"I wouldn't mind, but not every man wants a ready-made family, and of course he knows nothing of the boys."

Juliana sat back, clearly working out a plan. Niki laughed at her.

"This is not funny!" Juliana declared. "You

meet a man who makes you laugh and smile for the first time since Louis died, and we have no way to find him or even know if he's available. It's just too wretched!"

Niki only shook her head. "Wretched or not, it's a subject we have to drop for the moment."

"Why?"

"Christmas is a week from tomorrow. What do we have planned?"

"Were you able to shop?"

"A little. How about you?"

"Yes. Let's sneak up to my room right now, and I'll show you what I found."

The women did not need to sneak about. Gar was still fishing with the boys, who were probably getting cold but also having too much fun to care.

Indeed the women had more than an hour to make plans before the threesome arrived, all looking for hot drinks, the boys not seeming the least bit suspicious that Christmas had been the main topic while they were fishing.

Chapter Nine

Niki slept in her own room this night. She had gone in with the boys at bedtime, joined them in their bed, and talked to them until they fell asleep, but she then moved to the next room for her own rest.

The house grew quiet. It was a cold night, and her blankets were warm, but sleep was eluding her. Niki saw the piece of paper that Edward had given her on the table by her bed. She reached for it and, the lantern still burning low, moved into better light to read. For long minutes she just studied his handwriting. She liked the way he wrote his d's, and then realized he had two of them in his name, giving him years to perfect that letter.

A verse from Proverbs suddenly caught her eyes. *Trust in the Lord with all thine heart, and lean not unto thine own understanding. In all thy ways acknowledge him, and he shall direct thy paths.*

Niki knew she had not done this. Indeed

she had rarely acknowledged God before choosing a path, unable to feel she had a choice.

And what of now? How will I know what do to? How does one know Your will for one's path?

Niki thought about God and the things Edward had said to her. She felt she knew God, but not as Edward did. And what of her boys? Did she not want better for them? She didn't think they had ever questioned her about God or the existence of a higher being. Why would they? The Lawtons never went to church, and Niki hadn't attended since she'd been on the move. The boys had no exposure in that area.

Niki glanced at the paper again, and this time her thoughts went to Edward. She liked that he was taller than she was. She liked that his hands were large and well cared for. His teasing eyes came to mind, and Niki felt her heart squeeze a bit.

I find a man I'm attracted to and what do I look like? A snobbish male aristocrat and then a servant!

Working not to think about it, Niki blew the lantern out. She made herself lie still and willed sleep to claim her. For all she knew, Edward Steele was married. If that was the case, she had no business having such warm thoughts about a married man.

❧ ❧

The five of them were on an outing. Gar led the way, the boys behind him, with Juliana and Niki bringing up the rear. They were going to find a Christmas tree.

"I think it should be a Christopher tree," that little boy stated innocently.

Gar and Juliana laughed, but Niki flinched a little. Did he really know so little of the season?

"Hurry, Mama," Richard called out to her as they darted off the path into an area that looked promising.

Niki plunged ahead, her mind on Gar Lawton. He was unlike any gentleman she'd ever known. It never occurred to him to have a servant come along to cut the tree they chose. Such an adventure was only enjoyed to the fullest if one did all the work oneself. And of course, the boys went along. They had lived with the Lawtons for the last three years of their lives and thought the sun only rose in the sky when Gar got out of bed in the morning.

Niki knew that he and Juliana loved the boys like their own, but was their influence the best for their impressionable little hearts? And what of her responsibility? She knew very well that Gar and Juliana were not the ones who would have to answer for how the boys were raised. As their mother, the job and duty were squarely in her lap.

"What have we here?" Gar suddenly asked, and Niki thought he'd found the perfect tree. Bringing up the rear, she was the last to see that they'd gathered near a bush.

"See the nest," he said to the boys, and Niki tried not to feel like an extra. Would she ever spot such special little things, or would she always be looking in the bushes for the men who followed her, anxious to keep her sons safe?

"What bird lived here?" Richard asked.

"I think it looks like an old robin's nest," Juliana replied, giving her opinion.

"Where are the birds now?" Christopher wanted to know, looking around a bit.

Gar discussed it with the boys, and Niki, unable to miss the fact that her sons' full attention was on Gar, listened along with them. When they moved on, Niki joined them, but her thoughts were in a very different place.

In only the last few days she had begun processing thoughts through new channels. Things that had been before her all along now took on a new and clearer meaning. She knew the boys would miss her if she went away again, and even though they always welcomed her back with great love and affection, she also knew that their world was complete without her. A part of her was relieved by this, but another part was horribly grieved.

And had she really accomplished her purpose? Her husband's mother had been intent on keeping the boys and raising them herself. Mrs Bettencourt was even willing to have Niki out of the picture completely, offering her any amount of money to travel and live her own life. When Niki had realized the plan, she'd done everything in her power to stop her. But hadn't the elder Mrs Bettencourt still accomplished her purpose, at least in some way? She wasn't raising the boys, but Niki wasn't with them either.

The thought so distressed Niki that when a tree was found, it barely registered in her mind. Gar began to cut it, keeping the boys well back. Finally Juliana's voice got through.

"I'm freezing, Edgar," she said in a no-nonsense voice. "As soon as this tree is cut, I'm headed back to the house."

"All right, love." He glanced at his wife, Niki now beside her. "Niki looks cold too. Take her with you."

Niki smiled at him, mentally agreeing. She was cold, but it went far deeper than the sensation on her skin. When Juliana turned for the house, Niki gladly accompanied her, but long after they were wrapped in quilts by the fire, hot cups of tea in hand, Niki was still cold.

≈ ≈

"Look, Mama!" Richard called to his mother when he heard her come across the roof. "Uncle Gar found the Little Dipper!"

"May I look?" Niki asked, smiling at him in delight.

"Here you go." Gar stepped out of her way. "Have a seat."

Niki gasped with delight when she took the offered chair and put her eye to the scope. It was an amazing view of the Little Dipper in a crystal clear sky on this cloudless night.

"We can't let a clear night like this pass, can we, boys?"

"No," they both agreed.

Niki took a little more time and then stood up.

"That was fabulous," she said sincerely. "I'm so glad I came up."

The boys took some moments telling her what else they'd seen, their voices filled with the excitement they felt.

"Are you both warm enough?" she asked them when she could get a word in. She was already a little chilled in her light coat.

"We're warm."

"I'm warm."

They answered in their own way.

"We'll not be much longer," Gar promised the young mother. "And we'll find you as soon as we come indoors."

"Thank you," Niki said, even as she thought about the way he reassured her. Had she sounded tense? Had she hovered and made him think she was worried?

"How are they doing?" Juliana asked when Niki joined her in the small sitting room. The fire was delightfully warm, and Niki sat near, pulling a large coverlet over her. Denley suddenly appeared to offer her hot tea, which she gratefully accepted.

"They are having a marvelous time. I was even able to see the Little Dipper."

Juliana perked up over this.

"I haven't seen the Little Dipper in ages. Maybe I'll head up."

"Go, by all means."

Not at all sorry about being left to herself, Niki stared into the fire and thought about life with the boys. She wasn't worried about being on her own with them. They never ran out of things to do or talk about. The fear was over being found out and having nowhere to hide and protect them.

Before her thoughts could roam much further, the family came back inside. The boys made a beeline for their mother, their cold little persons climbing onto her and trying to get beneath the coverlet.

"Snuggle close," she encouraged them. "We'll get warm together."

"Mama," Richard was the first to speak. "We want to sleep on the roof some night."

"Not yet," Christopher put in, "but when it's warmer outside."

"That sounds very interesting. Who had that great idea?"

"I did," Richard told her. "And Chris liked it too, and so did Uncle Gar."

"Am I to join this adventure?"

"You can't," Richard said plainly. "You'll get cold."

"What's to keep you from getting cold?"

"We'll sleep next to Gar."

Not until that moment did Niki realize that the Lawtons were very quiet. She looked across at them where they shared the roomy davenport and found them smiling at her.

She shook her head at Gar's mischievous grin and listened again to what the boys were saying. An hour passed before she told them it was bedtime. Waiting until they'd kissed Juliana and Gar, Niki sent them on their way.

"We need to talk," she told them both, her voice firm. "If you're going to bed, that's fine. I'll just come to your room." She stopped and looked at them, her eyes saying she was quite serious. "Nevertheless, I'll check here first."

Gar and Juliana shared a look as she left,

neither one even thinking about moving from that spot.

❧ ❧

"Are you leaving?" Richard asked as he watched his mother fold his small shirt and lay it on the dresser.

Niki looked at him.

"No, Rich, why do you ask?"

"We heard you tell Gar and Juliana that you wanted to talk."

"And I do." She sat on the edge of the bed. "But not about my going away. I don't plan to leave you boys again."

"But sometimes things change," Richard put in.

"Yes, they do." Niki knew she had to be honest. "But this time I'm not going to leave without you."

Both boys looked at her.

"What are you thinking?" Niki asked, but they couldn't answer her. Richard said nothing, and Christopher only shrugged. Niki read their faces and could find no distress, so she kissed them goodnight and made her way back downstairs. Gar and Juliana were as she'd left them.

"Are they all tucked in?"

"Yes. They asked if I was leaving them again."

"Are you?" Juliana asked.

"No. They heard me tell you I wanted to talk and made assumptions." Niki didn't keep speaking, but her friends waited. "I guess I shouldn't have said that we need to talk," she continued, her voice calm and even. "It's you two who need to talk."

"Why is that?" This came from Juliana.

"Because I can tell that you're bothered about something, and I wish to know what it is."

Juliana looked to her husband, but he was still staring at Niki.

"Jules knows nothing of this," Gar began. "That is to say, I haven't discussed my realizations with her, but I've had some thoughts just since you arrived back. I did plan to ask you about them."

"Is there any reason you can't do that now?" Niki wished to know.

"The only reason that comes to mind is that I haven't figured out a way to ask gently, and I have no wish to be harsh."

Niki didn't expect this, but neither was she going to run from it.

"I don't bruise that easily, Gar. You may state what's on your mind."

"So be it," he said, still aware of the way his wife watched him. "It's just occurred to me that old Mrs Bettencourt has gotten her way. I mean, she hasn't had control over the boys as she wished, but neither have you been able to be with them. And I think that is a crime."

Niki smiled. "Only just today I had that same thought. I'm glad you had it too, Gar, because I'm standing by my decision not to be separated from them again. I said that to you my first morning back, but I didn't know if you took me seriously, so I'll say it again: If I feel a need to leave here, I'll take the boys with me. I know that no one's heart will go unaffected, but I feel it's what I must do."

Juliana's hand came to her mouth. Covering his own hurt, Gar reached for her.

"Please don't cry, Jules," he begged.

"I can't stand the thought of not seeing them."

"We will see them," Gar stated confidently. "We'll either go to them or have Niki and the boys back here or wherever we live." Gar shifted so he could look into her eyes. "Don't let it make you sad."

Niki ached for the tenderness of a man in her life. Gar looked at Juliana as though she were priceless to him. He was a bit older than she was and had never believed he would find love. When he'd spotted Juliana, he'd lost his heart completely. The only thing missing had been children. They'd never been able to have any. Niki's children had filled that empty place. She could only imagine how painful it would be to take the boys away.

"I'm sorry, Niki," Juliana apologized, trying to control herself.

"It's all right, Jules. Think of how I must feel every time that coach takes Denley and me away."

Her friend nodded in real sympathy.

"So what does this look like right now?" Gar asked the only question on his mind. "Are you and the boys leaving soon?"

"I'm not planning on that. Hopefully we won't need to move for some time, but it has occurred to me that come spring we might need to relocate for a while. That isn't to say we won't be back, but it might be for the best.

"One of these days I'll have to put them in school, and that will certainly limit where we can be, but for now, we might need to keep moving to be safe."

The Lawtons understood. They always knew it would come to this but had not been able to imagine the actual event.

"Do you think I'm doing the right thing?" Niki asked, suddenly filled with doubts.

"Yes." Juliana surprised her by being the one to answer. "The boys need you. We can't tell them about their father, and much as we love them, you are their mother. If you were not able to care for them, it would be a different story. I wish with all my heart that they could stay forever, but you're their mother."

Gar was nodding to all of this, and Niki's heart knew no end of relief.

"Will you give us some warning?" he suddenly requested.

"Certainly, and I don't believe it will be any time soon. I want to relax and enjoy Christmas, and beyond that, this last trip drained me. I feel worn out, my brain sluggish. Unless we're spotted, I don't plan to move for several months."

Details as to where and how had not

been worked out, but it didn't matter. The Lawtons knew of her plans and would support her. For the moment, she couldn't ask for anything more.

❧ ✒

Christmas morning was wonderful. Niki had found a Bible in the library and began by reading Luke 2 to the children. They sat very quietly, even knowing that gifts awaited, and Gar and Juliana seemed to enjoy the biblical account as well. Niki changed the subject when Christopher wanted to know what a virgin was, but other than that, it was a very special time.

Snow had dusted the ground overnight, and the boys were ecstatic. Just as soon as gifts were opened, Denley helped the boys into their outdoors things, and they went outside with their mother to play.

There was a sense of safety at Kendal-in-the-Forest. The house was large and well built, but it was more than that. The woods were lush and felt protective. Niki knew that she couldn't put too much stock into such feelings, but with all the traveling she'd done, it was hard not to.

As Niki was taking in the trees and still-falling snow, a small, wet snowball suddenly splashed into the side of her head. Her thoughts had been miles away, and she'd completely missed the fact that the boys had worked to build an arsenal of snowballs, all of them filled with leaves. Niki started on her own pile, and while far behind theirs, did her best to defend herself.

Watching them from the window, Juliana smiled at the sight. She was completely unaware that Gar watched the scene from another room, tears coming down his face as he told himself it would probably be their last Christmas together.

❧ ❧

It was mid-January before Niki was able to awaken in the morning without feeling beaten down by fatigue and worry. She had rested for nearly a month, clearing her mind of everything and simply trying to regain her balance in the unsettling life she'd found herself.

And all this time her mail had piled up. With no inclination to read letters from anyone, she had not been even the least bit curious as to who had written or what anyone had to say.

Her mail always came to her by a very circuitous route. She had several people outside of the Lawtons who were on her side and willing to help. Those people had gotten word to friends and the very small number of family Niki had left to inform them that she was out of France and moving around. It was through these people that her mail was forwarded and finally arrived in her hands. She might not get a piece for several months after it was written, which kept her awfully behind on news, but it was worth it to keep the boys away from their paternal grandmother.

Niki scrambled out of bed long enough to retrieve the stack of letters and then scooted back under the covers to read them. She made herself comfortable on the pillow and hoped someone would arrive with tea before too long.

The first letter was from Vernay, a man who lived in France and had been a good friend of her husband's. He didn't have much to say, and Niki wondered if he didn't feel rather obligated to keep in touch. She doubted she would write back to him and hoped that he hadn't been convinced by Patrice Bettencourt, Louis' mother, to help her find the twins.

The next letter was of greater interest. Niki's Aunt Mary was in touch. She hadn't had communication with her in a very long time, and she wasn't even a true aunt—the relation was rather distant—but her letter, written in a lovely hand, captivated Niki from the start.

Dearest Niki,

It's been a very long time. I hope this letter finds you well, but I can't imagine anything is in place with the way your mother-in-law has treated you. I hope you don't find me intrusive, but I was in London recently to do some Christmas shopping and saw Lyssa Seadon. She informed me of your situation. I have been praying for you ever since, but right now I feel as though I want to do more.

Please consider our home in your travels. We are quite tucked away here, and in case you've lost track, all of our children are grown and in their own homes. You would only have to put up

*with the two of us, and we would love
to see you and your precious little boys.*

Niki read on in some surprise, thinking
back to when she'd last visited her Aunt
Mary. It had been many, many years, but
the memory was a good one. The letter
closed:

*No matter what you decide, please
know that I hold you close in my heart
and prayers, believing that God has a
plan for you and the boys.*

*Much love to you now and always,
Aunt Mary*

Niki didn't reach for the rest of her letters
for quite some time. Mary's words had done
strange things to Niki's heart. How many
weeks had she been at Kendal-in-the-Forest and not sought out a church? Old fears
died hard, but so did stubbornness, and
she was realizing that she had been leaning
on herself for far too long. If she and the
boys went to Aunt Mary's, maybe she could
learn more.

A knock on the door interrupted these
musings as Violet, Juliana's personal maid,
came with the tea tray. Niki accepted it

gratefully and enjoyed a full cup before the boys found her. They wanted to snuggle for a short time, but wrestling soon ensued, and Niki almost found herself with a lap full of hot tea.

"Go and dress," she commanded them, rescuing all involved. "We shall breakfast downstairs as soon as you're ready."

The boys left with only a bit of complaint, and Niki went back to Mary's letter. She read it again and then folded it carefully for later review. She skimmed a few more letters, but none held her interest as Aunt Mary's had.

The boys were back before she was ready, having already been downstairs and found her missing. Niki threw herself together, promising herself a long bath later, and went to join her children at the breakfast table.

ᔕ ᔕ

More than a week later, Gar found himself in the mood to carve wood. His gifts at Christmas time had been small wooden soldiers for the boys—nearly an army of them—and lovely intricate bookends for

Niki, all carved by his own hand. Those done, he proclaimed he had nothing in reserve and must carve more.

"But, Gar," his wife concluded, "Christmas is past, and there are no more birthdays until the fall."

"You never know when you might need a gift," he reasoned as he kept his head bent over his work.

Juliana left him to it, keeping the boys from his workroom when they came looking for him.

"We want to go in the woods with Gar," they pleaded, trying to convince her.

"Well, dears, he's busy," she replied gently but firmly. "You'll have to talk me or your mother into it."

The boys looked more than a little doubtful, but when Juliana mentioned it to Niki, she looked game.

"I think a romp in the forest sounds lovely."

"You do?" Richard questioned. "It's muddy."

"I think I can survive a bit of mud," Niki told them, crossing her eyes for good measure.

The twins ended up grinning at her and

grew even more excited when Juliana said she would go along as well.

The women let the boys lead, trailing after their laughter and shouts of excitement.

"I've made a decision," Niki quietly told her friend.

"The letter from your Aunt Mary?" Juliana guessed. Niki had already mentioned it.

"Yes. She's invited us to stay with her."

"And you're going?"

"In March."

For a moment Juliana stopped and faced Niki. She smiled at her friend, even though her heart squeezed in pain. Her first inclination was to look after her own heart, but she knew that wasn't fair.

"Are you a little afraid?"

"A little. I've depended on the two of you for so long now that I'm not sure what I'll do."

"Well!" Juliana became all at once logical. "We're not going anywhere without telling you, so what you'll do is come right back to us."

Niki hugged her almost fiercely.

"Tell Gar for me, Jules," she whispered. "I don't think I can."

"I'll take care of it."

The women separated and moved after the boys. Both were covered in mud, and very soon the women were not much better. Nevertheless, they laughed and enjoyed themselves. If the laughter was strained at times, no one commented; both knew the recent decision was for the best. Crying wouldn't change a thing.

১ৎ ৯৲

Her plans made, Niki sat down that night with paper, quill, and ink. The letter was simply put and gave nothing away.

Dear Aunt Mary,

Thank you for your kind offer. I shall come and bring the boys. We shall arrive in mid-March. We will not stay if this will not work. It's doubtful you'll be able to get a letter back to me in time. Once we arrive, do not hesitate to tell me if you've changed your mind. Even if we can't stay, it will be lovely to see you.

Thank you again,
Niki

Collingbourne,
England

Chapter Ten

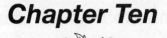

March 1813

Edward Steele sat comfortably back in the coach as it took him toward Collingbourne. His brother, Henry, had been ready to join him for a brief shopping trip but realized he had some pressing unfinished business on his desk.

None of Edward's needs were very urgent, but his friend and brother-in-law, Thomas Morland, was soon to have a birthday, and he wanted to look for a gift. Benwick, the local merchant, could always be trusted for his wares, and Edward headed there first. If the trip afforded a stop at Gray's tearoom before he left town, well, that was only a bonus.

Dressed warmly, since middle March could be on the cool side, Edward kept the curtains down until they arrived in town. He'd told the coachman where he wanted to go, and when he saw that they'd pulled up in front of Benwick's, he moved toward the door. The coachman beat him to it, holding it wide for him to emerge.

"I think you'd better wait," Edward requested.

"Yes, sir."

His hat in place, he stepped toward the door, his mind already wondering what he might find. The chaotic order of the interior never failed to fascinate him. Over the years he'd found the mundane and the unusual and, on occasion, the spectacular. Hoping for just such a find today, he began his search along the shelves.

He hadn't gone very far when he heard voices. For a moment he couldn't place their location and then realized they were from far below him. Glancing down and to the end of the aisle, he saw two little boys. They were talking excitedly in a mixture of English and French, and they were studying Edward's Hessian boots.

Edward watched them for a moment, but they never looked higher than his knees. Not able to resist, he went toward them and hunkered down to their level.

"Hello, boys. How are you?"

"You have Hessian boots," one of them said, not wasting time with niceties.

"Yes, do you have some?"

As though they'd been waiting to tell someone for years, they began to speak about it to Edward, still in the amusing mixture of French and English.

"We want Hessian boots," one child said.

"But Mama refuses," the other filled in.

"She says they're too expensive."

"It's because we're going to grow."

Edward nodded a bit, trying to take in the disjointed sentences even as he studied their identical faces with their perfect skin and straight, blond hair. Edward had decided they were beautiful just as they stopped and looked up at him.

"I'm Edward," he began, putting out his hand. "And you would be?"

"Christopher," that child supplied, shaking Edward's hand with a bit of awe.

"Hello, Christopher. And you would be?"

"Richard," the other boy said with a smile, liking this man who, though younger than Gar, was nevertheless kind as he was.

"How old are you, Christopher and Richard?"

"Five," they said together.

"Five is pretty old, but I'll tell you boys something: I didn't have Hessian boots when I was five either."

"You didn't?" They looked as stricken by this as they were by their own plight.

"No. I was older before I got my first pair."

"How old?" Richard wished to know.

"I can't remember exactly, but older than five."

Edward watched as the two adorable faces turned to each other, exchanging a glance of exasperation and camaraderie. Edward wanted to laugh as he watched them. He was just getting ready to question them again when he realized he was being watched. He glanced up to find James Walker looking at him, a huge smile on his face. Edward pushed to a standing position, his knees creaking a bit.

"Hello, Walker. Are these yours?"

"No, but Christopher and Richard are staying with us for a while."

"Grandchildren?"

"No. Mrs Walker's niece is also with us."

"Well," he said, looking back down to the boys, who were studying his feet again. "You're sure to have fun."

"Indeed," Walker agreed. "Mrs Walker always wanted twins and can't get enough of these two. We'll see you later, Edward. Come along, boys," Walker instructed. Edward waved when they looked his way. He smiled as they stole a last glance at his boots.

Edward went back to his search for a gift and found what he was looking for, but he wanted to laugh every time he remembered Christopher and Richard.

ᔆ ᔆ

Pembroke

Alexander Tate told his wife, Cassandra, sister to Edward Steele, that he had a headache. A fall from a horse a little more than a year before had brought to Tate a time of blindness. For this reason Cassandra was always a little concerned when his head pained him.

"Shall I read to you?" she asked solicitously, coming near the sofa where he lay in the music room and taking his hand.

"No, I don't think so."

"A cool cloth?"

"No." His voice was quiet, and Cassandra stood in indecision.

"I know it's not your favorite, Cassie," Tate suggested, "but maybe if you played softly on the piano . . ."

"Of course I will," she told him without hesitation, heading to that instrument just seconds later and getting situated before the keys.

Tate settled himself a little more comfortably and waited for the music to begin. Cassandra chose a soft piece, a lullaby, because she thought Tate might wish to drop off to sleep. Playing the piano was not her favorite pastime—she didn't care for her level of skill—but she made an effort to please her husband.

About halfway though the piece, Cassandra glanced at the man prone on the davenport and noticed that although his eyes were closed, his smile was huge. Wondering how he could look so pleased when he was in such pain, she continued to watch him. She looked to the music from time to time, but her eyes searched her husband steadily. For this reason Cassandra knew the exact moment he caught himself and schooled his features.

Seeing it, Cassandra had a smile of her own. Ever so gently and softly she finished the piece, her fingers as light as she could make them.

"Something else, dear?" she asked gently.

"Please," Tate murmured, well satisfied with himself on hearing the rustle of pages.

Without warning, Cassandra pounded the keys with a boisterous piece, not worrying about missed notes, timing, or tempo. As she watched, her husband shot into a sitting position on the sofa and turned to gawk at her. Cassandra's look was sweetness itself, and Tate knew he'd been found out.

Laughing at his own little joke, Tate came to his feet to approach her, but Cassandra had other ideas. She came off the piano bench in a flash and put the piano between them.

"*I know it's not your favorite, Cassie, but play something softly on the piano,*" she mimicked him, her eyes flashing with something between humor and vexation.

"Come now, Cassie," Tate coaxed, laughter filling his voice as he tried to get close to her. "You have to admit that it was a little bit funny."

Cassandra bit her lip to keep from laughing and said, "I thought the funny part was your sitting up in surprise."

"What gave me away?" Tate asked, hoping she wouldn't notice the way he moved relentlessly after her.

"I saw that huge smile when you didn't think I was looking. And don't you come near me, Alexander Tate!"

"We can't have that." He was still chuckling. "I think this constitutes a fight. We've got to kiss and get over it."

"Absolutely not! I thought you actually had a headache. That was a terrible thing to do."

"I might get one if you don't kiss me."

"If you get one, you deserve it."

Tate was done stalking her. They had circled the piano during the entire conversation, and now he was through. He rushed at Cassandra, whose legs were much shorter, but she dashed around the davenport to avoid him. Tate stood in front of it, his eyes telling Cassandra he was up to the challenge.

"You're not going to get away," he said when she glanced toward the door. "I won't let you."

"I'm angry at you. Don't speak to me."

"It's not talking I want to do."

Again she bit her lip to squelch a smile and looked around for ways to avoid him. It was a terrible joke on his part, and she was not going to reward him with a kiss or anything else.

Tate made his move while Cassandra was trying to gauge her distance to the door. One moment she was standing alone, and the next moment he'd manacled her wrist with one large hand.

"Let go of me, Tate," she commanded.

He ignored her, scooped her into his arms, and returned to the front of the davenport to sit down, neatly placing her next to him. His arms around her, her hands against his chest, Cassandra looked up at him.

"Can I have that kiss?" he asked.

"Are you going to lie to me again?"

"Not until the next time," he said, taking her so by surprise that she laughed before she remembered she was supposed to be angry.

Tate smiled down at her, his eyes alight with love.

"Will you forgive me?"

"Yes." She smiled back, unable to help herself.

Cassandra's hands moved from his chest to his face, her small hands warm against his cheeks as they kissed. "I'm glad you don't have a headache," she said after a time, her heart too tender to bear a grudge.

"I shouldn't have done that, but you never play for me, and I do enjoy it."

Cassandra made a face. Tate shook his head.

"I'm never going to convince you, am I? I *like* the way you play, Cassie."

"I'll work on it," she granted for the moment, but he could see that her heart was not in it.

Tate didn't comment before kissing her again. In the midst of their embrace, Cassandra thought he might be using the wrong tactic: If he promised to hold and kiss her, she just might want to play.

რ. რ

Newcomb Park

"What did you find?" Henry asked of Edward as soon as he arrived home from town.

"I'll show you," Edward said, leading the way to the round table that sat in the middle of the foyer. Pushing the flower arrangement aside, he set a wooden box down, flipped the catch, and opened it to reveal a geologist's kit.

Henry bent over the box and inspected the rocks, guide book, and various tools. It appeared to be a very complete and well-made set.

"Do you think he'll like it?" the younger brother asked.

"Yes, very much," Henry said, his eyes still on the items in the box. "Even Lizzy will like it," he added, referring to the sister who had married Thomas Morland less than a year before.

Edward looked pleased. He had spent a generous amount but knew the gift could be from both of them.

"I think I'll ask Cassie to wrap it. She's good at that."

"That's a good idea; then you can check on her too."

"Why would I need to do that?"

Henry's brows rose.

"Did I not mention to you that I thought she looked pale and tired on Sunday?"

"No, you didn't."

Henry frowned again. He was not a man who spoke every thought—he knew there was no need—but at times communication was important. This was just such a time. For several days his youngest sister, Cassandra, had been in his thoughts, but he'd not mentioned it to Edward when he meant to.

"I'll go and see her and Tate later today," Edward filled in, feeling as though Henry needed to be rescued. "Don't give it another thought."

Henry nodded. "When I take my ride in the morning, I may head to Pembroke too, but do let me know if you see Cassie."

Edward agreed and watched Henry move on his way. He was a different man from a year ago. Henry Steele, the oldest of the family, had always cared about his family, but no one had been able to tell. Now he was much more verbal, and all of his family knew of his deep love for them.

Still reflecting on his brother's positive changes, Edward tucked the geologist's kit into a safe place and went in search of lunch. Ready to relax with the newspaper, he would take his time over the meal, but he'd head to Pembroke as soon as he was done.

~ ~

Pembroke

"Did I just see Edward leaving?" Tate asked Cassandra as he joined her in the garden that afternoon.

"Yes. He came by to say hello."

Tate studied his wife's face.

"Is everything all right?"

"I think so." Cassandra looked a little confused. "He confessed to being concerned about me."

"In what way?"

"My health. He wondered if I was feeling all right."

"And are you?"

"Yes, I'm fine. I'm just not certain what Henry might be seeing."

"How did Henry get into this?"

Cassandra explained the conversation her brothers had shared earlier that day. Tate looked surprised but also watchful. His wife's brothers had known her a good deal longer than he had. It was true that they no longer lived with her, but as her husband he'd be foolish to ignore something they might have seen.

"What's this?" Tate asked, spotting the wooden box at her feet.

"Oh, a gift for Morland's birthday. Edward asked me to wrap it."

"I'll take it inside for you."

"Thank you."

Tate went on his way with a smile from his wife. Cassandra went back to the flowers she was inspecting, but her heart wasn't in it. Edward's visit had been kind but also unsettling. Cassandra moved among the flowers for a while longer but soon gave up, went inside, and tried to bury herself in a book.

ॐ ॐ

Thornton Hall

Marianne Jennings shifted the infant at her breast, bouncing him slightly so he would go back to eating, her eyes studying his dark hair and soft, beautiful skin.

William Jennings II was one month old. Arriving on time and with little fuss, he was nothing short of miraculous to his parents and greatly loved by his four older siblings.

The three oldest children in the family were not technically his siblings; they were wards of her husband, William Jennings I, but from her heart's standpoint, Thomas, James, and Penny had never been anything but family.

Catherine Anne Jennings, who would enjoy her second birthday during the summer, was William's full sister. Talking nonstop and dropping to her stomach to take the stairs at lightning speed, she often seemed to be in two places at once, and when she wasn't making them laugh, she was making them tired.

With five children in a 16-year age range, life was busy. Marianne looked forward to times when she could feed little William just to gain a few minutes of peace and quiet.

This afternoon he was done all too soon. Marianne had no more put him back in his cradle when Thomas came looking for her. He wanted to go riding with friends, and Catherine, who had trailed him, wished to go along as well. Thomas reached down to take her in his arms.

"If you go with me, who will be here to play with William when he wakes up?"

Catherine looked at him with wide eyes.

"You'd better stay and help with the baby," Thomas suggested.

Catherine nodded in compliance and wanted down. When she toddled on ahead of them, Marianne looked to Thomas with amused eyes.

"That was swift thinking."

Thomas, tall now and very grown-up, grinned at her before heading downstairs. Catherine's nanny, Sophie, had followed after her young charge, but Marianne still followed everyone down to the main floor, wanting to check on James' and Penny's plans for the afternoon.

A conversation with Jennings from the night before suddenly came to mind. He'd asked why she seemed tired lately. Marianne smiled and thought that he'd have to follow her around someday to find out.

∽ ∾

Sunday morning saw Henry and Edward in the carriage headed to church. Henry's eyes were trained out the window on this sunny March morning, but Edward was studying his Bible.

At times Henry glanced at his brother and

wondered whether he was memorizing a verse. The younger Steele would study a page and then look away. He did it all the way to the church building and even in the pew before the sermon began. Henry, who was very happy with quiet and his own thoughts, didn't think to ask him about it until after the service was over.

Edward explained, "I'm working on some verses in Ephesians."

"Have you got them down yet?" Henry asked as the men walked outside.

"Just about. I enjoyed the fact that Pastor Hurst referred to Ephesians 6:13."

"Which verse was that?"

"It ends with 'having done all, to stand.' That verse is the one right before Paul lists the armor of God."

"I recall it now."

The men were well onto the gravel yard that spread out in front of the church. They squinted against the sunlight and heard small voices.

"It's Edward!"

Leaving Henry for the moment, Edward walked toward the voices, smiling hugely when he saw Christopher and Richard coming his way, both dressed up for church but not in matching outfits.

"Hello, Christopher; hello, Richard. How are you?"

"You're not wearing your boots," Christopher mentioned, his brow furrowed a bit.

"No, not today. Shall I wear them tomorrow?"

Both boys nodded, thinking this a grand idea.

"We still don't have any," Richard told him, his face showing his woe.

"You have a nice suit of clothing on today, though," Edward encouraged, and watched Richard look down at his jacket as though seeing himself for the first time.

Christopher launched into the fun things they were enjoying at Blackburn Manor, James Walker's home, telling Edward about rides with the pony, reading with Aunt Mary, and playing on the veranda when it rained. Edward was laughing over their descriptions when the boys' mother approached. Edward looked up and saw Niki, everything inside of him freezing for long seconds and making him breathless.

"Mama!" the boys began at once. "It's

Edward. He has Hessian boots like we want."

"He didn't wear them!"

"Boys," Niki said in a soft voice that wasn't nearly as deep as he remembered. "We're speaking English today."

"We forgot" were the next words from them, and Edward stood by, unable to stop staring at this woman.

This was not a Niki Bettencourt he'd ever imagined. This Niki was soft and feminine, and her hair was blond and beautiful, just like the boys'. Edward was still staring like an idiot when the boys took off, leaving them on their own.

"Your sons?" he asked quietly.

"Yes."

Edward nodded but couldn't speak. How was she old enough to have five-year-olds?

"Does this answer a few of your questions?" Niki asked.

"Yes, but it begs a thousand more."

A small smile came to Niki's mouth as she nodded in understanding.

"You smiled," Edward said, his own mouth lifting at the corners.

"Niki does," she stated simply. "Osborne doesn't."

"Are you all right?" Edward asked, his voice unable to conceal the concern he felt.

Niki nodded, finding her heart oddly touched.

"And Denley?"

"He's very well."

"Is he here?"

"At Blackburn Manor, yes."

"I don't believe the Walkers have ever spoken of a relative named Niki."

"It's a rather distant relation; Aunt Mary and I cheat a little with the aunt and niece part."

Edward studied her, unable to help himself.

"The royal air is gone," Edward said, a bit of wonder in his voice.

Niki laughed a little. "Osborne is rather full of himself. It just comes naturally with that suit of clothing."

"Which one is the wig?"

Still smiling, she said, "Osborne wears a wig."

Edward nodded, his lungs still searching for air. "Your children are beautiful."

Edward was unprepared for this smile. Niki Bettencourt looked as though she'd been handed the moon.

"I certainly think so," she admitted, her eyes soft as she glanced around to find them.

"Where is Mr Bettencourt?" Edward asked before he could stop himself.

Niki's eyes came back to his.

"He's dead."

"I'm sorry," Edward returned most sincerely, wondering how recent it might be.

Silence fell for a moment, but then Edward realized he needed to know one more thing.

"Are you with Walkers for a time?" he asked just as the boys arrived back. They didn't interrupt, but even with a glance Edward could tell they had something on their young minds.

"That's the plan," Niki suddenly said, and Edward nodded, wondering if he could wait until midweek to have his questions answered.

"Mama," Richard tried.

"Just a moment, Rich," she said to him before turning back to Edward.

"My brother meets with Walker most weeks," Edward supplied. "I may tag along."

"Maybe I'll see you," Niki said, her eyes kind, her demeanor calm.

"Goodbye, boys," Edward said, nodding to Niki, and moving on his way.

Henry was already at the coach. He hadn't missed Edward's long conversation with Niki Bettencourt, but neither did he question him during the ride home. He waited until they arrived back at Newcomb Park and sat down for lunch.

Chapter Eleven

The Manse

"Did you see her twins?" Judith Hurst asked of her husband. Their youngest, Robert, rested in her arms. "I'm worn out with one baby. What would two be like?"

"Twice the fun?" Pastor suggested, his brows rising in humor.

Judith laughed but also shook her head, not sure she agreed.

"They're beautiful children and seem very sweet, but I can't imagine being widowed so young."

"Can you imagine being widowed now?"

Judith looked at her husband and pastor.

"You always say things that make me think, Frederick."

"Isn't that good?" He was smiling a little.

"That all depends on how tired I am."

"And with a newborn, you're weary all the time."

"I fear so," Judith said, smiling at Frederick before looking back to the tiny person in her arms.

Pastor moved into the dining room, Judith slowly following, to find their four older children all waiting in their places for lunch.

"May I hold Robert?" Jane, the oldest girl, asked hopefully, but her mother encouraged her to eat first.

The Hursts spoke of the morning and the different families in the congregation. The children had some interesting insights on their father's sermon, and as always, Pastor was all ears.

"Father," Jeffrey, the oldest child, asked in the midst of much discussion, "is it hard to concentrate when Mrs Sheridan's baby cries during a main point?"

"No, because he cries each week, but when the unexpected happens—like John falling from the pew about two weeks ago— that sets me back."

The whole family laughed at this memory, and John looked shy and embarrassed. His father winked at him, and he smiled a little.

Margaret had a question about the sermon, and the conversation shifted to that topic. Happy for the diversion, young John went back to his meal, hoping he would never fall from the pew again.

≈ ≈

Newcomb Park

"You seemed rather preoccupied on the ride home, Edward," Henry commented. "Did I see you speaking to Walker's niece?"

Edward looked at his older brother, his mind still trying to comprehend that Niki had shown up in Collingbourne of all places. He had been certain he would never see her again.

"Don't wish to speak of it?" Henry guessed when Edward stayed quiet for a moment. Henry's words seemed to release him.

"I have the most amazing story to tell you, Henry. I know I can count on your discretion."

"Why, Edward," Henry teased, "you know what a chatterbox I can be."

Edward laughed as he began, never dreaming that Henry would interrupt, but not long into his story the oldest Steele stopped his brother.

"You can't mean to tell me that Mrs Bettencourt was hidden in her disguise?"

"That's exactly what I mean to tell you."

Henry shook his head in disbelief. "I may not be overly distracted by women in general, Edward, but not even I can miss how attractive and feminine she is. However did she pass unnoticed?"

"Easily. I was the only one who seemed to give her a second glance."

"But what of her needs and privacy? What did she do?"

"I don't know exactly. We never shared a room."

Henry took a moment to process this.

"Where were her children?"

"I don't know, but I'm hoping to find out. If you're headed to meet with Walker this week, I'd like to go along."

"And you think she'll answer your questions?"

"Yes, I do. I mentioned joining you, and she was gracious about the possibility."

Henry's mind tried to conjure up a masculine image of Niki Bettencourt, but he couldn't manage it.

Edward smiled as he watched him.

"Are you certain about all of this?"

Edward laughed. "I will admit that at times I felt as though I was dreaming, but it was all very real."

"And is she all right?"

"She said she was."

"Edward." Henry suddenly became very stern. "Do you have feelings for this woman?"

Looking stunned, Edward asked, "As in romantic feelings?"

"Precisely."

"No, not at all."

"I watched you stare at her," Henry argued. "As did half the church, I might add."

Edward laughed. "If you could have seen her the way I last saw her, you would understand."

Henry sat back in relief. They did not know enough about this woman for Edward to fall for her. Henry was utterly relieved to learn that Edward had kept his head about him.

"So are you going to Blackburn this week?" Edward asked.

"Wednesday. Want to come along?"

"You know I do."

"On one condition," Henry surprised him by saying.

"Name it."

"That you tell me what she says."

Edward's head went back when he laughed. It was not like Henry to be overly busy, but clearly this had fascinated him. Edward, hoping only that he would learn the whole story himself, was happy to agree.

Ռ ௲

Brown Manor

Anne Weston and Lizzy Morland laughed as Anne's daughter, seven-month-old Sarah Weston, crawled between them, happy to give smiles and wet kisses to either woman.

"She's always so happy," Anne stated with pride. "She doesn't even fuss at nap time."

"That's amazing," Lizzy said dryly. "Even I fuss at nap time."

Anne laughed before asking how she liked being married.

"It's wonderful to be married to and living with the man you love," Lizzy told her, and she meant it. "I can't imagine starting as you did, Anne. It amazes me."

Anne smiled. "There were times when I wondered what I'd done, but do keep in mind, Lizzy, that Weston is a marvelous person. He's not spoiled like so many gentlemen. He's kind and takes delight in the happiness of others."

"Well, I can see that you're happy," Lizzy said, envy filling her heart as she watched Anne with Sarah. She tried to squelch the emotion, but it lingered off and on throughout her entire visit.

During the ride home in the carriage, Lizzy worked to dispel the black cloud coming over her. She wasn't very successful. Even after she arrived back at Ludlow, she could not drive off the feeling.

Usually Morland heard her arrival and came to greet her. Today he did not. Lizzy was slightly relieved. She was down at the moment and didn't want to burden her husband with her poor attitude.

Besides, she told herself, *Morland's birthday is tomorrow, and the family is coming for supper. You've got things to do.*

Lizzy learned that this was easier said than done. When her husband finally tracked her down in the small salon, she was trying to concentrate on the menu and making a complete mess of things.

"When did you get back?" Morland

asked as he bent to kiss her. Lizzy was at her desk, and Morland took a nearby chair.

"Not long ago."

"I was in the study. Did you not look for me?"

"No, I thought I should work on this menu for tomorrow night."

Morland had seen the paper and now watched his wife's face. There was more going on than his birthday the next day, but he didn't start there.

"How are Anne and Sarah?"

"They're fine." Lizzy's voice took on a wistful quality. "Sarah must be the loveliest child in all of England."

"She's beautiful," Morland agreed, having seen her on Sunday. "Tell me, Lizzy, did you find me a birthday gift?"

"Yes," Lizzy answered, looking surprised.

"Are you fearful that I won't enjoy it?"

"No, I think you will."

"How about the party? Is it too much for you?"

"It's only the family," she said by way of explanation.

"Then what's wrong?" Morland came out and asked.

Lizzy studied her nails for a moment.

"I was trying to hide it from you," she finally admitted.

"Hide what and why?"

"I came home from Anne's in a terrible humor, and I didn't want you to know."

"Why is that?"

"Because it's wrong. I have no reason to be unthankful."

Morland finally caught on. She wished for a baby of her own. She had spoken of it several times, but he'd forgotten for the moment.

"I was reading in 1 Samuel this morning," Morland suddenly told her, "the first chapter. I was struck by Elkanah's words to Hannah when she had no children. He said, 'Am I not better to thee than ten sons?' "

Lizzy stayed quiet, listening to her husband.

"I was also struck that we know the end of the story. We know that God honored her request and gave her Samuel and other children. We don't know the end of our own story, Lizzy. We might have children and we might not.

"And I was thinking that if we didn't, and God asked of me, 'Am I not worth more to you than ten sons or daughters?' I would want to say 'yes, Lord, You are.' Does that make sense?"

Lizzy nodded.

"I don't wish to make light of Hannah's plight—she was in terrible pain—and I know that question was asked of Hannah by her husband, and not of me by God, but it's still a good way for me to measure my attitude."

Morland fell silent then and let Lizzy take it in.

"Thank you, Morland," Lizzy said, her heart a mix of relief and pain. She was thankful that he'd understood without a lot of words but almost wished she could cry her eyes out in self-pity.

"Come here," Morland said softly, holding his hand out and waiting for Lizzy to sit in his lap. She snuggled close against his chest and felt him press a kiss to her brow.

"I love you, Morland."

"And I love you, Lizzy—more than I can say."

Lizzy tipped her head back to look into his eyes. Before he kissed her, she saw every bit of love written there.

Blackburn Manor

"I've been meaning to ask you a question since Sunday," Mary Walker said to Niki on Tuesday morning while the boys played in the yard.

"What is it?"

"Have you and Edward Steele met before?"

Niki smiled and said, "As a matter of fact, we have."

"My goodness, Niki, what a small world. Where was this?"

"On my last illusory trip."

Mary's mouth opened in surprise.

"How did he know you on Sunday?"

"He knew I wasn't a man. He saw through it." She glanced at the boys. "He's the first person to figure it out."

"Did he say how?"

Niki actually laughed at the memory.

"He said he had three sisters."

Mary laughed with her.

"*Does* he have three sisters?" Niki asked.

"Yes, and I suppose that would make some men more astute. I can believe it of Edward."

"What's he like?"

"He's a dear. Walker has Bible study with his older brother, Henry—another fine man."

"I could tell that Edward had something special, Aunt Mary. I just didn't know how to ask him about it. He gave me a list of verses from the Bible."

"Do you want to ask me any questions?"

"May I?" Niki looked pleased, turning a little to get a better view.

"Certainly. Should I get my Bible?"

"I don't know." The younger woman looked uncertain all of a sudden.

"Why don't you ask me, and if I don't know I can get my Bible or we can check with Walker."

"I guess my question was over the fact that Edward studied his Bible so much. I've hardly studied the Bible at all. I want to, but I don't. Why is that?"

"When you wrote to me several years ago and told me that you'd trusted Christ for salvation, Niki, what church were you and Louis attending?"

"We weren't."

"Then who told you about Christ?"

"A neighbor. I was miserably pregnant with the boys, and she came to visit me each week. We started talking, and she told me that I could have peace with God. She read the verses to me, and I prayed, but I don't know if it was enough. I still don't know."

"Niki, have you ever heard of the phrase 'proving works'?"

"No, never."

"Good works do not save us. There is no number of good deeds we can do to earn heaven, but after we believe in Christ, we are changed. Good works, or proving works, are what tell others that Christ now lives in us and that we're different.

"It doesn't sound as though anyone has ever told you. The mighty act of Christ's death on the cross and our belief in His act is not where it ends. It conludes with a life of devotion to Christ, a life of putting our old selves aside and becoming what Jesus Christ wants us to be. Am I making sense?"

"I think so. Would I have learned this had I gone to church?"

"I certainly hope so. You'll learn it at our church."

"I enjoyed Sunday," Niki suddenly confessed. "I didn't know there were verses that commanded children to obey their parents. There's so much I don't know."

"Do you have a Bible, Niki?"

"No. I've traveled too much. I don't afford myself the luxury of taking books along."

"Having your own copy of Scripture is a luxury, but it's also important. We need to get one for you soon. You need to understand the God you put your faith in, so you know what He expects of you. The way to know Him is to study His Word."

Niki was suddenly back in the coach, traveling from Lisbon to Coimbra and watching Edward read his Bible. He seemed to be a man with such peace and confidence. Niki was certain the cause could be traced back to his reading of the Bible.

❧ ❧

Ludlow

The meal for Morland's birthday was a smashing success. The family gathered in great humor to celebrate, and the conversation turned to younger days at the Steele home.

"I don't remember that, Edward," Cassandra told him in no uncertain terms. "I think it was you and Lizzy who sneaked into mother's room and tried on jewelry."

"I would never do such a thing," Lizzy protested, but she received no sympathy. Indeed the table erupted with laughter and disbelief.

Nevertheless, that particular episode was debated for some time. Not until there was a slight lull did Tate get a word in.

"Come now, Henry," he urged. "You've not dragged any of your secrets out. I want to hear them."

Henry smiled and said, "I was angelic, didn't you know?" If the laughter had been loud over Lizzy's declaration, it nearly shook the room over this. Without missing a beat, Henry's siblings took delight in reminding him of some of his escapades. For such a serious child, he had been a bit wild as a young teen.

"If I recall," Lizzy put in, "Henry got in the most trouble for being on horseback when he was supposed to be home."

"I think you're confusing me with our dear sister, Charlotte," Henry said.

"Not fair, Henry," Morland admonished. "She's not here to defend herself."

"Well, then, let's trot out her deeds," Edward suggested. "We can blame it all on her and make ourselves feel much better."

"What I wish to know," Cassandra interjected, changing the subject completely, "is if Charlotte and Barrington sent you a gift, Morland?"

"Yes," the guest of honor answered.

"What is it?"

"I didn't open it."

Cassandra looked surprised.

"But you must!" she proclaimed, and heard her husband start to laugh. "You never mind, Tate! Now listen to me, Morland—a present that arrives by post must be opened on the spot."

"But it came two days before my birthday," Morland explained.

Cassandra patiently wagged her head in his direction, the pity she felt for him clearly showing on her face.

"It doesn't matter."

"Have you not heard these rules about birthday gifts, Morland?" Tate interjected. "She has quite a number of them."

"They never worked on Mother," Henry reminded his youngest sister. "She always made you wait."

"And I have forgiven her," Cassandra said

piously, putting the room into laughter once
again.

Cassandra looked across at Tate, who
was smiling hugely at her, her look of innocence changing to laughter with the rest of
the family.

Lizzy suddenly pushed her chair back,
gaining everyone's attention.

"All this talk of gifts has made me excited. Shall we, Morland?"

He smiled by way of reply as all came to
their feet with plans to exit to Ludlow's
largest salon in order to watch Morland
open his birthday presents.

ๆ๛ ๛

Newcomb Park

Henry and Edward were still at the breakfast table on Wednesday morning when
Henry received a note. He read it to Edward.

"This is from Walker," Henry said. " 'Some
business has come up, Henry. Will it work
for you to come on Thursday? Let me know.
Walker.' "

This read, Henry looked across the table
to Edward.

"What will you do?" Edward asked, squelching the disappointment he felt. Niki and the boys had come to mind several times since he'd seen her on Sunday.

"Go tomorrow. Does that work for you?"

"I think so. Should you let them know I'm coming with you?"

"I don't think so. Although there are no guarantees that Mrs Walker or Mrs Bettencourt will be there."

Edward shrugged a little.

"If that's the case, you can join Walker and me."

"Thank you, Henry."

With that the subject was dropped, at least verbally. Edward found that the trip to Blackburn Manor lingered in his mind the rest of the day.

ဢ ⴰ

Pembroke

Cassandra woke slowly, trying to figure out where she might be. She blinked a few times before realizing she'd fallen asleep while reading in her room.

This was so unlike her that she sat up in surprise, looking down to where her book had fallen to the floor. She picked it up and stood stretching a little, trying to fully wake up.

Where her next thought came from, Cassandra would never know, but an odd feeling hit her so strongly that it could not be ignored. Setting the book aside, Cassandra exited her room and went to her desk in the small study she'd claimed for her own.

She studied the days of her calendar and began to smile. Unless the dates before her had her completely confused, she was going to have a baby. For a moment Cassandra sat and smiled, letting the delight of it sink in.

Her next thought was of her spouse. Tate had gone for a ride, not planning to be long. Cassandra glanced at the clock, wishing she'd known what time she fell asleep. She paced around inside for a time, hoping to hear Tate return, finally gave up, and walked outside. She'd been milling around for 20 minutes, trying not to look anxious, when she saw Tate heading her way.

"Well, this is a nice welcome," he said gently, coming off the horse to hand the reins to a waiting servant.

Cassandra smiled up at him and asked if he would walk with her for a time.

"You don't mind that I smell a little like that horse?"

Cassandra's answer to that was to take Tate's hand. She was so excited that she couldn't look at him as they walked, but he glanced down at her often.

"I think you have something to tell me," he guessed once they'd rounded the house and were at the rear. The foliage on that side of Pembroke was nothing short of spectacular, but Cassandra barely noticed.

"Are you going to keep me in suspense?" Tate tried again.

"No, I just thought we could walk to the bench over here and sit down."

"All right."

Cassandra could wait no longer. The moment they sat down, she turned to Tate and confessed, "I think we're going to have a baby."

Tate looked surprised by this sudden announcement, but that didn't stop his smile.

"You said 'think,'" he mentioned, his face thoughtful. "What did you mean by that?"

"Well, I've looked at the dates, and I think it might have happened."

"How do you feel?"

"Fine, but my stomach has had a hollow feeling lately, and just today I thought that might be the reason."

Not caring if he smelled like a horse or not, Tate put his arms around his wife. Cassandra sighed when he hugged her but looked up in surprise when she felt him stiffen. She suddenly found herself being held by the shoulders, Tate's serious face watching her.

"I chased you around the music room this week." Tate's tone said he was not happy.

"That's true; you did."

"What if you had tripped?"

"I probably would have skinned my knee."

Tate did not look relieved.

"We will be very careful from now on."

Cassandra had to think about this. She didn't recall anyone else being careful. Indeed, unless problems arose, the expectant women she knew carried on as usual. One look at Tate's determined face, however, and Cassandra knew that now was not the time to mention this.

"Do you suppose that this was what Henry saw in you?" Tate suddenly asked.

"I don't know, but it might explain why I looked pale and tired to him."

"Shall we tell Henry first?" Tate suggested.

"Yes, but let's wait just a bit. I'd like it to be our little secret."

Tate had no argument for that. Neither wanted to move for the next hour. They sat quietly and talked about the changes a baby would bring, as well as the joy and excitement their family would share.

"I just have one question for you," Tate finally put in. "When the baby gets a birthday gift by post, will he be required to open it right away?"

Cassandra's laughter sounded all through the yard, and Tate, unable to stop himself, could only kiss her.

Chapter Twelve

Blackburn Manor

The coach carrying Henry and Edward arrived midmorning and found Walker outside, the twins nearby.

"Good morning," Walker greeted as the men emerged, not missing the way the boys ran to Edward when they spotted him.

"Good morning," Henry greeted in return, but Edward had already hunkered down to talk with Niki's sons. In a matter of moments, they were speaking to him with rapt attention, and Walker smiled at the sight.

"Have you come to join us, Edward?" Walker asked when Edward pushed to a standing position.

"Unless a better offer comes along, and I think it has. The boys want to show me the horses."

"A sight not to be missed," Walker said graciously, although his eyes gleamed with amusement.

Henry met the twins, taking in their rapt little faces and feeling his heart melt a little. Watching as they looked to Edward as soon as it was polite, he knew that Edward had worked his charm once again.

"We'll see you later," Henry told his brother, smiling a bit. He stood quietly while Edward, Christopher, and Richard began to walk in the direction of the stables.

"How are they doing?" Henry asked out of genuine care.

"Remarkably well. It's as though they've been here for weeks. I'm weary from hours of play, but I wouldn't miss any of it."

"Edward will wear them out."

Henry might have laughed at his own words if he could have heard the twins just then. They were once again on the subject of Hessian boots, and Edward was just barely keeping up.

"I thought we were going to talk about horses," he finally put in, and with that, the boys were off on a new subject.

Edward listened in amazement. One of the things that struck Edward was how silent Niki could be. That begged the question as to where these boys learned to rattle away as though it were their last day on earth.

"This is our favorite," Christopher informed Edward once they were in the barn. "His name is King. Uncle Walker rides him."

"He's a fine horse," Edward agreed, taking in the proud head and neck on the black-and-white stallion. "What horse do you ride?"

"We don't ride yet." Richard was the one to volunteer this information. "But we go in the pony cart sometimes. Mama drives."

"Does she? Well, that must be fun."

Edward sat down on a bench outside the building, a bit of sunlight coming through the clouds. It hadn't rained yet, but the sky was mostly overcast.

The boys sat on either side of Edward, falling quiet for a moment. When he glanced at them, however, he noticed that they kept stealing glances at his boots.

"Shall we go for a walk," Edward suggested, "or do you want to sit awhile?"

The boys were off the bench so fast that Edward laughed. Rather loath to move from his sitting position, he rose slowly from the bench and began to follow the small blond boys, who seemed to know where they were going.

They weren't even a stone's throw from the barn when Edward spotted Niki heading their way. Edward removed his hat as she approached, greeting her loudly enough that the boys turned and saw her.

"We're going on a walk!" they told her, rushing over to be close.

"With Edward!"

"Sounds fun. May I come along?"

The boys were all for this, and in very short order Edward and Niki were walking side by side, the boys skipping and dawdling ahead of them in turn. They were oblivious to the adults at their heels, and when Edward sensed this, he began to question Niki.

"Where do the boys stay while you're traveling?"

"With friends."

"Clearly friends you trust," Edward commented.

"Most assuredly."

"But you're in Collingbourne right now. Did something happen?"

"No. I just felt it was time for a change."

The answers were noncommittal. Edward

somehow thought she would volunteer more. He was quiet for a moment. As he was asking himself if his questions should be more specific or if he should drop the idea of learning more, Niki volunteered a question of her own.

"Is that all? I assumed you'd want to know a good deal more."

Edward chuckled. "And I was wondering if I should be more specific or give up pressing you."

"Ask anything you wish. When we were in Portugal, my only fear was that Pomeroy's men had hired you to gain my confidence."

"Who is Pomeroy?"

"A French agent, hired by my mother-in-law."

Edward came to a stop so he could look at her. Niki looked back, her face open as she watched him. From the corner of his eye Edward caught that the boys had stopped and were looking at them. He made himself move on, Niki falling into place beside him.

"Why would she do such a thing?" Edward asked, his voice telling of his confusion.

"She wanted the boys. She still wants

them. She desires to raise them for her own."

"I think now is the time I'll ask you to tell me the whole story." Edward glanced toward her. "Will you, Niki?"

"Yes, as long as the boys aren't nearby."

Both Edward and Niki watched as they stopped to look in a hole, but when they moved again, she began to talk.

"My husband, Louis Bettencourt, died suddenly. The boys were very young—just babies. The doctors said it was his heart. I was crushed and shaken, but my mother-in-law was devastated. She wouldn't eat for days. I felt sure she would die as well, but some weeks after the funeral, she rallied and became more herself. What I didn't realize was that she had lain there in her bed and made plans to take my sons from me.

"That first year we nearly lived with her at her estate outside of Paris. We had our own home, but it seemed to give her comfort to have us near, and she was usually very kind. But after a year had passed—the boys were just past their first birthday, and I had stopped wearing black—she encouraged me to go and do some things, telling me to leave the boys in her care.

"I didn't see it then, but she wanted me absent from them as much as possible. I did travel some, but I missed them so much that I was often back before planned. Then she asked me to visit a friend who had written that she was unwell. I did as she asked, and through one pretext or another, I was gone for more than two months. The boys barely knew me when I returned, and I hadn't been back in her home a week when she asked me to travel again. I was ready to say no, but she cried and told me how unwell she was, and as Louis' wife I must visit this elderly aunt."

Niki had to stop. The pain of that time came back to her with surprising force. She had been so naive and trusting.

"You don't have to go on," Edward said quietly, thinking that it must have been awful.

"I want to," Niki said, finding it true even as memories flooded back. "I returned as swiftly as I could, but it was too late. Mrs Bettencourt had taken the boys and moved to an undisclosed place. Only servants were left at the estate, and it looked as if she'd disappeared from the face of the earth and taken my sons with her.

"At first I was immobile with my grief. I didn't know what to do or where to turn. My father wasn't well and died shortly after this time, never knowing that his grandsons had been taken. When that happened, I realized I was fully alone. I knew I would have to find the boys on my own. And that's what I did."

"Mama!"

"Yes, Chris."

"The creek is ahead."

"All right, go on but do not get wet. Stay well back until we get there."

The boys shot off with energy to spare, and Niki picked up the pace a bit to keep an eye on them.

Edward could see that the rest of Niki's story would have to wait. His mind scrambled with the facts she'd offered. As they joined the boys alongside the slow-moving, still very cold stream that ran through the Blackburn property, he asked what he thought to be a safe question.

"How are you old enough to have five-year-olds?"

Niki smiled. "I was married when I was 16 and had the boys a year later."

"How old was your husband?"

"Significantly older, more than 12 years."

Edward looked thoughtful, and Niki couldn't help but wonder what he was thinking.

"Edward," Christopher suddenly called. "Come and see the water."

Edward moved ahead without seeing the surprise on Niki's face. She followed a little more slowly, and by the time she reached the banks of the creek, the three "men" had hunkered down to look for fish, careful to keep their knees out of the mud.

"Let's cross the bridge!" was Christopher's next suggestion.

"Come on, Edward," Richard begged, and this time Niki spoke up.

"Tell me they are not calling you Edward," she demanded.

Edward only smiled at her and went after the boys, who had already reached the small footbridge.

"Come with us, Mama," was the next call, and Niki lengthened her stride to keep up. She wanted to talk about this discourtesy immediately but could see that she was the only one distressed by it. She crossed the bridge behind the threesome, and for a time just listened.

"Look at that fish! Did you see it?"

"I did see it," Edward told Richard. "It was big."

"We don't like to eat fish," Christopher informed him, "but Gar does."

"Does he?" Edward asked, his voice giving nothing away.

"Do you know Gar?" Christopher asked.

"I don't believe I do," Edward had to tell him.

"He takes care of us when Mama travels." Richard supplied this.

"With Juliana," Christopher added, pulling at a weed with his small fist.

"They keep us safe so no one can take us from Mama."

Edward had all he could do not to look at Niki. He didn't think the boys knew of this and wondered if she'd overheard.

"Look at this rock!" Richard suddenly said, his hand going out to grasp the stone that filled his fist.

"Let me see," Christopher demanded, but Richard held it away from him. "Let me, Rich," Christopher tried again.

"No."

Niki stepped in, holding her hand out. "Please, give me the rock."

Richard did so, but not before glaring at

his brother. Niki didn't miss this, and, without even glancing at the rock, addressed her angry son.

"What's the problem, Richard? Why wouldn't you allow Christopher to see your rock?"

"I found it."

"What does that matter?"

The little boy's lip protruded a bit, and he looked on the verge of tears. Niki waited patiently for an answer, but none was forthcoming.

"Did you think Chris would lose it?"

"No."

"Then why can't he see it?"

"It's mine. I found it."

"It would still be yours," Niki said logically. "It's in my hand right now, but it's still yours."

Richard began to calm. He looked at his brother and then back to his mother's hand. "I'm sorry, Mama. I'm sorry, Chris," he stated repentantly.

Niki gave him the rock. As soon as it was in his hand, his twin crowded close for a look. Richard let him look before glancing up at his mother.

"That's much better, Rich. Thank you."

Her approval went a long way. The little boy smiled up at her in relief and even handed Christopher the rock to hold.

Edward had stood back during this exchange. He'd wandered a slight way off but returned when he found Niki's eyes on him. The boys walked farther along the creek bed, Christopher looking for a rock of his own. Once again Edward found himself able to have private conversation with Niki.

"Did Richard surprise you with his observation?"

"Completely. I assumed they didn't know a thing."

"Are you bothered that they know?"

"I'm not certain. I rather wish Gar or Juliana had warned me. I'll have to find a way to ask the boys about it."

For a moment they walked in silence, but Edward still had too many questions to remain mute.

"Why all the moving around, Niki?" Edward asked. "How does that keep Mrs Bettencourt from finding the boys?"

"She tries to track them through Osborne," Niki began, and then realized it was much larger than this. Before she could go on, Edward had another question.

"What of these friends, Gar and Juliana? Doesn't Mrs Bettencourt go after them?"

"No. She doesn't know they exist. You see, I never mentioned having a friend named Juliana Wood, since I hadn't thought about her in years. We hadn't seen each other since we were in school. After Mrs Bettencourt had taken the boys, I chanced to run into Juliana. She had married Edgar Lawton by then, and I met him as well." Niki paused and tried to gather her thoughts, suspicious that she sounded as disjointed as she felt. "When I told Gar and Juliana what I was going through, they offered to help. Well," Niki continued, choosing her words, " 'help' doesn't actually describe how involved they have become. And you can only understand that if you realize that Gar Lawton is unlike any other man I've ever met. He's a complete eccentric. He thinks moving about and keeping the boys safe is a great adventure. They've moved six times in the last three years, both in France and England, just to accommodate the boys and me. Pomeroy's men have never found the Lawtons. They follow Osborne, but he always loses them before he gets back.

"And added to all of that, the Lawtons, Denley, and I all have other friends involved. These friends get mail to a central place so we can retrieve it, and that also helps me keep the boys safe."

"Why do you not just confront your mother-in-law?"

"I tried that, but it did no good. My search took me back to the estate outside of Paris, and Mrs Bettencourt was actually there. To my chagrin, the boys were not. She had lost all charm at that point and told me with complete confidence that I would never see my sons again, and she would raise them as her own.

"The authorities did next to nothing, telling me it was my word against hers. From that point, I began to follow her. When I discovered where the boys were, months had passed. Gar, Juliana, and I sneaked in and took them away in the night. It was horrible. I don't know how my mother-in-law had managed it, but they were terrified of me. They cried for their grandmother for nearly a week before they began to settle. It was some time before we became a family again. They were so little and frightened all the time. They'll never be able to tell me what they went through, and short of my death, I'll never allow her near them again."

Edward thought it the most astounding story he'd ever heard. It was nothing short of beastly to take a woman's children from her. Edward had seen Niki with her sons, albeit briefly, but enough to recognize that she was a kind and loving mother. The elder Mrs Bettencourt could not have been thinking with anyone but herself in mind.

"So you go about disguised as a man," Edward said thoughtfully.

"Denley and I came up with that, since it seemed to throw my trackers off the path."

"Why not just stay tucked away with the Lawtons?"

"Because no one is safe forever. People talk. Servants and delivery folk share inconsequential details that seem harmless at the time, but they all lead to clues when you're tracking someone. Mrs Bettencourt has the resources to keep looking forever, which means I have to be very careful."

"How long will you stay here?"

"For as long as I can."

"Do the Walkers know the details of your plight?"

"Yes. Aunt Mary hasn't even written her children to tell of my visit. The smallest thing can lead to discovery."

"And if you have to leave here?"

"We'll go back to the Lawtons."

"What if they're found out?"

"They'll move."

"Then where will you go?"

"Wherever they are."

Edward looked at her.

"You have every detail in place."

"I have no choice."

"But what of a normal life, Niki?" Edward couldn't help but ask. "What of school for the boys? When will they know a real home?"

Niki's smile was a bit sad.

"No home is worth our separation. When the boys are a little older and not so vulnerable to abduction, I'm sure I'll be able to do things differently, but not now. Not yet."

The boys were coming back to join them. Christopher's feet were wet, and he was cold. Niki had a few words with him about stepping into the water, but even at that it was time to return to the house.

Again Niki listened as her sons chatted away to Edward, seeming never to run out of words. They talked to him all the way back to Blackburn Manor, until Denley appeared and ushered the boys away to wash and change.

"They're so talkative," Edward commented, his eyes twinkling. "And I know they don't get it from you."

Niki laughed a little.

"Gar talks a great deal, and so does Juliana. They've been with them most of their lives."

Several things came to mind when Niki said this, but the sad note Edward heard in her voice caused him to fall silent. When Henry arrived on the scene not a minute later to meet Niki and tell Edward he was ready to leave, the younger Steele felt as if both he and Niki had been rescued. It was a lot to take in, and suddenly Niki looked tired too.

The Steele brothers soon said their goodbyes and exited. Henry was quiet in the coach, but almost the moment they arrived home, he asked Edward for every detail.

ॐ ॐ

Newcomb Park

"She must have an impressive level of unlimited resources," Henry said over dinner that evening before they could even begin to eat, causing Edward to laugh.

"We spoke of Niki Bettencourt for an hour this afternoon. Have you been thinking about her all day?"

"Off and on, yes. I mean, to live as she does, she must have income from somewhere."

"True, but that never came up."

"Is this Lawton fellow a relative, did you say?"

"No, he's married to Niki's old school chum."

"Have you always called Mrs Bettencourt, Niki?"

Edward smiled. "No, I first called her Mr Osborne."

"You know what I mean, Edward. I just noticed that you call her Niki."

"I do, don't I?"

"When did that start?"

Edward tried to think and ended up shrugging, unable to remember.

The conversation moved on to several topics, including a letter from their sister,

Charlotte Barrington of Bath. Edward attended to Henry's comments and even had thoughts of his own to share, but the fact that he called Niki by her nickname lingered in his mind for the remainder of the evening.

ॐ ॐ

Blackburn Manor

As she tucked the boys into bed that night, Niki's movements were slow and thoughtful. She knew the boys were tired and ready for sleep, but she also knew that she would not get much rest if she didn't question her son about his comment to Edward.

"Hey, Rich," Niki asked, her voice calm and undemanding, masking the small flutter of emotion that moved inside of her. "Do you remember what you told Mr Steele today?"

"About what?"

"About why you stay with Gar and Juliana."

"Oh, yeah, so we'll be safe."

"What has Gar told you about that?"

"I don't know," the little boy answered, looking uncertain.

"He said that we can't trust everyone," Christopher put in, his eyes on his mother. "He said that if we wandered off, someone might think we didn't have a family who cared, so they might take us home and put us in their family."

"And you would cry if that happened," Richard added, now understanding what his mother wished to know.

"I would cry," Niki said, her hand smoothing his hair. "My heart would be broken."

"We'll stay very close," Christopher reassured her. "We'll be very careful."

"Do you have to go away now?" Richard asked.

"No, I'm going to be here," Niki answered, realizing that she'd always done this. She'd always taken extra time with them the night before she had to leave. "I don't want you to be afraid, but I'm glad you're being careful."

"Uncle Walker says that we don't have to be afraid because God watches over us."

"That's very true. He does."

"Do you believe in God, Mama?"

"Yes, I do. Do you, Chris?"

"I think so. I've never seen Him."

"Well, someone once told me that God

can be seen in all He created. Did you know that the Bible says He made the earth and every person and creature that lives on it?"

The boys looked fascinated by this, and Niki searched for words to explain, realizing how few she had.

"In the first book of the Bible," she knew enough to add, "it tells all about what God created. Would you like me to read it to you sometime?"

The boys nodded in interest, but Niki saw again that they were tired. She kissed them and blew out the lantern, her face looking serene. But as she let herself from the room, her heart wondered if one night a week she should bring them to bed early and read to them from the Book of Genesis.

Chapter Thirteen

The nightmare that woke Niki a few hours after she sought her own rest left her sweating and trembling. She knew it was a dream. She knew the sounds and images were all in her mind, but that didn't stop her next move.

Reaching for her robe, she exited her room and went to check on her sons. Not until she stood next to their bed and saw firsthand that her mother-in-law had not come and snatched them did her heart begin to calm. She stood for some minutes, her body shaking a bit.

I told the boys not to be afraid, but I don't even know how to trust You, Niki's heart confessed. *I see that they're safe—I see it with my own eyes—yet I still tremble.* Niki's heart fell silent and she breathed deeply. *Talking to You is new for me,* she admitted. *But I thank You that my sons are still here and safe. Please don't ask me to give them up again. Please help me to keep them safe.*

Niki stood for long moments, working to pray and trust. She might have stood even longer but turned when she heard a noise and saw lantern light at the door. It was Denley. Niki bent low to tuck the covers around the boys a little tighter and joined her servant in the hall.

"Are they all right?"

"Yes."

"Are you all right, Mrs Bettencourt?"

"I had a dream, a nightmare, but I'm all right now."

"Would you like me to go in with the boys for a time?"

"No, we're safe—I realize that. I just needed to see them. Thank you, Denley."

Denley gave a small bow and moved down the hall. Niki stood until his lantern light disappeared and her own eyes grew accustomed to the dark once again. Hoping she hadn't disturbed anyone else, she returned to her room and lay for a time in the dark.

She settled against her pillow, thinking about God being in all places at all times. It didn't take long for her to see that right now it was more than she could mentally manage. She curled up on her side and told herself to sleep.

❧ ❧

Pembroke

"What are you doing, Cassandra?"

Arms full of books, Cassandra turned to look at her husband, feeling very surprised at his reproving tone.

"I'm organizing some of my books. I've been meaning to for ages."

Tate took the large stack from her arms, including the two she held in one hand.

"I don't want you lifting or doing heavy jobs," Tate declared, setting the books on a shelf.

Cassandra stared at him. Had he really meant that? Did he know how silly he sounded?

"It's just a few books," she said quietly, watching his face.

"I want you resting. The books will always be here."

Cassandra, whose looks usually gave away every thought, continued to watch him with little expression on her face. When Tate looked back, she tried again.

"You don't wish me to do this at all, or was I lifting too many books at one time?"

Cassandra had not meant to sound sarcastic, but the narrowing of Tate's eyes told her that she hadn't pulled it off.

"I don't want to see you doing this at all," Tate emphasized, his voice low and quite serious.

"Can we talk about this, Tate, or is your mind made up?"

"My mind is made up," Tate said swiftly, even as the look on his wife's face gave him pause. He thought Cassandra would be all for this. He thought she would enjoy nine months of resting and being a lady of leisure, but her face and her voice were saying otherwise.

Nevertheless, Tate reasoned, *it's for the best.*

However, an hour later when Tate couldn't immediately find Cassandra, he began to have doubts. He looked around the mansion—a large place in anyone's estimation, and even larger when looking for someone—and finally found her in their bedroom. To his astonishment, she was cleaning and organizing again.

"Cassandra," he asked sternly this time. "What are you doing?"

Cassandra turned with a few undergarments draped over her arm.

"I'm cleaning out this drawer. It's overflowing with things I don't wear."

"I thought I made myself clear," Tate said, even going so far as to remove the shift and petticoat from her grasp. "I want you to rest."

"I thought that was just about the books," Cassandra said quietly, hoping he wasn't really going to press her on this.

"I want you resting. Period."

Cassandra felt anger rising within her. That this was utter nonsense was only too clear to her, and she planned to tell her husband just how she felt! Her mouth was opening to do just that when Hastings, Tate's man, came to the door looking for him. Cassandra watched him leave, realizing that she was much too emotional at the moment.

Just remembering to tell her maid where she was headed, Cassandra grabbed a light wrap and took the back stairs. She walked out the rear door of Pembroke and onto the veranda. Not noticing the lovely blooms all around her, Cassandra began to walk in the garden, working to pray and calm down.

She traversed the grounds amid hedges and shrubs, walking swiftly but not really taking heed of anything around her. Her mind was nowhere near settled when she looked up to see Tate heading her way.

The sight of him made her angry all over again. Cassandra stopped, spun in the opposite direction, and walked on. She wanted to discuss this with Tate in a reasonable manner, but she feared if she talked to him right now, she would say things she did not mean.

Thinking he would understand her need to be alone, Cassandra was visibly startled to suddenly have him overtake her. She jumped and turned to face him, the scare making her even more upset, a fact proven by how red her cheeks had become.

Tate didn't immediately notice. Instead he made the mistake of asking for the third time in one day, "What are you doing?"

"I'm getting away from your nonsensical

rules," Cassandra said ruthlessly, shocking her husband into silence.

Cassandra took his silence as understanding and started on her way once again. She didn't quicken her pace but kept steadily on, taking several minutes to realize Tate was still with her. She stopped and faced him.

"You're angry," he said in surprise.

"Yes, and if we talk right now, I'm going to say things I'll regret."

Tate stared down at her. His heart had tried to tell him he was going too far, but he'd ignored it.

Again Cassandra took his silence for compliance or understanding and resumed her walk. Tate stayed with her, but Cassandra didn't stop or try to speak. She felt tears fill her eyes and used the back of her hand to swiftly wipe them away.

Tate saw the movement. If there had been any anger left, it drained away in view of his wife's distress. He didn't try to engage her in conversation but kept a steady pace by her side as she walked. In time she slowed, and Tate cast looks in her direction. Cassandra did the same.

By the time they had made a large circle

and were back at the rear of the house, Cassandra was ready to sit down. Tate joined her on the bench, the very bench on which Cassandra had shared her news with him.

"Are you all right?" Tate asked after a moment of silence.

Greatly calmed but a little wary, Cassandra answered, "If you're going to tell me that I can't go for walks, I'm going to move back in with Henry and Edward until the baby's born."

For some reason this amused Tate. He laughed a little, bringing his wife's eyes to him.

"We haven't handled this very well, have we?" Cassandra asked.

"No, I'm afraid we haven't. I thought you would want to rest and lie about."

"Why did you think I would?" Cassandra asked, wishing she'd been calm enough to ask him about this to begin with.

"I don't know. I certainly never imagined you wanting to organize and stay so busy."

"Why is it so important to you, Tate? Why must I rest?"

Tate shrugged a little, at a loss for words.

Cassandra waited.

"I thought it would be best for the baby. And for you," he finally confessed.

"How many expectant women have you been around?"

"None, I guess. I just imagined how it would be. Anne Weston had to rest."

"The doctor did not send her to bed until she had signs of strain. Until then she just lived her life. Marianne Jennings did the same thing. I believe Lydia Palmer did as well, and that's not even mentioning Judith Hurst. None of their pregnancies had complications, at least not serious ones, and for the most part they just lived their lives. I was planning on doing the same."

The couple fell silent, Cassandra thinking Tate would have something to add, and Tate musing over what his wife had shared. Cassandra gave Tate a little time but then asked if he was still upset. Before he could answer, Hastings came from the house and approached.

"Yes, Hastings?"

"Mrs Morland is here, sir."

"Tell her we'll be right in."

"Yes, sir."

Cassandra looked at her husband, regret filling her for the way she'd been angry with him.

Tate looked back at Cassandra and shook his head. "We'll talk about this as soon as Lizzy leaves, all right?"

"I'm sorry I was angry at you."

"And I'm sorry I wouldn't slow down long enough to listen to you."

Tate slid his hand between them on the bench and Cassandra reached for it. Husband and wife rose from the bench together and headed indoors.

𝕰 𝕽

Blackburn Manor

Niki dismissed the boys from the breakfast table, as they were both finished with their meal. She asked them to remain indoors, but they made sure she was coming to play with them soon. With a promise to do just that, Niki sent them on their way.

"They certainly talk a lot, Niki," Walker said quietly when it was just the three adults. "Where do they get that? I know it's not from you."

"Edward Steele said that very thing to me

yesterday. I think the boys chatter because Gar and Juliana allow them to."

Walker looked thoughtful, and Niki watched him closely.

"I'm sorry they disturbed your breakfast."

"It's not that, Niki, but a person who chatters incessantly reveals a restless heart. I know they're still very young, but it would be good if they could understand the importance of being quiet. They need to learn how to be comfortable in silence and have the right thoughts about it."

"How do I go about teaching them that?"

"I think taking time to sit and work on it would be helpful. Have the boys sit, and tell them they can't speak or wiggle about. I also think that learning a Bible verse might help."

"Which verse?"

"Can I get back to you on that?"

"Of course," Niki answered as she reached for her teacup, her heart still thoughtful. After only one sip she added, "I don't think I've ever memorized a verse. You might have to show me how to teach them."

"We'll keep it easy," he assured her.

Little conversation was shared as they

finished their meal, but as soon as Niki went to check on her sons, Mary Walker spoke to her husband.

"How do you think she's doing?"

"I think she's doing well. What do you think?"

"I think she's remarkably sweet. I wish she and the boys would stay forever."

"I wouldn't count on that, Mary—not unless she can learn to relax."

Mary Walker's eyes widened.

"You don't think she's relaxed?"

"Not very often. She worries after the boys—and with good reason—but it's more than that."

Mary waited for her husband to elaborate, but he didn't. She could have pressed him on the subject, but something held her back. With a mental shrug, she realized it didn't matter. Just being aware of Niki's tension was helpful. Mary would pray about that very thing, but she would also be watchful of it herself.

ズ る

"Do you boys know what this book is?" Walker asked of the twins.

The boys looked at the Bible that he had open in his hands, and Christopher said, "It's a Bible. Mama read to us at Christmas."

"I'm glad to hear that. Did she also tell you that God has written this book so we can know about Him?"

"We know about God," Christopher volunteered.

"What do you know, Christopher?"

"Mama prays to Him."

"Yes, she does. Why do you think she does that?"

The boys shrugged, not ready with an answer.

Walker looked to Niki.

"Do you want to tell the boys?"

"Certainly. I pray to God for many reasons, but especially because the Bible commands us to pray and also so I'll learn to trust Him. I ask Him to take care of me and my family."

"That's an important thing to do," Walker praised her. "And it's also important to memorize verses from the Bible. And so today I want you boys to learn a verse with me. Do you think you can do that?"

They looked a little confused, but Walker continued.

"The Bible is organized into books, chapters, and verses. The book I've turned to right now is one of my favorites. It's called the Book of Proverbs, and I'm in chapter eight of the book. Can I read the sixth verse to you?"

Rather fascinated now, the boys nodded and leaned a bit closer.

" 'Hear; for I will speak of excellent things, and the opening of my lips shall be right things.' What was the first word I read?"

" 'Hear.' "

"What's another word for 'hear'?"

" 'Listen.' " Richard knew right away.

"Very good, Rich. There are many other good words in this verse, but for right now I just want you to memorize, ' "Hear," Proverbs 8:6.' Can you say it with me?"

" 'Hear,' Proverbs 8:6," Richard said, but Christopher remained quiet.

"Can you try it, Chris?" his mother asked, watching his small face.

"Is it 'listen' or 'hear'?" he asked.

"Either one," Walker told him, "because both remind us to stop talking and pay attention."

Understanding dawned on the little boy's face, and all at once he became very interested. Walker spent the next ten minutes with the boys, going over the verse and telling them a little bit more about the Bible. Both boys were very receptive.

Niki didn't have a lot to say, but she had the distinct impression that if she suggested reading to the boys from Genesis before bed, they would be all for it.

❧ ❧

Pembroke

The day had run away from them. Tate and Cassandra's plans to talk had been interrupted time and again. Now Tate climbed the stairs for bed, knowing it would have to wait until morning. Cassandra had retired an hour earlier and was sure to be asleep.

Tate slipped quietly into the bedroom and shut the door, suddenly realizing he was wrong. Sitting with the lantern turned low, a book open on her lap, her hair falling in soft waves around her shoulders, Cassandra sat against the headboard of the bed, quietly reading.

She didn't hear her husband right away,

and Tate, wanting to stand and watch her for a moment, didn't speak. Several seconds passed before she looked up.

"I didn't hear you."

Tate pushed away from the door.

"I thought you would be asleep."

"I think I did sleep for a bit, but then I woke up and you still weren't here."

"Tibby cut her hand in the kitchen. Hastings saw to it, but I had planned to speak to him about the holes in the drive tonight, so I waited."

"You must be tired," Cassandra said as he sat on the edge of the bed.

"A little."

The couple looked at each other.

"I love you," Tate said after a moment.

"I love you," Cassandra said.

"Earlier today I asked you to take it easy. I thought I would be able to relax about your activities as long as I knew you were taking this seriously and not taxing yourself, but then I realized that's rather insulting. You do take this seriously, and you would never do anything foolish to endanger your life or the baby's."

"That was a nice compliment."

"But it's true, isn't it, Cassie?"

"Yes. I want this baby very much. If I feel uncomfortable or tired, I'll tell someone or rest, but I think staying active is very good for both of us, and that's what I planned to do."

Tate leaned to kiss her, but he didn't speak.

"You're not saying anything."

"I'm still working it out."

"What's to work out?"

"My wanting to worry about this."

"Well, I won't get angry at you again," Cassandra told him. "I'll do my best to listen."

"But you'll move home to Henry if I'm a pest."

Cassandra smiled and Tate laughed a little. They kissed again, the conversation ending on a light note. Both, however, were still aware that Tate was going to have to work this out in his heart.

೧ ೫

Thornton Hall

"How are you?" Marianne greeted Niki as the boys ran off to play with Penny.

"I'm doing well, Marianne. Thank you for

asking. And thank you for inviting us. The boys are so excited."

"It's our pleasure. Come in and get comfortable."

"Thank you."

Niki told herself not to be nervous. Mary, Marianne's mother, had said that Marianne would be very understanding if she didn't wish to speak of her circumstances, but Niki worried nonetheless.

"Mama!" Catherine was suddenly at the edge of the room.

"Yes, dear," her mother said with a smile, seeing that Nanny Sophie was close at hand.

Niki smiled as Catherine spoke several sentences of gibberish, a few intelligible words thrown in for good measure, and then went on her way.

"She's adorable," Niki said, laughing in delight.

"She keeps us busy."

"Is the baby asleep right now?"

"Yes. I'll probably have to feed him before too long. I hope you won't mind."

"Not at all."

"Was it fun nursing twins?"

Niki smiled. "I don't know if 'fun' is the word I would use to describe it."

Marianne smiled, liking this grown-up Niki very much. Prior to her visit, she hadn't seen her in years.

"Mother was telling me that you've been moving about a lot lately. Has it been nice to rest at Blackburn for a time?"

"Very nice. Your parents are so warm and gracious. They're very good at including us but still taking time for themselves."

"I know they're enjoying the boys."

"Your father taught them a verse."

"Which one?"

Again Niki smiled.

"They'll have to say it for you."

And with that, Niki's hesitancy fell away. The two talked like old friends. Memories of when they'd been together as children came rushing back, and in little time they were laughing about days and incidents from long ago.

Niki felt herself relaxing more as each minute passed, realizing that she'd worried over nothing.

❧ ❧

"Are you pleased that Walker invited us to lunch?" Henry asked his brother on the way to Blackburn. The church service had been over for nearly 30 minutes.

"Yes. Why do you ask?"

Henry looked across the carriage at him, his gaze steady but his look unreadable.

"What is it, Henry?"

"You're going to marry Mrs Bettencourt. I hope you realize that."

Edward had all he could do to keep his mouth closed. He was utterly flabbergasted that his staid, seemingly unemotional, unromantic brother had said such a thing.

"I've shocked you," Henry said mildly.

"To say the least! Why would you say such a thing, Henry?"

"Because something changed in you this week, and then again in the last few days. You were interested in Mrs Bettencourt's being here, but you didn't let your guard down until I told you what Walker said about her believing some years ago. And that was all before this morning."

"What happened this morning?"

Henry's brows rose as if to say it was more than obvious.

"You could barely keep your eyes off of her."

Edward gazed out the window. There was little sunshine but still plenty of light to see the passing landscape. Edward tried to concentrate on it, but all he could see was how lovely Niki had looked that morning in a light blue dress that accentuated her hair and eyes.

No other words were spoken, and before Edward was ready, the coach arrived at Blackburn Manor and Henry went in to join Walker. Edward feared that he would feel awkward, but he hadn't counted on the boys.

"It's Edward!" they exclaimed, throwing themselves at him in delight, words pouring out of them the moment he hunkered down to their level.

"Your verse, boys," Niki said when she came on the scene, causing the boys to grow silent.

Edward glanced up at her and then back at the twins.

"Have you learned a Bible verse?" Edward asked.

They both nodded.

"Say it for me."

"Listen" came from Christopher. Richard said, "Hear."

"Just the one word?"

"Yes."

"Very good. What's the reference?"

The boys knew that as well, and Edward smiled at them in approval. Bertram appeared, signaling for lunch to be served, and Edward let the boys lead him toward the dining room. Five minutes later they were all seated. Walker prayed, thanking God for the meal.

What followed was astounding to Edward, as he listened to his brother take charge of the conversation. Edward did little more than sit and observe.

"I haven't been to France in some time, Mrs Bettencourt. In what part did you live?"

"I lived in Abbeville and also outside of Paris."

"It's beautiful country."

"Yes, it is."

"I know your husband was French, but I don't think I've heard why you have a French given name."

Niki smiled.

"My parents loved France and the language. They lived in England but visited all the time. I was actually born in Paris, so they thought it was only fitting that I should be Nicola."

"What if you had been a boy?"

"Armand."

Henry smiled at her, and Niki smiled back.

"Why don't you tell Henry your salvation story, Niki," Walker suggested. "I'm sure he would enjoy it."

"It's not very long." She sounded apologetic.

"That won't matter."

Niki nodded, feeling somewhat embarrassed, but she was able to begin by not looking at anyone.

"I was expecting the boys. Louis and I lived on a quaint street in Abbeville. We had a neighbor who was kind, an older woman. She came to visit me every week, and something about her was special. I never asked her about it, but one day she asked me if I had peace with God.

"Louis and I had just quarreled, and I felt wretched with the twins so near. I can't say that I had peace with anyone at that moment, and out of superstitious fear that my children would be harmed by my anger, I listened to her.

"I had not been raised in church but had been taught to respect all religions and beliefs. I'm not sure I was fully listening to her until she spoke of forgiveness. I wanted forgiveness, and she said Jesus Christ would forgive me if I repented. This wasn't easy for me, but she graciously taught me, and I prayed with her. I meant it with all my heart, but I saw very little of her after the boys were born, and I've had no chance to learn about the Bible since." Niki stopped but swiftly added, "I don't blame anyone but myself for that. I haven't taken the time to learn."

"How has it been for you here?" Henry asked. "Have you learned some things since arriving in Collingbourne?"

"Yes, thank you for asking. The sermons have been most enlightening, and I've studied with Aunt Mary and Walker too."

"The boys have learned a verse," Mary put in.

"Did you learn a verse?" Henry asked them.

"Yes."

"May I hear it?"

Christopher and Richard gave their own version of the verse and looked at Henry.

"I don't think I know that verse," Henry said when he realized it was only one word. "Can you tell me where it's found?"

"Proverbs 8:6."

"Very good," he said, smiling at them before the meal continued.

At the moment Henry happened to find his brother's eyes on him. That Edward was surprised by his talkative mood was only too obvious. The older Steele shocked his brother again when he smiled gently at Edward and went back to his meal.

Chapter Fourteen

"Your brother is nice," Niki commented once they were outside. Mary had suggested a walk, but when all was said and done, only Edward and Niki had gone.

"Yes, he is—also full of surprises."

"How is that?"

"He was just a little more chatty today than I expected. He's usually rather quiet."

"Well, we know that doesn't run in the family," Niki teased.

"I think I've just been told I need to learn the verse."

Niki only laughed as they continued to walk in the huge backyard at Blackburn Manor.

"The boys seem to be adjusting well," Edward commented when the silence grew long.

"Yes, I think you're right. It will be hard when we leave."

"You sound as though that's happening rather soon."

"It's hard to say, but I'm sure it won't be too long."

"Why?"

Niki stopped and looked at him, disappointment filling her that after all this time he still didn't understand.

"Don't give me an answer I already know, Niki," Edward put in before she could speak. "Why do you need to keep on the move?"

"You know the answer to that, Edward," she said, disappointment swiftly giving way to anger. "I must protect my sons."

"Protect them, or teach them your fears?"

"What is that supposed to mean? Do you think I've made all of this up?"

"Of course not. I mean only that you can't keep running. You must see that."

"I have no choice. Mrs Bettencourt will take the boys if she finds them."

"What will she do, overpower you and Denley or perhaps kill you both?"

Niki stopped and stared at him. She hadn't let herself ever picture a confrontation with her mother-in-law. That lady held too much power over her emotionally, and Niki had never tried to reason it out.

Without another word Niki continued her stroll, Edward in step beside her. It was embarrassing to be so transparent to Edward, but she wasn't sure it mattered. He'd already seen her at her worst.

They walked on in silence until they got to the deep grasses of the meadow. Niki stopped and just stared across the field, Edward's presence beside her forgotten.

Edward knew she was thinking. He had turned completely to look at her, and she hadn't even noticed. Edward smiled as one finger went to her mouth and she began to nibble on the nail.

Edward reached up and pulled it away, bringing Niki's surprised eyes to his.

"I don't recall that Osborne bit his nails," he teased gently.

"Nail," Niki corrected, holding up the single digit. "Osborne had more control, but Niki bites this nail."

Edward smiled at her in a way that had a strong effect on Niki's heart. She didn't think he meant anything personal by it, but she suddenly wanted him to touch her. She wanted him to take her hand or hold her in his arms. The thought caused so much emotion to run through her that she felt herself blushing.

As for Edward, all he saw was the way she schooled her features. He was opening his mouth to ask her whether she was all right when he noticed that the skin directly beneath her collarbone had gone quite red. Edward's gaze went from the blush to Niki's eyes, but they gave nothing away.

"You're blushing," he stated quietly, his eyes studying her face. "I don't believe I've done anything to cause that, so I can't help but wonder what you're thinking just now."

Niki didn't answer, and at the same time the adults heard the boys approaching. Edward glanced to see the twins running across the yard toward them but quickly looked at Niki.

"What goes on behind that calm face, Niki?" Edward asked before glancing to see that the boys were approaching fast. He looked back into her eyes. "Too bad I don't have time to find out."

Anything Niki might have said would have to wait. The boys had covered the ground in good speed, pleased to have their mother and Edward together. They had a plan: Edward could take them to the creek if their mother gave permission.

Laughing at their enthusiasm, Niki granted her permission and even agreed to go with them. Not until they were on their way and she'd found Edward's eyes on her two different times did she regret her decision.

❧ ❧

Richmond

Morland and Lizzy were visiting Morland's aunt, Penelope Long. Lately she was not in the best of health, wanting visitors only for a short time, but today she was perky and ready for a newsy chat.

"So tell me, Lizzy," she asked, a twinkle in her old eyes. "Do you enjoy marriage to Morland?"

Lizzy smiled. "Very much, Aunt Penelope."

"And you, Morland? Does marriage agree with you?"

Morland only smiled at his dearest living relative, earning a chuckle from her.

"You look so well together. I think your babies will be beautiful."

Not wanting to think about it, Lizzy's heart dimmed a little, and she hoped her face gave nothing away.

"I have something for you," Penelope announced, suddenly changing the subject, much to Lizzy's relief. "Go over there, Morland, to that side board, and bring me that tea caddy."

Morland did as he was told and returned with an unusual object.

"Now this," Penelope said as she took a pear-shaped tea caddy from his hands, "was a wedding gift. You see the ornate brass *L*? Well, that stands for Long of course, but we'll just pretend that it stands for Lizzy. I want you to have it, Lizzy. It's actually made out of pear wood."

"Thank you," the bride said with pleasure. "It's beautiful. I'll treasure it."

"How is Cassandra enjoying marriage?" Penelope asked, and Lizzy went with the change in subject yet again.

Penelope had several questions for Morland, but nearly everything had been directed at his wife. Babies and children had been mentioned several times, but Penelope had not pressed the point. Morland, however, checked with his wife the moment they left in their carriage.

"Are you all right?"

"Yes."

"Are you quite sure?"

Lizzy looked over at him.

"Everyone assumes we'll have children."

"Don't you?"

"Not since I've started to worry about it."

"Worry won't help us conceive. In fact, it will probably have the opposite effect, not to mention it's wrong."

Lizzy nodded, knowing how right he was. She did not want to be weak in this area and worked to remember that God was in control. If He had a baby for them, it would happen. She needed to be thankful for all His provisions and not worry about things out of her control.

Lizzy worked this out in her mind and then looked over to find Morland's eyes on her.

"What are you thinking about?"

"That pretty nightgown you had on last night."

"I don't recall that you said anything last night."

"I should have."

Lizzy smiled a little.

"Do you want me to wear it tonight?"

Morland grinned and Lizzy laughed.

Even sharing the same seat, Morland felt she was too far away. He pulled her close and wrapped his arms around her for the remainder of the ride.

∞ ∞

Tipton

Frank and Lydia Palmer sat in the small salon in their home, their children around them. The oldest was Frank—then Walt, Emma, Lizzy, and Oliver, ages 15, 13, 10, 7, and 21 months respectively. There was family news to be shared, and even though Oliver was too young to take it in, the children always wanted to include him.

"We're going to take a trip together," Palmer announced without introduction and then waited for everyone to calm down.

"Where?" Walt got in. "Where are we going?"

"Well, the Jenningses have had such fun at Weston-super-Mare that we are going to give it a try."

"Sea bathing?"

"All of us?"

"I can't swim."

"When do we leave?"

"I don't have a bathing costume!"

Palmer found order again and calmly explained. "We'll go this summer—July or August—when the weather is warmer, and all details will be worked out, sea bathing and all."

This brought a smile to everyone's face, and Palmer and Lydia grinned at each other, pleased that the children were so excited.

"Are the Jenningses going to be with us?" Emma wished to know.

"I don't think so," Palmer answered.

"We could ask them," Lizzy suggested, shifting Oliver in her lap. "Penny loves to sea bathe. I know they would want to come."

Palmer and Lydia looked at each other. It was a fun idea, but they hadn't thought of it. They looked back to find all of the children smiling at them. The children knew that when their parents didn't answer right away and exchanged a look, they were at least considering the possibility.

"I think they're onto us," Palmer said, not bothering to whisper.

Lydia could only laugh, and the children laughed with her.

❧ ❧

Blackburn Manor

"Did you say Edward is here?" Niki asked Mary to repeat herself.

"Yes, he's come with Henry."

Niki nodded, telling her heart to calm down. She hadn't seen him since Sunday and didn't expect to see him until the following Sunday. Having him arrive midweek was exciting and unsettling.

"Did he come to see the boys?" she asked.

"What do you think?" Mary asked, her mouth smiling a little.

"I don't want to think about it at all," Niki admitted. "What should I do?"

Mary ducked her head and looked out the window to the backyard.

"I think you should go out and see if the boys are behaving themselves."

Niki smiled.

"Is he out there with them?"

"Did I say that?" Mary asked, doing her best to look innocent.

Niki only laughed, sent for her wrap, and headed that way. She told herself it was only normal to check on the boys; after all, she was their mother. But in truth, Denley had been seeing to that for her at the moment. The boys were, nevertheless, pleased to see her, and Edward smiled in his warm way, causing Niki to calm a little.

"I didn't know you were returning today," Niki said after the boys had been reminded about their verse.

"Well, Henry was coming." Edward sounded calmer than he felt. "And the boys were disappointed on Sunday not to see my boots."

Niki's eyes dropped to his feet.

"And that is the only thing I'll hear about for two hours after you leave."

Edward's brows rose before he looked down at the boys.

"I was in Portugal last year. Do you know where that is?"

"Gar showed us on the map," Christopher told him.

"Well, I saw something when I was there. Would you like to guess what it was?"

The boys took a few guesses about animals and birds, but Edward shook his head.

"I saw three boys, just about your size, and they had no shoes on their feet."

Richard and Christopher's eyes grew large.

"They couldn't afford shoes of any kind," Edward explained. "Even if they had to walk on the hot cobblestones, they had to do it in bare feet."

The boys looked at each other.

"I think it's all right to be excited about something you want," Edward finished, "but we can't forget to be thankful for what we already have."

Edward smiled down at the boys and then looked back to Niki, who looked troubled. In that instant Edward realized what he'd done. He took a step closer to her and dropped his voice to a whisper.

"I'm sorry, Niki. I had no business pushing in like that."

"That's not it. I just never know how to tell them things. I don't know what to say. I could tell that they listened to you."

"And they listen to you too. You're doing fine. They're wonderful boys. I just felt responsible because I came wearing my boots."

"That was actually very sweet of you," Niki said, and for several moments in time their eyes caught. Edward made no move to look away, and Niki couldn't have moved if she tried.

When the couple noticed that the boys were standing and watching them, neither could have said, but both realized it at the same time and swiftly moved their attention to the small people at their feet.

"What shall we do today, gentlemen?" Edward asked, his voice a little quiet. "Have you ever learned to shoot a bow and arrow?"

"Edward," Niki began, but he only turned to her and smiled.

"We'll make sure the dogs are inside."

"That's a great comfort," Niki muttered, thinking that she would have to come along for her own peace of mind.

She need not have worried. Walker had arrows with rounded tips. They struck the target but were too dull to penetrate it. Certainly someone could have been harmed, but it wasn't likely.

Niki sat back and watched the excitement for more than two hours. The boys laughed until they couldn't stand up, and Edward's antics and facial expressions were delightful. By the time Henry was ready to leave and they made their exit, Niki knew she was more than a little smitten.

ɔ ɕ

"Unless I miss my guess, you and Mrs Bettencourt had fun today," Henry commented the moment the coach started for home.

"Yes, we did."

Henry waited, but Edward had nothing more to say.

"That's it? You're not going to tell me more?"

"Well, because I suspect you watched from Walker's study window, I assume you know it all."

"Not in the least. What did she say? What did you say?"

Edward had to laugh.

"Henry, I've never seen you like this."

"Yes, you have."

"When?"

"With Morland and Tate."

Edward snorted. "Not by half. You never asked Lizzy and Cassie these questions."

"Well, of course not! They're my sisters."

"And your point would be?"

"I can't ask them personal details."

Again Edward had to laugh. His own brother a romantic! It was too funny.

"I'll have the final laugh, you know," Henry said next.

"Is that right?"

"Yes, it is. I'll remind you of this conversation on your wedding day."

"Henry," Edward said, serious now. "Why do you think I'll marry Niki?"

"You're just right for each other. She's been hurt and needs you to take care of her and those little boys. You can live close by here in Collingbourne, and the whole family can help keep them safe."

"I take it Walker has been sharing with you?"

"Yes, he's told me quite a bit."

For a time, the occupants of the carriage fell quiet. Edward was the next one to speak.

"You haven't asked me if I love her."

"You might not right now, but you will."

"Again, you speak with remarkable confidence."

Henry only shrugged before saying, "Mrs Bettencourt is not the type of woman about whom you have bland feelings. You'll fall for her and make a wonderful match."

And to that Edward had no reply. Henry was right on one account: His feelings for Niki were anything but bland, but what he should do with those feelings and how the lady herself felt was altogether a mystery.

🙰 🙰

"I need a favor, Henry," Edward requested nearly a week later as the two men sat in the carriage taking them to Pembroke for the evening.

"Anything."

"Don't tell the family that you've found me a wife."

"Of course not, Edward. It never entered my mind to share that conversation with anyone but you."

"Thank you."

"Were you disappointed not to see her on Sunday?"

"I was, yes. Rich told me that Chris was

not well and his mother had stayed with him."

"Those boys like you, don't they?"

"They seem to."

"I meant what I said, Edward. I won't say anything, but I can't promise you that Cassie has been blind through all of this."

Edward nodded.

"Are you headed to Blackburn tomorrow?"

"Yes, would you like to join me?"

Edward smiled this time. "What do you think?"

Henry didn't reply, but his smile matched his brother's.

ର ଯା

Pembroke

"This meal is excellent, Cassie," Edward commented about halfway through. "I compliment you."

"Thank you, Edward. It's one of Tate's favorite dishes."

"My, my, Cassie," Edward teased, "still acting like a newlywed. You've got to be careful, or you're going to spoil the man."

"Is that envy I hear?" Tate put in.

"I think it might be," Edward said with a smile.

"Well, I have a way to take care of that," Cassandra told him, her eyes sparkling a little.

"I'm not sure I want to know."

"Well, I'm going to tell you anyway. You need to get married."

"Not at all," Edward came right back. "Henry needs to get married, and then I can enjoy the food his wife orders from the kitchen."

"Did you hear that, Henry?" Tate said. "Even if you marry, you won't be getting rid of him."

"I'm not sure I need to be overly worried about that."

Henry's voice was so dry that the other three family members erupted in laughter. Cassandra gazed fondly at her oldest brother, thinking he was wonderful but having to agree: She couldn't imagine Henry married. Edward, on the other hand, would do very well with a wife. Cassandra was about to raise this issue again, but Tate mentioned something he'd read in the paper. The subject around the table turned political.

Edward gladly participated, more than a little aware of where Cassandra wanted to take the conversation. He didn't know if she had Niki in mind, but he wasn't willing to find out. He had no idea what he was doing right now and wasn't in the mood to discuss it with anyone outside of Henry.

For a moment his thoughts drifted to the possibility of seeing Niki the next day. His heart squeezed a little at the thought. He had all he could do not to shake his head. His heart was getting very involved—there was no doubt about that. If only he knew how that lady felt about him.

"How does she feel about that?" Henry asked, and Edward's eyes flew to him.

"She's fine," Tate answered calmly, not seeming to notice Edward's distraction. "Aunt Harriet had a particular plan in mind, but she's flexible."

"So how much longer will she be traveling?"

"Another four to six weeks."

Edward mentally shook himself. If he didn't pull himself together, Cassandra would not be the one to give him away; his own thoughts would do the job.

"Shall we have coffee and dessert in the

salon?" Cassandra suggested, and the men rose to join her.

The four went back to their conversations about lighthearted subjects until dessert was gone and several cups of coffee had been enjoyed. Tate turned to his wife and raised his brows. She smiled at him.

"We have news," Cassandra started but found herself at a loss.

"Are you going to tell them?" Tate asked her.

"I think so. I just don't know how."

"Just say it."

Cassandra blushed, and her brothers smiled at her.

"I knew something was on," Henry said quietly, rising to his feet to go and hug her. Edward was close at his heels.

"Are you taking good care of yourself?" Henry asked once he had retaken his seat.

Cassandra laughed.

"I think you stumbled onto a private matter, Henry," Edward said, catching the look between husband and wife.

"I'm doing better," Tate put in, surprising his brothers-in-law, "but for a time there I thought Cassandra would be moving back in with the two of you."

Edward and Henry enjoyed hearing the story, and then Edward had a question.

"Have you told Lizzy?"

"No. We wanted you to be the first to know."

"She'll be very pleased, but she'll also wish it was her news to share."

"Did she tell you that, Edward?"

"No, Morland did. He said she aches for a baby and thought they would have one started by now."

"I wasn't planning on it," Cassandra admitted. "It's very early, so we're not sharing the news too much, but I can't honestly say I was eager for it. I wonder why Lizzy is."

"She's a little older than you are," Henry reminded her. "And she cared for Morland before you even met Tate. She's been ready for a very long time."

Once again Henry had surprised his family. His insight and caring had been quiet and hidden for too many years.

The conversation went in all directions in the next few hours. The men talked until Tate noticed that his wife had fallen asleep by his side. The three of them finished the subject they were on, and then Tate bid his wife's brothers goodbye and gently bore her to bed.

The image of Tate lifting Cassandra into his arms lingered in Edward's mind all the way home. He couldn't help but wonder if he would ever have an excuse to take Niki in his arms.

The thought alone made his heart sigh.

Chapter Fifteen

Blackburn Manor

"Look at that!" Christopher cried as he crowded close to a rock that would more than fill his hands.

Niki and Richard joined him on the creek bank.

"That's a big one," Niki agreed. "Try to lift it, Chris."

Christopher tried first, and then Richard. Both boys were unsuccessful.

"Let me have a go at it," Niki volunteered, causing her sons to laugh.

"It's too heavy, Mama."

"You can't!"

Niki ignored them. Groaning and carrying on in a way that made the boys laugh hysterically, Niki lifted the rock—which she didn't find all that heavy—and threw it into the creek.

Screams of delight and gales of laughter rose in the air as they were all splashed with water. Niki grabbed a few more rocks and threw them in for good measure, showing the boys her muscles and laughing at their enjoyment. By the time she was done, she was laughing so hard that she collapsed on the grass. The boys came after her, and in a moment they were lying with their faces close together, mud spatters and all.

"We're so dirty, Aunt Mary will never let us back in the house."

"You have mud on your face," Richard told his mother.

"I'm sure I do. You look like a raccoon."

They spent a little time crossing their eyes at each other before Niki pushed to her feet. She took the boys farther down the creek bank, and they went on their knees in order to lean close to the water to find schools of little fish. This was how Edward found them.

For the first time the boys did not run to him but called and waved him over to see the fish they'd discovered. Niki had time to push to her feet, wave at him, and move a little ways away, careful to keep her back to him at all times.

"Of all the days not to have a hankie," she whispered furiously to herself, examining the dirt on her hands and the front of her dress, knowing her face and hair would be just as bad.

"How are you?" She suddenly heard Edward behind her and stiffened.

"I'm fine," she answered cheerfully, still presenting her back.

"Did I interrupt?" he asked.

"Not at all. The boys are still looking for fish if you care to join them."

Niki didn't hear anything else and assumed Edward had gone to the creek side.

"I take it you're as muddy in the front as you are in the back."

His voice, even closer than before, startled her into turning around. The minute Edward saw her mud-splattered face, he smiled. Niki did anything but.

"I think it's only fair to tell you, Edward Steele," she replied, her voice tight with frustration, "that no man has ever seen me at my worst the way you have."

Having experience with three sisters, Edward knew he was on thin ice, but he had to say something.

"In that case, I consider myself honored."

"I don't know how."

"Well, you must be a little bit comfortable with me."

"Or one of us has horrid timing."

Not able to help himself, Edward grinned at her. Dreadfully embarrassed, Niki didn't want to smile back but allowed a small one to peek through.

"What were you doing?" Edward asked, his voice kind.

"Just looking at fish."

"You can tell me if I interrupted."

"No, not at all. Boys, did you want to show Mr Steele anything?"

"We found fish."

"Mama threw a rock! It was big."

With that they were off, talking nonstop in French. Niki was tempted to quiet them, but this time she stood back and let Edward handle it.

"Slow down so I can get this straight," Edward begged after a moment, also using French. "How big was the rock?"

"Big!"

"Huge!"

The boys took Edward to the place and showed him the rock that could be seen in the middle of the creek bed. Edward looked at it before turning mischievous eyes to Niki.

"Huge," he said softly, and Niki's grubby fingers came to her lips in an effort to cover laughter.

She kept quiet and continued to watch the three of them, a new truth dawning on her with every passing second.

Edward glanced her way at one point and found an odd look on her face. When he could find an excuse, he sent the boys ahead so he could talk to her.

"Everything all right?"

"No, it's not," she said baldly. "It's only just occurred to me that they think you're a tall five-year-old."

Edward began to laugh.

"It's quite true!" Niki insisted. "No matter how many times I tell them they must call you Mr Steele, you're still Edward. They can't see anything else. I've never seen them react this way to anyone."

"Well, how many men have they met?"

"Not many, now that I think on it."

"And they call Mr Lawton, Gar, don't they?"

"That's true, but they never speak to the Walkers in an informal manner."

"They don't look like tall five-year-olds."

Niki heard the tease in his voice and turned her head so he wouldn't see her smile, all of which was fine with Edward. He thought her profile adorable, making her look younger than ever, especially with the mud.

Edward said the next thing that came to mind. "I don't think I ever asked you why you married at such a young age."

Niki smiled a little and walked after the boys, who were a little farther down the creek bank.

"You would have your answer if you had known my parents. They had a touch of bohemian in them and rarely said no to me about anything. My mother died when I was 12, but my father and I often traveled together. When I met Louis on a trip to Paris and fell in love, Papa was delighted. My parents had met and fallen in love when they were very young, and he assumed that was the way everyone should do it."

"Is that the way you want the boys to do it?"

Niki looked at him.

"You have a way of asking questions that stops me in my tracks."

"I didn't mean for that."

"No, it's all right. I just haven't thought about it. I long for the day when the boys are old enough to fend for themselves and not be vulnerable to capture." Niki shrugged a little. "In my quest to get them to that point, I've never even thought about their marrying."

"And it doesn't have to be thought about today. I just asked what came to mind."

"Even with just a few moments of thought," Niki went on immediately, "I would say no. I want them to take more time. For the most part, Louis and I were happy, but not all was perfect. Had he lived, we would have had many things to work on."

"As do all marriages."

"True, but I think our problems would have turned serious. I'm not sure Louis would have ever believed in Jesus Christ. He didn't like to be told what to do, and one must be willing to put oneself under authority, or so the Scriptures have led me to believe."

"Has that been hard for you?"

Niki sighed.

"At times. Trust does not come easily for me."

Edward wasn't quite sure how to reply to this, but it didn't matter: His mind was on something else she'd said.

"Did you say that your husband did not like to be told what to do?"

"Yes. He wasn't harsh with me, but if his mother demanded something of him, he would push his heel into the dirt."

"She taught him well, didn't she?"

Again Niki looked at him, her brows raised in surprised admiration.

"You've certainly taken little time to understand my mother-in-law. At times word has come to me that my keeping the boys has enraged her. She's very accustomed to having her way. No one, and I do mean *no one,* tells Patrice Bettencourt what she can and cannot do."

"She sounds like a formidable adversary."

Niki took a deep breath and admitted quietly, "In truth, she frightens me."

"You're safe here."

"Not if she finds me."

"Even then." Edward gently pushed the point, but Niki didn't seem to hear him. They had reached the boys, and Niki saw that their clothing was only getting worse. She had chosen older pants and shirts for each of them, and her own dress was ancient, but enough was enough.

"Chris, Rich, I think we'll return to the house."

"Must we?" Christopher complained.

"Yes. It's time to clean up a bit."

The boys did not move.

"Come along now," Niki urged them, and with ill-concealed displeasure they rose to their feet and accompanied her.

Watching them, Edward thought an element of thankfulness was missing for their having an outing at all, but for two reasons he didn't voice his misgivings: They were not his children, and if the slight droop in Niki's shoulders was any indication, she already had enough on her plate.

❧ ❧

Ludlow

"Lizzy, I'm going to have a baby."

The words Cassandra had whispered to her sister lingered long after she'd left for Pembroke. Lizzy had not been expecting to hear such news, but she was completely thrilled for her sister. And considering how much she wanted a child of her own, surprisingly unenvying.

Lizzy's yearning for a baby was still strong, but it didn't diminish her joy at the prospect of becoming an aunt. Lizzy smiled as she visualized Cassandra growing round in the middle. For a moment, Sarah Weston came to mind. Cassandra and Tate's baby would be just as adorable, and Lizzy knew she would fall instantly in love.

A moment later, Lizzy sat up straight in her chair. She had to tell Morland! But where had he said he was going?

"Here you are," Morland said with satisfaction as he strolled calmly into the room Lizzy occupied. "I couldn't find you."

Morland had barely entered the room before Lizzy rushed across the room to hug him.

"I have news!" Lizzy told her husband, still holding onto him.

Morland looked down at his wife's face, his heart filling over the joy he read there.

"Lizzy, are you pregnant?" he asked hopefully.

"No, but it's the next best thing. We're going to be Uncle Morland and Aunt Lizzy."

"Charlotte and Barrington?"

"No, Cassie and Tate. Can you believe it?"

"Cassie?" Morland asked in surprise, shaking his head a little. Cassandra was the youngest in the family, the one they had always tried to baby. For a moment, Morland couldn't imagine her with a baby of her own.

"You don't look excited," Lizzy mentioned, trying to read his expression.

"I am," he assured her, "but it takes a little getting used to. Our Cassie, a mother. I can't take it in just yet."

Lizzy smiled at him.

"You're looking very pleased," Morland said when he caught her eye.

"I'm just so excited for them. It's going to be wonderful."

"Are you struggling that it's Cassie and not you?"

"No, I'm all right. I think God has children in mind for us, but not just yet."

Morland bent so he could kiss her nose. Lizzy wrapped her arms around him, and they held each other close. They had been married nearly eight months, and they had been some of the happiest months of

Lizzy's life. She knew she would be plagued again about motherhood and God's timing versus her own, but for the moment, she was choosing to rest.

Aunt Lizzy, she said to herself, hugging Morland just a little bit tighter and thinking the name had a lovely ring.

ᔕ ᔕ

The Manse

"What are you looking for?" Pastor Hurst asked his wife on Sunday afternoon when he found her in their bedroom, paging through her Bible. Lunch was over, the baby was asleep, and the older children had been asked to engage in quiet activities for the next few hours.

"That verse you referred to at the end of the sermon. Robert was beginning to fuss, and I missed the reference."

"Get me started," her husband prompted.

"It was something about 'faces harder than a rock.' "

"Jeremiah 5."

Judith turned to that chapter and began to read out loud.

" 'Run ye to and fro through the streets of

Jerusalem, and see now, and know, and seek in the broad places thereof, if ye can find a man, if there be any that executeth judgment, that seeketh the truth, and I will pardon it. And though they say, the Lord liveth; surely they swear falsely. O Lord, are not thine eyes upon the truth? Thou hast stricken them, but they have not grieved; thou hast consumed them, but they have refused to receive correction. They have made their faces harder than a rock; they have refused to return.' "

Judith stopped and looked up at him.

"I can't remember why you read this."

"I was making a point about the patience of God. The children of Israel failed so many times. Even when He punished them, God was gracious, but they kept on sinning."

"I don't recall ever reading these verses before."

" 'Rock-hard faces' is a vivid phrase, isn't it?"

"Yes." Judith suddenly laughed. "It was actually helpful to have Robert deciding that he needed to be fed on the spot. His face very clearly told me that he was unhappy over not having his own way." Judith shook her head. "We want our own way from a very early age, so I'm not surprised that the Israelites had trouble getting it right."

Judith looked into her husband's face.

"You look tired, Frederick."

"I am. I'm going to nap."

"I think I'll join you."

Without further ado, the couple got comfortable in bed. They talked a bit more about the morning and the sermon, but extra rest was too necessary these days. Hoping that little Robert would sleep for at least another hour, Pastor and Mrs Hurst fell sound asleep.

এ এ

Blackburn Manor

"What did Pastor Hurst mean this morning when he said we need to be saved every day?"

"He's been introducing us to that concept off and on for several months now, Niki," Walker told her after lunch. "He's not intending to cast doubt on our eternal salvation, but heaven-bound believers need God to rescue them—to save them—each and every day from their sinful thoughts and choices.

"The first time I heard it, I was completely confused. So many of the New Testament books are written to believers, and yet He tells them to be saved."

Niki looked completely at sea. She tried to put this together in her mind but didn't succeed.

"Can you show me some places?" she asked after a moment.

"Yes," Walker answered, even as he rose and went for his Bible. Turning to the fourth chapter of Ephesians, he resettled in his armchair.

"Starting at verse 22 it talks about their former way of life, so we know these are believers, but then verse 25 tells us to put away lying, verse 27 tells us not to let Satan have a place in our lives, and verse 28 talks about not stealing but instead working hard.

"These are verses to folks who have already believed in the Lord Jesus Christ, Niki. They are still tempted to lie and be lazy. What Pastor Hurst wants us to see is how much we need to be saved every day from those old patterns. Not eternal salvation, let me repeat, but daily salvation, so we can live the life Christ gave us when we put our faith in Him."

"So it's not because I've lost my salvation. It's about sinful habits."

"Exactly."

Understanding lit Niki's face. She had complicated it in her mind, but this was simple. This she could grasp.

"Thank you for telling me."

"I pray every day to be saved from my daily sins and old habits, Niki. Mary does too."

Niki looked over at her aunt, who smiled at her.

"I'll have to work on that," Niki told her.

"Do you have any idea how proud I am of you, Niki?" Mary suddenly asked.

Niki shook her head no.

"I'm very proud. I know all of this has been so hard, but you keep working at it."

"I'm afraid I'm not making much progress."

"That's not true," Walker said. "You've made progress just in the weeks you've been here. Don't let your heart tell you lies."

Niki nodded, wondering how often her heart did just that.

"Niki, I need to ask you something," Walker interjected. "But it's not really my business."

"I don't think I'll mind."

"All right, but if you do, just tell me."

"I'll do that."

"Are you somewhat interested in Edward Steele?"

"Interested in what way?"

Thinking she would know just what he meant, Walker shrugged a little and said, "I don't know exactly. I just wondered if he's a little special to you."

Niki smiled.

"Edward Steele is the first man since Louis' death to make me laugh and forget some of the pain. He's not a man my heart can ignore."

Walker and Mary exchanged a swift glance, one that Niki didn't catch. By the time she looked back at them, they were both smiling at her in very real pleasure.

"Why do you ask?" she wished to know, having read something in their faces.

"We find ourselves wishing that you'll be around for a time," Mary confessed. "We thought Edward might be reason enough."

To this Niki only smiled. She didn't have

an answer to that question and was glad they didn't press her. In her mind, Edward was more than enough reason to stay in Collingbourne, but as in the past, the decision to stay anywhere would probably be taken out of her hands.

❧ ❧

Collingbourne

"We have to shop for baby things," Lizzy told Cassandra as the coach entered town on Monday morning, her eyes on the list in her hand.

Cassandra protested. "No, not yet, Lizzy. We'll have everyone gossiping about the possibility, and they'll be outright guessing."

"We'll be subtle."

"You can't be subtle in Collingbourne. It's too small."

"I can manage. You'll just have to study the way I do it and learn something."

Cassandra shook her head and muttered, "By the time we leave for home, my condition will be all over town."

But Lizzy was not convinced. She was quite excited about shopping for baby items and was certain she could do it without drawing attention to herself.

"We'll start at The Mill."

"Why The Mill?" Cassandra asked.

"They have the best fabrics."

"How are you going to buy fabric suitable for a baby's needs and not give this away?"

Lizzy opened her mouth to reply and then closed it.

Cassandra waited.

Lizzy stared at her sister, her brow furrowed.

"I thought I was going to study the way you do things and learn from you," Cassandra inserted.

"Yes, well, I might have been a bit hasty with that," Lizzy said, sounding comical to Cassandra, who began to chuckle.

"We could just go to tea at Gray's and call it an outing, Cassie," Lizzy suggested, and that put her sister into full-blown laughter. Lizzy, shaking her head at her own arrogance, laughed with her.

The women did end up shopping at Benwick's, taking their time and actually finding a few things, but it was nothing like Lizzy had envisioned.

They enjoyed a leisurely tea at Gray's and then headed for home, laughing all over again at Lizzy's plan and the way Cassandra was supposed to watch and learn.

Chapter Sixteen

Blackburn Manor

Juliana's letter began, *We've been discovered.* Having seen who the letter was from, Niki had gone to her room for privacy. She now sat down slowly on the bed, her eyes taking in the words.

A man by the name of Ellenborough has been put on your case. He's a chap from London with an excellent reputation for finding anyone he's hired to locate. He was here poking about, and for that reason we're moving. When we get resettled, we'll come to see if you need to join us in our new place. As always, you and Denley know how to reach us should the plan fall to pieces.

The letter went to Niki's lap, and for a long time she sat staring at nothing. For a short while she had believed that she had left the past behind. For long hours and sometimes

days, she'd forgotten that Patrice Bettencourt was hunting for her and the boys.

A sigh lifted her chest even as she tucked
the letter away and went in search of her
servant. He would need to be informed and
start making trips into town. They didn't
have to leave Collingbourne, but they would
have to be more cautious.

As Niki exited her bedroom, her mind
quite naturally went to Kendal-in-the-Forest. She loved that home and its location.
The boys did too. She wanted to cry at the
thought of never being there again.

"When will this end?" she whispered quietly, making her way down the hall in search
of Denley, the one person who had been
with her through it all.

∼ ∽

"Let me see it," Denley said to Christopher, whose tears were very close to the
surface. "Ah, yes, you did pinch it, Master
Christopher. Shall we find a cool cloth to
put on it?"

The little boy nodded, trying to be brave
even as his right index finger throbbed no
small amount.

"I'm sorry, Chris," Richard repeated.

Christopher looked at the person identical to himself, but he wasn't angry. The two little boys walked side by side behind Denley, who was the soul of gentleness and patience. The boys should not have been playing with the garden tool they'd found lying in the grass, but they had, and now Christopher was in pain.

Looking at Richard's small face, Denley thought Richard's pain might be just as great as Christopher's because he had been the one to close the handles and cause the pinch.

"Denley—" Niki was suddenly in front of him as he crossed the veranda, not seeing the boys in his wake. "I need to speak with you."

"Right away, Mrs Bettencourt."

These words were no more out of his mouth than Christopher threw himself at his mother. He didn't cry but buried his face against her and held on for dear life.

"What's this?" Niki questioned the top of his head, but Richard did all the talking. Niki heard him out and would have scolded them but thought Christopher's hurt finger might be punishment enough. If their faces were any indication, they had learned their lesson.

"Go with Denley now and get that taken care of. Then I must speak to Denley. After that, we'll sit quietly and I'll read to you."

Niki lingered on the veranda until Denley returned. Wordlessly she handed him the letter.

"Do you wish to leave?" he asked, returning the paper to her hand.

"No, but I think this merits some activity in town."

"How often would you like me to go?"

Niki had to think about this, and for the next several minutes the two put together a plan. From there, she went in to read to her sons. Privacy had become a way of life with Niki, and for that reason, it never once crossed her mind to tell Mary or Walker about the letter.

❧ ❧

Pembroke

"Cassandra Tate!" her husband said from behind her, nearly upsetting her balance. "Get off that chair."

Cassandra climbed down, trying to look

nonchalant and innocent but not quite pulling it off.

"Now, I think I've improved," Tate began severely as he crossed the room toward her. "I'm not watching you every moment as though you're going to break, but do not expect me to stand back and watch you climb onto pieces of furniture, pregnant or not."

Cassandra stood beside the chair, torn between guilt and laughter. She knew Tate would not find this funny, so she said nothing.

"What were you doing?"

"I couldn't reach the book I wanted."

Tate's expression of long-suffering almost broke her resolve not to laugh.

"You have a houseful of servants and a very tall husband."

"I didn't think of that," Cassandra admitted, and Tate caught the twinkle she had worked so hard to hide.

"You think this is funny, don't you?" He looked astounded.

"No," Cassandra lied, her eyes growing large with the effort.

Tate leveled her with a look, and Cassandra glanced away, her fingers going to her mouth.

"Which book?" he asked, keeping his ire close at hand so he wouldn't laugh with her.

Cassandra pointed.

When Tate fetched the volume, she thanked him but took it without looking up. She waited for him to leave the room, but he stood there resolutely. After what felt like a long time, Cassandra glanced into his face. That he was now fighting laughter was more than obvious, and Cassandra's smile went into full bloom.

"I wouldn't have fallen," she said when his arms came around her.

"You're probably right, but I don't think I'm willing to take the chance."

"You have been better," Cassandra encouraged him. "Not much like a hen at all."

"A hen?" Tate looked flabbergasted at being described this way.

"Did I say hen?" Cassandra asked, trying to look innocent all over again.

Tate wanted to be outraged, but he was suddenly taken with her face. He studied her freckles and beautiful eyes, all the while remembering that she was the sweetest woman he'd ever known. It didn't take long to completely forget that she'd been on the chair.

Cassandra, certain she was still in trouble, was more than happy to see her husband's head lowering. When their lips met, Cassandra sighed. She would have to stay off of chairs in the days to come, but if Tate was going to kiss her for the crime, climbing onto any stool close enough was going to be a temptation.

❧ ❧

Blackburn Manor

"Go, Niki," Mary encouraged her. "The boys will be fine, and you need an evening out."

Niki hesitated, looking down at the invitation again. Marianne and Jennings had invited her for an evening of cards, an adult evening, scheduled in two days' time. Niki wanted to go, but in truth, unless she was traveling, she was with the boys. Thinking about leaving them in Denley's care, much as she trusted him, felt odd.

Having gone through several moments of mental gymnastics, Niki looked up and saw that her Aunt Mary was waiting for an answer.

"Are you and Walker invited?"

"No, she's asked us to have the children here. In fact, all but the baby will be spending the night. Your boys will love it."

Niki nodded and forced herself to say, "I'll go."

"Good. You can send word anytime you like."

Before she could change her mind, Niki sent word but then stood in the foyer for a long time after her aunt went on her way. She wanted to be near the boys almost constantly since hearing from Juliana but knew that she shouldn't live in that kind of fear. She was finding that old habits died hard.

In fact, Niki's next thoughts were for the boys. She had to force herself not to search for them. Denley had said he would keep track of them for a few hours, and Niki knew she could trust him.

She did wonder why she couldn't relax if her trust of Denley was so great. Not wanting to give it much thought, she went to her room in order to write a letter to Juliana. Right now she was willing for anything that might take her mind from wanting to worry.

❧ ❧

Denley had not planned on visiting the library, but word traveled swiftly at Blackburn Manor. He had only had the boys outside for a short time when word came to them that Edward Steele was in the library, studying maps and charts.

The twins begged Denley to go and see him, but that man only agreed to check with Mr Steele.

"If he wants to be left in quiet, we will not disturb him. Do I make myself clear, young masters?"

The boys nodded in agreement, but Denley wondered if, in their excitement, they'd really taken it in. They walked quietly enough into the library but ran for Edward the moment they spotted him. Denley came swiftly in their wake and waited for Edward to look at him.

"We do not wish to disturb you, Mr Steele, but the boys wanted to say hello."

Edward thought, *I was beginning to think they would never find me,* but said, "I'm glad they did. Why don't you leave them here with me, Denley? We'll have a great time with this atlas and the maps."

"Very well, sir. Shall I call for them after a time?"

"There's no need. I'll make sure you're around before my brother is ready to leave," Edward told him, watching Denley bow before leaving the room.

"What have you boys been doing today?" Edward asked when they were alone.

"We went on a walk outside, and then we saw you."

"Is this a French or English day?" Edward asked, having caught a little of both.

The boys looked at each other.

"Mama didn't tell us," Christopher informed him.

"What did you speak yesterday?" Edward tried.

The boys both shrugged, and Edward laughed a little. He sat on one of the soft davenports, an atlas in his hand, and without need for an invitation, the boys sat on either side of him.

Edward opened the book, aware of their small bodies close to his and feeling things in his heart that had never been there before. It occurred to him for the first time that if Niki went away, she would take these boys with her. His pain over her departure would not be doubled, it would be trebled.

"What's this?" Christopher asked, pointing to the map of Asia.

"That's China. It's many miles from here."

"Has Mama been there?" Richard asked.

"I don't know. You'll have to ask her."

"Have you?"

"I have not. I've been here," Edward said,
turning to the page that showed Africa.

The boys were very impressed by this,
and in the next hour Edward took them on a
finger-walking tour of his travels. He didn't
mention that he'd been to several of those
places in an effort to keep their mother safe,
but those days were surprisingly fresh in his
mind.

James Walker had a fine globe, one that
sat in a very large, ornate stand in the middle of the room. When the atlas had been
exhausted, the three "travelers" went to the
globe to crowd around it and find Edward's
travels all over again.

At one point Edward showed them some
land on the top of the globe. Richard
couldn't see, so Edward lifted him into his
arms. Perched on his right arm, Richard
studied the globe for a time, but it wasn't
long before he tired a bit, and without giving

it a moment's thought, he laid his head on Edward's shoulder.

Edward didn't comment or do anything to dissuade the child. For several heartbeats he let himself enjoy the feel of Richard's soft hair against his neck, his warm weight against him.

This is the way Niki found them a few minutes later. Having run into Denley in the hall and asked about her sons, she wasted no time gaining the library.

In some ways she was now sorry she'd come. Seeing Richard's head on Edward's shoulder did the strangest thing to her heart. She felt as though she wanted to laugh and cry all at the same time.

The boys were excited that she had joined them. Even Richard wanted out of Edward's arms so he could show her the globe. In the midst of trying to find Bhutan, the boys remembered a map book that Walker had given them. They exited the library in a hurry and ran to their room to find it.

"They like you," Niki said, feeling awkward all of a sudden but wanting to say the words anyway.

"I hope so. I like them."

"I'm glad."

Silence hung for a moment, but Edward couldn't stand it.

"Does their mother like me?"

"You know I do," Niki answered, tentatively allowing her eyes to meet his. Edward boldly returned her gaze, but Niki felt too vulnerable and exposed just then. She moved to the door and opened it.

"I thought they would be back by now."

Edward didn't comment. He knew she was afraid. He was a little fearful himself. But he was also excited. He found himself awash with emotions and euphoria every time he was near her. To know that she was feeling some of the same things only added to the sensation.

"Here they are," Niki said with relief, glad that she hadn't been forced to look at Edward or say anything more.

By this time Henry was nearly finished studying with Walker, so Edward, Niki, and the boys had very little time together, but it was enough. Edward, leaving with his brother, and Niki, taking the boys off to play, both thought about each other for the rest of the day.

୨୧ ୨୧

Thornton Hall

Niki told herself that it had not been planned. She told herself that Marianne wouldn't do such a thing, but the truth of the matter was that she and Edward were the only singles at the party.

The Jenningses had also invited the Palmers, Westons, Hursts, Morlands, and Tates. Three tables had been set up to accommodate four players each, leaving two people free for a break or substitution.

It did not escape Niki that she and Edward were at the same table, but they were also with the Westons, a couple Niki found delightful.

"Nicola is the most beautiful name in the world," Anne Weston told Niki in the midst of one game. "I think our Sarah might have been a Nicola, had I thought of it."

"Thank you."

"Have you spent much time in France?" Weston asked.

"Yes, I lived there for years."

"Anywhere near Paris?"

"Just outside."

"Do you miss it?"

"I wouldn't mind visiting, but I actually prefer England."

The game continued with random pieces of small talk, but Niki found Edward on the quiet side. He was watchful and played his cards to perfection, but for Edward, he was oddly quiet.

When there was a break, both Weston and Anne left the table for some refreshment. Niki waited only until they were out of earshot to speak.

"You're very quiet tonight, Edward."

"Am I?" he asked in a noncommittal tone, his eyes on her.

Niki was growing exasperated and decided to say what she was thinking.

"Edward, what's come over you?"

"What do you mean?"

"I mean, you're behaving oddly. At no time in our travels did you look at me with such interest."

"I should hope not," he said with a grin. "You looked like a man."

Niki stared back at him but didn't comment.

"You don't look like a man any longer," Edward said quietly, his meaning more than clear.

"Stop staring at me, Edward," Niki now whispered in return. "You'll have me thinking about kissing you again."

"Again? Did you say *again*?"

"No," Niki lied without shame. "Of course I didn't say that."

Wishing the floor would swallow her whole, Niki became very absorbed with the score sheet on the table, refusing to look across at Edward. When she did, he was smiling at her. Niki felt it coming on but tried to ignore it. The blush, which always appeared just below her collarbone, was spreading quickly. Edward spotted it and his smile widened. Niki's hand went to her throat.

"Too late," Edward told her softly. "I can see that you're blushing."

Niki was opening her mouth to say something, but Anne and Weston were returning.

"Shall we change partners?" Weston asked when he neared the table, seeing his wife into a chair and taking his own.

"That might be fun," Edward agreed. "Then *again*," he added, "maybe we should stay as we are."

"No, let's change," Anne piped up. "I want to partner with Niki."

Niki didn't care. Either way, Edward was too close. She was still horrified by what she'd admitted to him, and clearly he was not going to forget it.

"Is it my turn to play *again*?" Edward asked when the cards came around to him, putting the emphasis on that word in such a subtle way that Niki was certain she was the only one to notice.

When she was willing to look Edward's way she found him at his most innocent until it was time to use that word. Niki found herself wanting to laugh at his audacity but knew she would have to explain herself if a giggle escaped.

"I'm sorry," Niki said to Anne when they lost three hands in a row. "I must not be concentrating."

"Not at all," Weston spoke up good-naturedly. "I think anything wrong in your game, Niki, can be blamed on Edward."

"What did I do?" Edward asked.

"I'm not exactly sure, but while Anne and I were away from the table, you had plenty to say to Niki. Now you're very quiet, which can only mean that you're teasing the life out of this poor girl."

Edward looked so comically insulted that Niki and the Westons laughed. Niki enjoyed looking at Edward now, her expression rather smug. *You've been figured out* was clearly her intent, and Edward was forced to smile.

Sitting at the next table, the Hursts and Palmers took in some of this scene. They noticed the way Edward and Niki smiled at one another and wondered, as Niki had, whether Marianne Jennings had been matchmaking when she invited the two.

"Would Marianne do that?" Pastor Hurst asked in disbelief.

"I hope so," Palmer surprised him by saying, shocking both Judith and his wife into hysterical laughter.

∾ ∾

Blackburn Manor

Niki slipped in the front door at a late hour, finding the house quiet. Bertram was there with a lantern, and she made her way upstairs but didn't go to her room.

Not able to help herself and not really trying, Niki headed for the boys' room. She stood quietly over their bed, her heart breathing a little sigh of relief as she saw that they slept peacefully.

It was an awful trap to be in—never trusting, tormented by fear—but at the moment Niki didn't know how to change. She finally sought her own bed and sleep, which came before she had any answers.

ॐ ॐ

Newcomb Park

"You're quiet this morning," Henry commented to Edward at the breakfast table. The younger Steele had taken a seat and begun to eat with little more than a word.

"Don't mind me, Henry," Edward said, and then fell silent again.

Henry's brows rose. It wasn't often that his brother was out of things to say. Henry waited several minutes, enjoying his breakfast and thinking, but when Edward remained quiet, he began to guess.

"Have I done something you don't like?"

"No."

"One of the girls?"

"No, nothing like that."

Henry finished his tea and poured more into his cup. At one time Henry would have been more than happy to leave Edward in his silence, but something was on his mind, and Henry wanted to know what it was and whether his brother was all right.

"Are you feeling unwell?"

"No, I'm fine."

"Are you tired from your late night?"

"No, but thank you for checking."

Henry paused but wasn't long in continuing. "Have you finally figured out that you're going to marry Mrs Bettencourt?"

Silence greeted this question, and Henry knew he had hit on the matter. He didn't push Edward but waited for him to share.

"She was at Thornton Hall last night," the younger Steele admitted.

"Were you able to speak to her?"

"Yes. I think she has feelings for me."

"I can believe that. What are your feelings for her?"

"They're very strong. They frighten me."

"May I give you some advice, Edward?"

"Please do."

"Go slowly. Your heart won't wish to, but you must. Get to know her very well; take your time. If you love each other, you'll be willing to wait until you're both ready."

"She has two sons," Edward spoke as

though Henry hadn't. "I would become a father as well as a husband in one day."

"You love those little boys, Edward. I've seen you with them. It's a serious undertaking, but you already care enough to get the job done properly."

Edward looked at his brother, realizing how valuable he was to his life. In just a few brief sentences Henry had set his mind at ease.

Go slowly. You already care.

Those simple lines took the confusion and muddle from his mind.

"Thank you, Henry," was all Edward had left to say.

Henry inclined his head modestly, poured another cup of tea, and reached for the newspaper.

Chapter Seventeen

Blackburn Manor

"All is quiet in town," Denley reported to Niki on Monday.

"Good. How did you handle the situation?"

"I took the list you gave me and wandered about as if I hadn't a clue."

Niki smiled at him, unable to help herself.

"Did you remember to find the items on the list?" she asked with a good deal of amusement.

Denley actually looked affronted.

"Certainly, Mrs Bettencourt," he intoned. "I even checked in for the post and was given a letter for Mr and Mrs Walker."

"I'm sure they will appreciate that."

Still looking a bit put out, Denley nodded and moved on his way. Niki looked after him, a small smile on her face. At times she thought him perfect; it was a small comfort to know he had feet of clay.

ॐ ॐ

"We've heard from Elinore," Mary told Niki later that day, referring to their oldest daughter. "Her husband is ill, and she's asked us to come and visit with the children while she devotes time to him. They're not babies anymore, but with their father ill, she thinks we'll be a nice diversion."

"When will you leave?" Niki asked.

"Well, that's just it, Niki. We don't know if we should go and leave you and the boys alone."

"Why ever not?"

"Do you feel safe about staying here?"

"I can assure you, Aunt Mary, that we will be fine. You must go to Elinore's. The sooner the better."

"Are you certain, Niki? If you need us, you must tell me."

Niki smiled and reached to hug her.

"You have been a lifeline for me, Aunt Mary, but you must go. The boys and I will be fine."

"Only if you're very sure—" Mary began but stopped when she heard Walker laugh.

"I'm afraid there will be no convincing her, Niki."

Both women watched him approach. He stopped before Niki and looked her in the eye.

"Elinore's needs are somewhat pressing, but nothing to yours. Mary is only trying to protect you."

"And for that I thank you, but I do wish you would go to your daughter. Please don't stay on my account."

"We won't," Walker stated, having seen that she was most sincere. "And if a need arises, you can always send word. Bertram will know how to reach us."

Niki smiled at him, and he bent to kiss her cheek. Niki's heart swelled with pleasure, even as she found herself hoping that she and the boys would never have to leave Blackburn Manor.

ॐ ॐ

Newcomb Park

"You didn't ask me to accompany you today, Henry, but I would like to go with you when you see Walker."

"I'm not going to Blackburn today."

"What do you mean you're not going?" Edward looked as surprised as he felt.

"The Walkers have gone to visit their daughter Elinore. They're not home."

"Where are Niki and the boys?"

"Still there."

For a moment Edward was quiet, but it didn't last long.

"Well, that's just fine!" He was more than a little put out. "How will I have an excuse to see Niki and the boys?"

Henry couldn't stop the amused sparkle that lit his eyes. Edward saw it and shook his head.

"It's not fair laughing at me, Henry. I didn't get to speak to her at all on Sunday. I was patient because I thought I would see her today."

"Well, I just learned of it myself; Walker sent word early this morning."

Edward didn't comment, but Henry read the discouragement in his eyes.

"You're trying to devise a way to go over there, Edward, and you know it won't work."

Edward looked at him.

"When did you become a mind reader?"

"You're the fourth of my siblings to fall in love. The players have all been different, but the script basically looks and sounds the same."

Edward had to smile. His brother's voice had been so dry and resigned. Henry gave him a smile of his own, touched him gently on the shoulder, and went on his way.

Edward watched him depart. As he turned away to find something to do, his sigh was quiet, heard only by himself. He thought he was quite alone in his thoughts concerning Niki, but in truth Henry had already decided on a plan to rescue him.

❧ ❧

"Where are we going?" Christopher and Richard asked their mother as the coach took them toward Ludlow on Thursday afternoon.

"We're going to visit Mr and Mrs Morland. Do you remember meeting them?"

"No."

"Mrs Morland is Edward's sister," Niki said, not remembering in time to call him Mr Steele. She shook her head a little; the boys were rubbing off on her.

"Will Edward be there?"

"I don't believe so, but we'll still have a

nice time, and I expect you to behave very well."

The boys looked into her eyes and found them serious. There had been a fight that morning. Niki hadn't been able to get all the details because the boys were crying by the time she got to them, but one had kicked and the other had bit. Niki had punished them both.

Not wanting them to think she was still angry, Niki gave the boys a small smile before turning her attention to the window. She was glad to get out of the house for a time—it was probably what the boys needed—but in truth she was not well acquainted with Mrs Morland and knew Mr Morland even less. Realizing that the couple was very close to Edward should have been a comfort to her. So why was she so nervous?

"Mama," Christopher broke into her thoughts, "I have to be excused."

"Oh, Chris, didn't you take care of that at Blackburn?"

"I have to again," the child told her, squirming a bit in discomfort.

"We'll be there shortly," Niki told him,

wondering if that might be somewhat embarrassing.

Thank you for having us, Mrs Morland, Niki pictured herself saying. *I hope you don't mind if I take my son to relieve himself.*

The thought alone made Niki hot around the collarbone. She was glad that the boys were talkative for the remainder of the ride, helping to take her mind from the inevitable.

ᔕᔕ ᔕᔕ

Newcomb Park

"Edward, you've done nothing today but lie around," Henry said over lunch. "And that was all you did yesterday."

Edward didn't comment but glanced up before spearing a carrot with his fork.

"Get out today, Edward. Go into town. Or better yet, go visit Morland." Henry's voice was a study in nonchalance. "He always cheers you up."

"He has a wife now," Edward said quietly.

"Yes," Henry's voice was dry. "A woman you barely know. One who just tolerates you."

Edward smiled.

"All right. I'll go see Morland."

"Good. If you think of it, Lizzy has a book I want. It's a field guide on bird life. She keeps it on the shelf in the library behind the large sofa."

"How do you know where it is?"

"That's where I looked at it last time we were there. She might know just where it is, but if she can't find it, try that area."

"All right."

The men didn't do much visiting to finish the meal, but Henry was more than satisfied. Edward called for his horse the moment he stood from the table, and Henry watched him ride away no more than 15 minutes later.

❧ ❧

Ludlow

"It was so nice of Morland to take the boys outside for a time," Niki said to her hostess as the women settled themselves in the library. "They're a bit fidgety today."

"Do you think that has to do with the Walkers being gone?"

"I don't know. It might. They enjoy them so much, and we'd fallen into a nice routine."

"They're the sweetest boys," Lizzy said with a sigh. "I'm glad I never have to punish them."

"You might not find it so difficult," Niki returned dryly. "Just this morning they made it very easy."

Lizzy laughed. "What happened?"

"Too many tears to gain all the details, but their answer to the squabble was a violent one. There was biting and kicking."

Horrified and laughing all at the same time, Lizzy raised her hand to cover her mouth. Niki only shook her head, laughing a little as well.

"Most of the time they do very well," Niki amended. "I don't mean to paint them in a poor light."

"I didn't take it that way. All siblings have their moments, as I'm sure you're aware."

"I'm an only child," Niki volunteered. "And my parents treated me as an equal from very early on, so having two boys so exactly alike has made for a time of learning."

"An only child? That's a life I can only imagine."

Niki smiled at her, thinking of her family and the closeness she watched them share.

It was that life she wanted for her own children, not the one she had grown up with.

"I think I prefer your way of doing things over mine," Niki admitted.

"Why is that?"

Niki's head tipped a bit in thought.

"I don't think I would have felt that way as a child; after all, I had my parents all to myself, but now I'm alone. Your parents are dead and so are mine, but you have all your siblings to share memories and joy and heartbreak. I'm very much on my own."

"And how difficult is that?"

"Around the holidays I feel it most keenly, and for the rest of the year I simply work not to dwell on it." Niki suddenly smiled. "I do have the boys, and there's no describing that joy."

"Right here, Mr Edward," the butler directed, suddenly opening the library door and admitting Lizzy's next guest.

Edward began to stride across the room, glad to find Lizzy in the library but not expecting to see Niki.

"Well, hello," he said, slowing up a bit to walk calmly over to join the ladies. "I hope I'm not interrupting."

"Not at all," Lizzy told him with a smile, so

glad that Henry's plan had worked. "We were just visiting. Join us."

"Thank you."

Edward took a seat on the opposite end of the sofa from Niki and turned to look at her. She looked back for a moment and then away. Edward forced his own gaze back to his sister and found her eyes kind with understanding.

"I hadn't realized," Lizzy went on easily, "that Mrs Bettencourt was an only child. She was just telling me about it. It's such a different life from ours, isn't it, Edward?"

"Yes." Edward worked to calm his heart and speak coherently. "I know there were times when we wished we were only children, but no one went so far as to murder anyone."

The women laughed at his words as well as his tone.

"You said something," Lizzy said, addressing Niki again, "about your parents treating you as an equal. What was that like?"

"It's much as you would imagine. I was asked if I wanted to do things, not told. I was given lots of choices and responsibility. If I grew angry or disturbed, they never saw that as rebellion. Everything was always discussed."

"Were you ever told no?"

"I can't recall a time. There must have been some, but I don't remember."

"But you're able to tell the boys no?"

"Yes, I try to be strict with them. I don't want them to have as many choices as I did. I was willful, even if my parents never saw it."

"Tell her how young you married," Edward put in.

"I was barely 16."

Lizzy looked her surprise. "And they agreed to this, your parents?"

"My mother was already dead, but, yes, my father did agree. To do anything else would have been contradictory to the very way they had raised me and lived their lives. I fell in love with Louis Bettencourt, and they saw that as the normal path of life."

"What were their spiritual beliefs? Do you know?"

"Not specifically, no, but I remember that they believed all faiths were valid as long as they gave you peace and happiness on earth. I don't think my parents believed in any kind of afterlife."

"It's interesting that given their beliefs, Niki, you believe in eternal life."

"That didn't begin until after I was married. I began thinking about life and death when I was expecting the boys. I saw such value in the lives I carried. Suddenly the thought of anyone just lying in a cold, dirty grave forever made no sense to me. I think God must have started to work in my heart at that time because I was saved a short time later."

"I'm glad you told me," Lizzy said. "I love hearing salvation stories."

"So does Walker," Edward said with a smile, thinking of how many times he'd heard Walker urging someone to share his or her story. "Before I forget," Edward continued, his eyes on Lizzy, "Henry is looking for a book you have."

"Which one?"

"Some sort of guide on birds."

"I think it's in my room," she said.

"Henry seemed to think it was on a shelf right here behind this sofa."

Lizzy shook her head. "I don't think so." She came to her feet. "I'll just go and see if I can locate it."

"I'll look here on the shelf," Edward volunteered and rose to do just that.

Niki had been quiet during this exchange. She could hear Edward behind her, his hands on the books, but she didn't turn. Neither did she hear his steps on the carpet, but he was suddenly there, bending over the back of the davenport to look at her, his face very close. Niki looked into his eyes, her heart thundering.

"I didn't think I would see you today," Edward said softly.

"Nor I you."

Edward looked into her eyes for a moment.

"Did you find the book?" Niki was out of breath.

"No. I found my eyes wandering back in this direction."

Niki tried to calm the frantic beating of her heart, but it wasn't working.

"Did you know," Edward went on softly, "that you look as charming from the back as you do from the front?"

Niki gave a small shake of her head but wasn't certain what he'd said. He was too close. She couldn't think.

Edward didn't want to think. He was

amazed that she was here. He'd almost gone to town at the last moment but changed his mind. If he'd done that, he would have missed her. And once he had arrived, he couldn't think straight. He'd taken a seat with all the calm he could muster and had tried hard to think of books and other subjects to distract himself, but it hadn't worked.

"I can't stop thinking about you," Edward finally said, coming closer.

When Niki saw that Edward was moving, her chin lifted ever so slightly. Edward kissed her without haste, and Niki kissed him right back.

"Again?" Edward asked when he'd put a fraction of space between them.

"Again."

Edward was still kissing her when he heard the door, but he didn't jump like a man caught in the act. He straightened slowly and walked around the davenport to sit with Niki.

"I think I have it," Lizzy told them, crossing the room to hand the book to Edward before retaking her seat. She had the distinct impression that something had gone on while she was away, but not for any reason would she have asked. She did notice, however, that Edward was sitting closer to Niki.

"I think this must be the book," Edward said and thanked her. "I'll see that Henry gets it."

"Tell him there's no hurry."

"All right," Edward said easily, still working to gather his thoughts. "Where are the boys?" he asked of Niki, wanting a reason to look at her.

"With Mr Morland."

"I believe they went outside," Lizzy put in. "The day is perfect for it."

"Shall we go find them?" Edward suggested, thinking that if he had to keep sitting there, he would begin to squirm.

Lizzy's smile as she agreed told him that she was onto him, and he thought that Niki looked ready to laugh as well. The threesome had no more stood when Morland came through the door, the boys in attendance.

"Edward!" they cried in unison as if it had been years. The pair bolted across the room to see him. They remembered to smile at their mother, but Edward was clearly the person they wanted to see.

"Mr Morland has a big tree, like you saw in Africa!" Christopher told him in excitement.

"We can show you," Richard offered.

"I would love to see it. Shall we bring your mum?" Edward asked, thinking it a stroke of genius.

The boys were even more excited about that idea, and in short order the adults—all of them—trooped after the boys to see this large tree. The day was ideal, and the six of them took their time until Lizzy suggested tea and refreshments. For this enticement the boys were willing to go indoors. Niki walked with them while they moved back inside, intent on questioning them.

"How did things go with Mr Morland?"

"We didn't kick," Richard told her.

"I'm glad to hear that. Were you well behaved?"

They nodded, not looking at all hesitant.

"Did you thank him for taking you outdoors?"

The boys looked at each other then, and Niki had to cover her mouth over the quizzical looks on their faces.

"Take care of it as soon as you can," their

mother put in and then let the matter drop. Suddenly she was weary from so much emotion in one day. The boys had argued, she was worried about her visit with Lizzy Morland, and then Edward had arrived. And all of that before the kiss. Niki wanted to go somewhere private so she could relive it in her mind and think about him, but that wasn't possible.

Forcing herself to attend to what Morland was saying, Niki put her own wishes aside. She was a little hungry, and the tea that had been prepared looked lovely. Even at that, Edward's kiss kept swimming back into her thoughts.

It would have done a great deal of good for Niki's heart if she had glanced at Edward. One look would have told her he was thinking about it too.

ɶ ɷ

Pembroke

Cassandra felt Tate's eyes on her, but she wouldn't look at him. The hour somewhat late, the two were reading in bed. She knew he was curious about her behavior, but she wasn't going to open the subject. Right now she hoped he would grow sleepy and forget about it.

"Are you all right?" Tate ventured, not sure he could sleep if he didn't question his wife.

"I think so," Cassandra hedged.

"But you're not sure?"

Cassandra was silent about that.

Tate watched her. He wanted to reach over and take the book from her hand, but instead he set his own down and turned a little more so he could stare at her.

"Don't do that!" Cassandra's voice was sharp.

"What is it, Cassie?"

Cassandra gave up and put her book aside but still didn't look at him. She was angry that he'd pushed the point, but she couldn't say as she blamed him. She had changed in the last few days, and had the situation been reversed, she would have had plenty of questions of her own.

"What is it you want to know?" Cassandra asked, hoping they were not on the same subject.

"I want to know why you don't want me to see you when you're undressed. You've been hiding from me behind doors and in darkness for three days."

Cassandra's heart sank. This was the very thing she didn't want to speak about. She glanced at her husband and still found him to be the man she fell in love with and married, but deep in her heart she didn't think he would understand.

Without looking at him, she admitted, "I feel fat. I feel thick around the middle."

"And that's why you're hiding from me?"

"Yes." Her voice dropped before she continued. "I think the freckles on my body stand out more now that I'm pregnant. I don't want you to see me."

Tate had been on the verge of growing impatient, but then she'd mentioned her freckles. Her freckles had almost kept them apart. He'd decided a long time ago that he would always be patient about her freckles, and this time was not going to be any different.

"I love your freckles," he said gently, meaning it with all his heart. "If you recall, I didn't get to see them when we first met, so I'm still making up for lost time."

Cassandra smiled a little. It was so like

him to say something sweet. She glanced at him, feeling a little better.

"So," Tate said slowly, "do I give you time with this, or do I push the point?"

Cassandra frowned.

"What do you mean?"

"I mean, are you going to work at believing me in the very near future, or do I need to show you how much I like your freckles right now?"

Cassandra bit her lip, a little uncertain. Tate watched her, reminding himself how gentle he needed to be.

"Why don't I scratch your back," Tate suggested.

"You don't mind?"

"Not at all."

Cassandra smiled at him and then rolled over so he could reach her. With a smile of his own, Tate began a gentle motion with his neatly-trimmed nails. They had been down this road before. He knew it was only a matter of time before she realized that doors and darkness were not needed: He loved every freckle she possessed.

Chapter Eighteen

From a window in his bedroom, Pastor Hurst saw the threesome alight from the carriage and walk into the church. He thought someone might have left a jacket or Bible on Sunday, but several minutes passed and no one emerged. He was done for the day and wanted to be home, but he knew that the Walkers were away, which meant that Mrs Bettencourt was on her own.

"Frederick," Judith said as she entered the room, finding his back to her. She was ready with a question but waited.

Finally he turned. "Can you make time to go over to the church?"

"Certainly."

"Right now?" he pressed.

"Yes."

With a word to the ever-faithful Phoebe, the two left the house and headed across the yard. Pastor held the door for his wife, who slipped in ahead of him and sat down in a rear pew. She watched as he approached the small family down front.

Niki Bettencourt sat with a son on either side of her, a few tears on her face. She heard Pastor Hurst coming and turned to him.

"Can I help you, Mrs Bettencourt? Or my wife perhaps? She's with me."

"I can't explain it," she said softly. "I was hoping if I came here I would somehow have the words, but it hasn't helped." Niki sniffed. "Chris asked me about Jesus Christ, and I tried to tell him how I had believed, but I've only confused him."

Frederick sat near the huddled family.

"Which one of you is Chris?"

"I'm Chris," he volunteered. "Mama never cries. I didn't mean to make Mama cry."

"You're a very kind boy, Chris," Frederick said, seeing some of his own son, John, in that small, sweet face. "I'm sure she appreciates that."

Richard looked from the pastor to his mother, his own face pale with confusion. His brother had asked a few questions, and the next thing he knew they were headed to church on a Tuesday!

"Since your mother is crying right now, Chris, do you think maybe I can answer your questions?"

"I don't know."

"Would you like me to try?"

"Sure." The little boy was amiable but said nothing else. Frederick fought laughter and found that Niki was smiling a little too.

"Chris," she prompted gently, turning a little to see him. "Ask Pastor Hurst the question you asked me."

The little boy looked up at her, his face hesitant until Niki nodded in encouragement.

"All right," Chris said quietly, now turning to the pastor. "Why did Jesus have to die to save people? If He's God, why couldn't He save people and stay alive?"

"What a very good question, Chris," Frederick praised him. "And I'm glad you asked it. You see, the Bible says that sin has to be paid for. Do you know what I mean by that?"

"No."

"It means that someone must pay a price. If I were to steal something and go to jail, then I would be paying a price for my crime, wouldn't I? The Bible tells us that all sin is against God and that sin must be paid for in blood. That might sound confusing, but I'll tell you what I mean. A very long time ago, before God sent His Son, people who believed in Him would sacrifice a lamb or a goat, and by shedding the blood of that animal they would show God that they were sorry for their sins.

"But then God sent His Son, Jesus Christ, to die for the sins of all men, and when Jesus shed His blood, He paid the price for all the sins of all people. If Jesus had stayed alive, then His blood would not have been shed, and our sins would not have been paid for."

Both Frederick and Niki watched Christopher nod, his little face intent.

"But there's more to it than that, Chris, and I think that's what your mother has been trying to tell you. You see, just because God offers us forgiveness for our sins, that doesn't mean everyone believes. Your mother has chosen to believe, and you could believe too."

"I'm only five," Christopher felt a need to tell him.

"I'm glad you told me, Chris, but I have something to tell you. I believed in the Lord

Jesus Christ to save my sins when I was five years old."

Christopher's eyes got a little big with this announcement, and he turned to his mother. Niki nodded, a gentle smile on her lips.

"Aunt Mary said it's about agreeing with God, Chris," his mother said gently, "and believing Him. And salvation is for anyone who will do that."

"I'll do that," Richard said suddenly, surprising his mother and brother; Niki had nearly forgotten he was there.

"Do what, Rich?" His mother had to be sure he understood.

"I'll believe in God to forgive my sins." He suddenly looked hesitant, his voice growing very soft. "I sin when I bite Chris."

Niki put an arm around him, kissed the top of his soft head, and tried not to sob her eyes out.

"Shall I tell you what I did, Rich?"

He nodded against her.

"I told God that I needed His salvation. I prayed and thanked Him for sending His Son to die for me. I asked Him to save me from my sins, and He did."

"How do you know, Mama?" Chris asked this question.

"I know because God's Word promises that all who believe will be saved, but I also know because I was different inside. I never felt alone anymore, but more than that, I wanted to know more about God. It took me awhile to ask questions about His Word and get answers, but I wanted more of God."

"Do you *feel* saved every day, Mrs Bettencourt?" Pastor asked.

"No."

"And what do you do on those days?"

"I remember Scripture and God's promises to me. I let His Word remind me of the gift I've been given."

Pastor Hurst smiled at her, his heart pleased that she understood the way emotions could deceive.

"I can't read," Richard said quietly, bringing the adults' eyes back to him.

"But you can still believe," Niki said, feeling sure of herself and her words now. "You can pray and ask God to save you, and He will."

"Can I pray right now?"

"Yes. Do you want some help?"

The little boy surprised them by shaking his head no. They watched as he closed his eyes. Some time passed before he opened them, and Frederick spoke.

"Do you mind if I ask you a question, Richard?"

"No."

"What did you say to God?"

"I said that I'm sorry about biting Chris and sinning. I said I want to know Jesus like Mama does."

"And did you mean it with all of your heart, Richard?"

"Yes."

"I'm glad to hear that. A wonderful life awaits you, Richard. Not an easy life, but one where you know that God loves you and will never leave you."

The little boy smiled at him, and Frederick turned to the other little boy.

"What do you think, Christopher?"

"I don't know. I'm not sure."

Frederick nodded calmly. "I think you are wise to wait until you are sure, Christopher. Accepting salvation from God is a big step because God takes it very seriously, which means that we must take it seriously too."

"Did I take it seriously?" Richard asked.

"Well, Richard, time will tell. You won't do everything right the first time, but when our hearts have been changed, we live differently. Can I tell you something my father told me?"

The little boy nodded.

"When I was young, he took his gold pocket watch out and handed it to me. He asked me this question: Would you take good care of this if it was yours? I answered that I would. I thought he was going to give it to me, but he put it back into his pocket. He said that the gift of salvation from God was more valuable than anything in the universe. And even greater care than I would give a gold watch needed to be given to my salvation. I must never take it for granted or forget what God had given me. If you work hard to remember that in the days and months and even years to come, you'll know that you've taken it seriously, and God will richly bless you."

"Thank you," Niki said, still feeling very emotional but not crying.

"You're very welcome. I'm glad I could help."

"I think we'll go home now," Niki said to her sons. "I find myself a bit weary."

Niki rose to leave. Judith was still in the back, and Niki smiled when she saw her.

"I forgot that Pastor said you were here," she apologized.

"That's all right. Tell me, Mrs Bettencourt, can you join us for supper this evening? We would so love to have the three of you."

"Please call me Niki, and, yes, I believe we are quite free. What time would you like us?"

"Will six o'clock work?"

"Certainly, and thank you again."

"The pleasure is all ours."

Niki wasn't certain that she could feel her feet on the ground as she and the boys exited the building. Pastor and Judith waved them off and then stood just inside the church doors and looked at each other. Judith couldn't find any words. She simply wrapped her arms around her husband and held him tight.

❧ ❧

Thornton Hall

"Jennings," his wife called when she heard the door. "Is that you?"

"Yes."

Marianne came around the corner and met her husband in the middle of the room, where they shared a kiss.

"Are you just back, or did I miss your arrival?"

"I'm just back."

"You were gone a long time. Did you speak with Niki? Were she and the boys there?"

"They weren't at Blackburn, but Bertram told me they'd gone to the church. I went there, and they were just coming out."

"Of the church?"

"Yes." Jennings smiled. "It seems that the boys were asking some questions about Niki's faith, and she took them to the church to talk to them. She told me that Richard trusted in Christ."

Marianne's pretty mouth swung open.

"That's marvelous!"

"Yes, it is. I wish you could have seen Niki's face. She was glowing."

"What of Christopher? Was he there?"

"Yes, and although he looked happy for his brother, he didn't say anything."

"I want to hear the whole story!" Marianne said suddenly. "I think I'll send word and have them to dinner."

"Not tonight. They're going to the manse."

Marianne smiled. "You already invited them."

Jennings smiled in return and admitted, "I wanted to hear the whole story too."

When their children came looking for Jennings a short time later—they wanted him to go riding—Marianne was still chuckling.

❦ ❦

Blackburn Manor

Please help me to trust You, Niki prayed when she woke in the night with another bad dream. *You've saved Richard, Lord, and You've saved me. I know You love us—I can think the words in my mind—but my heart still pounds with fear.*

Niki forced herself not to go to her sons. She knew it had just been a dream. Denley and the other servants were aware of what was going on in the house. If there was an intruder, they would hear.

Continuing to pray and asking God to change her and work in her heart, Niki remained in bed until she fell back to sleep. The boys woke her in the morning when they climbed onto the bed; she had slept in a little. Niki's pleasure at seeing them was heightened because she'd done the hard work of trusting in the night.

≈ ≈

Collingbourne

Edmond Ellenborough stepped down from the carriage, his eyes taking in every detail with very little effort. He planned his arrival for a weekday, hoping the town would be busy. His hunch was correct. On this Wednesday morning the streets were teeming with people, horses, and carriages. Ellenborough, looking for all the world like a man without purpose, turned toward The Owl, intent on finding a room. His mission would be a little tricky if none were to be had, but that wouldn't stop him. Nothing ever did.

With barely a glance to one side or the other, Ellenborough moved on his way, thinking this might be one of the easiest trips he'd ever made. Even if nothing turned up concerning Nicola Bettencourt, an old friend lived nearby. The last time he and Henry Steele had talked, he'd invited Ellenborough to visit, should he ever be in the area. Never a man to enjoy much leisure, the relentless agent planned to make an exception in this case.

❧ ❧

Pembroke

"Well, now," Edward said softly when he and Niki had their first moment alone in the evening. "This is a nice surprise."

Niki's eyes turned teasing.

"Yes, it is. I didn't know that the Tates would be serving beef. I love beef."

With all he could do not to take her in his arms, Edward laughed. It didn't release the tension of wanting to touch her, but it let him hear her laugh, and for the moment that was enough.

"Edward." Christopher was suddenly at his side. "Did you see my rock?"

"I don't think I did. Do you have it with you?"

"Mama made me leave it in the carriage." He sounded disgruntled.

"Does it not fit in your pocket?"

"It does."

Edward raised amused eyes to Niki and

found hers trying to be stern. He knew he could get himself in trouble if he didn't step carefully here.

"Well, maybe you can show it to me later," Edward suggested.

"All right," the little boy agreed, clearly not thrilled with this idea.

"Remember what we talked about, Chris—about what's important and what's not?" his mother reminded him.

Christopher nodded and moved on his way.

"I need to thank you," Niki said suddenly.

"For what?"

"For not mentioning Rich's salvation in front of Chris. We were at the manse on Tuesday night and at Thornton Hall last night. Naturally everyone is excited, but I think he needs more time. And if Rich continues to draw as much attention as he has already, I'm afraid that Chris will try to make a commitment before he's ready."

"Well, I did speak to Rich, but I kept it private."

"I'm glad. Chris was the one who had the original questions. I know he's thinking about it, but I don't want to rush him."

"He's too bright not to catch on, Niki. We'll all keep praying for him. He'll come."

Niki looked up into Edward's confident eyes. He was the kindest man she'd ever known, and her feelings for him grew stronger every day. Niki kept looking—their height difference was only a few inches—so this wasn't hard to do. Looking away was the hard part. Edward's kiss from the week before came rushing back to her, and Niki wanted nothing more than to be alone with this man.

"I want you to know," Edward said, suddenly breaking into her thoughts. They weren't going to be alone for long, so he kept his voice low. "That those kisses were not without feeling."

"I didn't think they were."

"Then we need to talk very soon."

Niki nodded her agreement just before Tate and Cassandra approached.

"We've been talking to your sons," Tate informed Niki, a huge smile on his face. "Something about a runaway pony and some mud."

Niki's fingers came to her lips as she fought laughter. It had been on her mind to tell the boys not to mention that episode, but she'd never gotten around to it.

"Do tell," Edward said, his voice full of teasing.

"I don't have to tell," Niki informed the three of them. "A contrary pony and a mud puddle. Your imagination will do the rest."

"Was anyone hurt?" Cassandra asked.

"A few bruises," Niki said quietly and suddenly found Edward's gaze intent.

The Tates did not miss his attention.

"We have a game we told the boys about," Tate said smoothly. "We'll go and start it with them. Join us whenever you'd like."

"Thank you," Niki said, not looking at Edward as their hosts walked toward the boys, who were looking at books on the drawing room floor.

"Are you all right?" Edward asked almost immediately.

"Yes," Niki said, but her eyes did not come up and her collarbone began to grow pink.

"What happened?"

"Never mind."

"I don't want to never mind. I want to love and take care of you."

Niki could hardly breathe. He'd said the word that she'd tried not to think or ever hope to hear. She glanced at him, meeting his eyes and finding them full of purpose and caring, but still managed to look away.

"Let's just say I sat down rather hard."

"Oh, Niki." Edward's voice was full of compassion.

"It's all right," she said, touching his arm for just a moment before joining Tate, Cassandra, and the boys.

Edward came directly after her, frustration filling him even as he thought, *If she were my wife I could have intimate thoughts about her. I could know where she was hurting and take care of her.*

Edward quickly found that such thoughts accomplished little. They only added to his frustration because he and Niki weren't married. Praying for calm and patience, he joined the game that was in progress, trying to put the entire conversation out of his head.

❧ ❧

Ellenborough had all the information he needed. His work outside of town had paid

off, so by the time he arrived in Collingbourne, he had only a few details to con-
firm. He accomplished this in a subtle but
swift way and was now free to visit Henry
Steele.

He'd hired a coach and driver to take him
to Newcomb Park, requesting an open
coach that allowed him to sit back and enjoy the beautiful countryside. He had not
sent word ahead about his arrival, but he
knew Henry wouldn't mind.

Newcomb Park was beautiful. The
grounds, managed to perfection, only high-
lighted the very large home with its wide
windows and second-story balconies. Ellenborough hoped that Henry would be
home, but the view of the house was worth
his trip even if he wasn't.

Ellenborough was still taking it in when he
realized that Henry had just ridden in on
horseback and dismounted on the drive to
greet him, an unrestrained smile on his
face.

"Ellenborough! Welcome!"

"Thank you, Henry," that man said as he
climbed down from the carriage. "I was
hoping to find you home."

"Well, you did! Come inside and give me a few minutes to freshen up."

Remembering how much Ellenborough's brother, William—who had been Henry's first acquaintance with the family—enjoyed reading, Henry left his guest in the library and retired to his room. He wasted little time and was soon able to rejoin his guest. As he expected, Ellenborough was poring over the shelves and maps in this room, seeming most content.

"How are you?" Henry asked when the two had made themselves comfortable on the facing sofas.

"I'm very well, ready for a rest."

"So you're not in town on business?"

"I came on business, but the matter is all wrapped up. At the moment I am a man of leisure."

"Good for you. Tell me, Ellenborough," Henry cut to the chase, "any word on William's death?"

"No, and I've stopped looking."

When Henry looked his surprise, the older man explained.

"When you came to see me last year with Mr Tate, I realized how long it had been. I need to let it rest, as I hope William has."

Henry wasn't comfortable with Ellenborough's statement about a dead man but
wasn't sure if he should comment on it
specifically. Nevertheless, he did have
something to ask.

"Does it trouble you not to be working on
the case?"

"Closing my investigation was a good decision," Ellenborough told him quietly.
"That's not to say that I don't think about it,
but I feel a great rest that I haven't known
for a very long time."

Henry nodded, and for a moment there
were no words between them. Ellenborough looked thoughtful, and Henry was
working on what to say next. His guest beat
him to it.

"Do you live here alone?"

"No, but nearly. My sisters are all married
and living on their own. My brother, Edward,
still lives with me, but he had business in
town this morning. And speaking of town, is
that where you're staying?"

"Yes, at The Owl."

"Well, that must change. Transfer your
things here. You must stay with us."

"I don't wish to impose."

"No imposition at all. You can avail yourself of this library and truly be at your leisure."

Ellenborough smiled, his head turning to take in the room again.

"Now, that is a temptation."

"It's all settled then," Henry said as he stood. "I'll have your things sent for. You must stay as long as you wish."

And without further ado, Ellenborough agreed. Henry saw to the matter, and in no time the men were visiting once again, discussing books, London, and people of joint acquaintance.

When Edward arrived back, he was simply brought into the conversation with them. Having never met the man, he found himself as fascinated as Henry always was. As the hours flew by in good conversation mixed with times of reading, Ellenborough said he would remain until Sunday morning, completely unaware that both Steele brothers were praying that he would stay long enough to go with them to church.

Chapter Nineteen

Edward had told the boys that he would take them riding on Saturday. His horse took him in the direction of Blackburn Manor at midmorning, having left Henry and Ellenborough still at the breakfast table, completely naive as to Ellenborough's purpose in town.

For just a little while, Edward had forgotten about how he'd come to meet Nicola Bettencourt. Not even Henry was suspicious of Ellenborough's sudden visit, so the two men hadn't spoken of the possibilities.

With all of this blissfully missing from his mind, Edward rode up to Blackburn and was allowed entrance by Bertram. He was no more inside the foyer when Denley came his way.

"Hello, Denley. I'm taking the boys riding this morning. Are they about?"

"Yes, sir," Denley said with extra care, causing Edward to study the man's face.

"Is everything all right?"

Denley stood mute, working to frame a reply. Edward beat him to it.

"Tell me, Denley," Edward went on, his voice almost casual. "Is Mrs Bettencourt about?"

The hesitation was more than obvious before he said, "Mr Osborne is here right now, sir. Would you care to see him?"

"Immediately," Edward said firmly, his voice low.

Denley led the way upstairs to Niki's room, knocked, and was granted entry. Inside, Edward found Mr Osborne throwing things into a satchel, every movement shouting fear and desperation.

"Hello, boys." Edward greeted the little boys who sat on the bed watching their mother with sober faces. They scrambled for the edge of the mattress and threw themselves at Edward, who had hugs for each of them before sending them out of the room with Denley.

"No," Niki tried to stop them, but Edward intervened.

"They'll be close by," he said softly, not wanting to alarm. "Won't they, Denley?"

"In the next room, sir—just through this door."

The boys looked at their mother, their faces vulnerable and uncertain. Niki mustered a smile for them.

"Go ahead boys; go with Denley."

Denley wasted no time but took the boys away. Niki waited only until the door shut to have her say to Edward.

"We shouldn't have done that! The boys need to be with me. We're leaving, and you're not to try to stop me, Edward Steele. She's found us, and we've got to leave."

"How do you know she's found you?"

"That man, Ellenborough. He's tracked us down here."

Edward's heart stopped in his chest and then galloped on without mercy.

"He's at my house."

Niki looked so hurt that Edward reached for her. She was numb with shock or she would have pulled away.

"He's an old friend of my brother's. Neither one of us thought."

"I've got to get away." Niki began to pull from his arms.

Edward thought fast.

"Get dressed as Niki. You're going to my sister's so I have time to think."

"That's just what she needs in her condition, Edward, a houseful of people."

"Not Cassie's, Lizzy's."

Niki began to shake her head, and Edward captured her hands in his.

"You've forgotten how close I am to Morland, Niki, and he's married to my sister. They would be angry if we did not go to them."

Niki worked to take even breaths and stem the panic rising inside of her. She felt herself calming even as she heard herself agreeing.

"I'm going to make sure that Denley packs for the boys and for himself," Edward went on. "I'll tell them where we're going, and we will all wait for you downstairs."

After Niki nodded, Edward kissed her very gently. He started away but then stopped.

"You're not going to run anymore, Niki. The pursuit is over. Mrs Bettencourt can come. I have something to say to her."

Niki stood still as he walked to the door and exited. His voice and manner filled her with courage. Not wasting any time, but not rushing either, Niki dressed as herself and did as Edward had instructed.

℘ ℘

Ludlow

"You need to send word to the Walkers and tell them where you are and that you are safe. I'll send word home to Henry that we need to speak to Ellenborough."

Niki frowned at him in confusion. "Why do we need to speak to him?"

"Clearly he's been hired to find you, but I don't know exactly what that means. Has he been asked to track you no matter where you go or just report the last place you were seen? Either way, he needs to know that you're done running."

Niki stared at him, neither one aware of the couple that sat with them in the room. Morland and Lizzy had remained quiet after Edward had given them a brief explanation, wanting only to help in any way they could.

"What am I saying to the Walkers exactly?" Niki asked, not able to think very clearly. Running had been her only plan.

"Just that you're safe and that you'll be here at Ludlow until they arrive back."

Niki's eyes went to Lizzy, her helplessness and embarrassment clear.

"If you had gone anywhere else I would have been very angry," Lizzy wasted no time in saying.

Niki looked back at Edward and found his eyes full of amusement.

"What did I tell you?" he said.

Niki sighed and thanked the Morlands—it was the fifth time—before turning back to Edward.

"Are you sure you want to do this? You don't know what she's like."

"You're right; I don't. But the alternative is to let you and the boys walk away from me, and my heart won't take it. You're not alone here, Niki. If it takes my whole family, we'll protect you and the boys."

Niki nodded, relief filling her. She was so weary of running away but, until today, didn't think she had a choice.

Someone knocked on the door, and Denley appeared after Morland's call to enter.

"I'm sorry, Mrs Bettencourt, but the boys are asking for you."

"Of course, Denley. Bring them in and join us for a moment."

Seconds later the boys entered and ran

to their mother, who wrapped them both in a huge hug. It was to Denley, however, that she spoke.

"We'll be here until the Walkers return from their daughter's, and then it's back to Blackburn Manor. We'll not be moving about anymore."

Denley bowed, a small smile on his face.

"As you wish, Mrs Bettencourt."

Niki smiled as he left. "He hasn't wanted to move about for a very long time, but he's never complained."

"Wherever did you find such a man?" Lizzy asked.

"I'll tell you the story sometime," Niki said, not sure she wanted the boys to hear.

"Mama," Christopher suddenly asked, his small brow furrowed. "Are you going to dress as a man again?"

Niki smiled into his eyes and shook her head no before looking up at her hosts. The looks on their faces were comical.

"Maybe we can hear about that story as well," Morland said dryly, his eyes alight with humor.

The older occupants of the room all enjoyed a good laugh over this. The little boys laughed too, but for a very different reason.

Their mother looked like their mother again, and the panic and fear she'd been feeling had receded from her face.

ᕕᖺ ᕗᖺ

Every wise woman buildeth her house, but the foolish plucketh it down with her hands. He that walketh in his uprightness feareth the Lord, but he that is perverse in his ways despiseth him. In the mouth of the foolish is a rod of pride, but the lips of the wise shall preserve them. Where no oxen are, the crib is clean; but much increase is by the strength of the ox. A faithful witness will not lie, but a false witness will utter lies. A scorner seeketh wisdom, and findeth it not; but knowledge is easy unto him that understandeth.

Niki silently read these verses from Proverbs 14 and thought about building up her house and honest witnesses. It was a lot to take in, but she was glad she'd taken the time. Her letter was already written to the Walkers, and although Edward was still downstairs, he'd sent word to Ellenborough.

It was only a matter of time before they

met with the man, assuming he would come, and more than anything Niki wanted to trust God for the outcome. It was so hard not to fear Patrice Bettencourt, but she was working on it.

Help me to trust You, Lord God. Help me to remember how faithful You are, and how far You've already taken us.

Niki didn't have much time alone. The boys, still a bit spooked by all that had gone on that day, were looking for her again. She did not want to send them away, not when they were nervous, but she was thankful that she'd had time to read and pray and found herself asking God to remind her of His truths in the hours ahead.

ॐ ॐ

Henry accompanied Ellenborough to Ludlow. That man had been very quiet upon receiving Edward's letter, but he had shared it with Henry, who had offered to take him.

During the ride over and after they arrived, Henry stole glances at the older man's face. This had been the face he'd presented to Tate many months back, when they had met with him in London to present

Tate's case. It was no wonder that Henry had not been suspicious when Ellenborough had arrived at Newcomb Park. The working Ellenborough, the investigator, seemed a completely different man.

"Thank you for coming." Edward welcomed Henry and Ellenborough into the room that Morland had chosen for the meeting. Lizzy was also present, and the six of them made themselves as comfortable as possible under the circumstances.

"I want you to know first of all," Edward began, "that we have no wish to interfere with your investigation, Mr Ellenborough. But because you are a friend of my brother's, I felt I could give you a bit more information that might, in the long run, be a help to Mrs Bettencourt." Edward indicated Niki with a nod of his head.

"I'd like to hear whatever you have to say, Edward," Ellenborough stated, his face still serious. "But you do understand that I have been paid by Mrs Bettencourt's mother-in-law for a service, and I am bound by my word to do the job."

"Certainly. I would expect nothing else."

"May I ask a question?" Ellenborough suddenly inserted, his eyes on Niki.

That woman nodded.

"Are these children actually yours?"

Niki smiled, amazed at the peace she felt.

"Let me guess, Mr Ellenborough." Niki couldn't keep the smile from her face. "She's told you that I'm a nanny who stole them from her daughter—her daughter who conveniently died having them?"

A smile tugged at Ellenborough's mouth. "You've clearly heard the story before."

"That one among many others," Niki went on confidently. "And there are some aspects of the story that are true. She never had a daughter, only a son, and I was married to him. So it is true that my sons are her grandchildren."

"But you didn't want her in their lives, I understand."

"I took my children out of her grasp only after she abducted them from me. I was widowed, and she proceeded to hide them from me for a year."

Ellenborough's gaze narrowed. The Steeles were good people. He had always known that. Could they be fooled by this woman? It was possible, but Ellenborough considered himself a fine judge of character, and right now he was bitterly certain that he had been the one duped, and not by these people before him but by the senior Mrs Bettencourt. If he had known what she was about, he would never have taken the job.

"Mrs Bettencourt and her sons are going to be living here in Collingbourne," Edward put in before anyone else could speak. "If the older Mrs Bettencourt wants to come, she may do that. But she needs to understand that the boys will not be surrendered to her and that she may find herself having to answer to the law."

"I checked her out," Ellenborough said quietly, hating to admit to any professional flaws. "Everyone I spoke with confirmed her story."

"She has power," Niki said, unable to stop the shiver of fear that ran through her. "And she's relentless. Not in all these years has she given up."

"Did you go to France and meet with her?" Henry suddenly asked Ellenborough.

"Yes. Her missive to me wrung my heart. She begged me, certain that the children were here in England. She said she was old and desperate to see her grandsons before she died."

"And did you find her in ill health?" Niki asked without malice.

"No, but she even had a reason for that, stating that after I wrote back to her she had enough will to change doctors and was under a new treatment."

"She sounds as though she could have made a living on the stage," Henry said with a certain level of disgust.

Edward couldn't stop his smile. His brother had that effect on him.

"I haven't sent in my report," Ellenborough said. "I won't do that until I return to London and my secretary readies it."

"What will you say?" Henry asked, not caring if it was his business or not.

"That Mrs Bettencourt and the children are here. I'll be brief and to the point. My bill will be exorbitant, my usual fee, and my dealings with the elder Mrs Bettencourt will be concluded."

"And what of your dealings with the younger Mrs Bettencourt?" Again Henry spoke his mind.

Ellenborough looked at the lady in question. There was no missing her sincerity or Edward Steele's interest. He had always had a weakness for tall blonds and could hardly blame the man.

"I'll let Henry keep me informed," Ellenborough stated, his eyes going to both Edward and Niki. "I'll expect to be invited to the wedding, and if you ever need my services, I'll come at a moment's notice."

Niki managed not to blush and even smiled at him before asking in her sweet way, "Mr Ellenborough, would you like to meet my sons?"

Ellenborough's heart swelled within him, and he couldn't stop his answering smile.

"Nothing would give me greater pleasure."

❧ ❧

"Gar and Juliana are vagabonds; that's how they describe themselves. They don't keep servants long because they love to move about," Niki explained to Lizzy while they enjoyed a cup of tea. Edward and Morland had taken the boys on that promised ride. "Denley had just begun to work for them, and for some reason, the two of us fit together quite nicely. It's unusual, but then so is my situation. As a man Denley could get things for me that a female servant could not. He was willing to see to nearly every job, and of course a woman would never have worked when I went in disguise."

"What was that like?" Lizzy found herself captivated.

"Frightening. I was never very relaxed. I wanted to be with my boys, and the constant fear of discovery was draining."

"But the Lawtons always kept them safe?"

"Yes. They've been quite wonderful."

"Where are they now?"

"On the move, I'm afraid, because Ellenborough found them."

"How do they contact you, or you them?"

"We have a special place where we mail messages, a small town that no one has ever discovered."

"Well, I hope you'll write and tell them you're here to stay. Invite them to visit. I would love to meet these people."

"They would enjoy that so much." Niki looked as pleased as she felt. "I think they might even love Collingbourne if they haven't settled already."

"Is Juliana Lawton the woman who introduced you to Christ?"

"No." Some of the light went out of Niki's eyes. "Gar and Juliana don't see much need for God. They're very self-sufficient, and I'm not sure they grasp such things."

"We'll just have to pray that they see their need," Lizzy said simply.

Niki looked at her. "I like you, Lizzy Morland. I like you very much."

Lizzy twinkled at her. "I'm glad to hear that, Niki, but what I really want to know is whether you like my brother."

Niki smiled shyly but wasn't afraid to admit the truth. "I do like him. I like him very much."

"I can't tell you how glad I am to hear that."

"Did you doubt?" Niki decided to tease. "I can't think why anyone wouldn't like Henry Steele. He's a fine man."

Taken very much by surprise, Lizzy burst out laughing. She grabbed her napkin and put it over her mouth, but her giggles would not be suppressed.

Niki laughed with her. If the children had been anywhere near the vicinity, they would have come running to find out what they were missing, but the women were alone.

Thoughts of the children quelled some of

Niki's joy. Patrice would be on her way soon—she was certain of that. When the children were not in her presence, she was not completely convinced they were safe. Knowing this was a lack of trust, Niki resolved to try in the weeks to come to put that trust in place. She would find it to be the most difficult task of her life.

Chapter Twenty

By the time Patrice Bettencourt arrived in Collingbourne, the Walkers were home. Niki and the boys were once again safely ensconced at Blackburn Manor, where Edward visited and spent most of each day.

They had not announced their engagement nor even hinted at it, but the conversations that went on were all with a future in mind. Edward had not asked the question that was in his heart. They still had things to learn about each other, and facing Niki's mother-in-law was just one more aspect of that journey.

"She's here," Walker told his wife, Edward, and Niki on the third Wednesday of May. Denley had been making daily trips into town, so they knew that Patrice had arrived the day before. Since then the boys had been under very watchful eyes. Denley had been with them full-time, and two other men with the Walker household were available constantly. All three men were armed. No one wanted anyone to be hurt, but at this point no one was willing to take any chances.

"Mr Walker." Bertram was suddenly at the door. "A Mrs Patrice Bettencourt is here for Mrs Bettencourt."

"Thank you, Bertram. Please show her in."

There was nothing stupid about Patrice Bettencourt. She was a woman who knew what she wanted and how to get it. She did not expect to find Niki alone and played no games to the contrary.

"Nicola," the elder Bettencourt said as she nodded to her daughter-in-law, "thank you for receiving me."

"You're welcome," Niki replied with more calm than she felt, memories rushing back in a hurry. "Allow me to introduce my Aunt Walker and her husband. And this gentleman is Mr Steele."

Patrice nodded to all in turn and sat when she was invited to do so. She took her time finding Niki's eyes with her own and then spoke plainly, and in French for the first time. "We've come at cross purposes, Nicola. I'm sorry it's come to this point."

"As am I."

Patrice looked very relieved. "I was certain you'd feel that way. You must know how much I want to see the boys."

"Yes, I'm sure you do. What I don't know is why you would try to keep them from me."

"I was a different person then, Nicola. You must see that I was overcome with grief."

Niki stared at her. Patrice looked back, seeing already that this was not going to unfold according to her original plan. She had to hide her satisfaction that she had a backup plan in place.

"If I could turn back the hands of time," Patrice went on, her voice very contrite, "there is so much I would do differently."

"Such as?" Niki asked politely, feeling more in control by the minute.

"I would have spoken to you and not just acted. I would have explained how much I had planned for the boys; I'm sure you would have seen."

"But it would have all boiled down to my giving up my sons?" Niki asked, her voice telling Patrice that she had better step lightly.

"Of course not," she lied. "I never wanted to cut you out of their lives. I acted without thought, as I'm sure you have by keeping them from me."

"On the contrary, Patrice, I've given great thought to my actions."

"But surely I can see them now that we've talked." Patrice's voice was at its most reasonable. "You will let me visit with them today, won't you, Nicola?"

"Visit with them, Patrice, or take them?" Niki asked, not sure where the question had come from but suddenly needing to know.

"Visit with them, of course. I know how much children need their mothers."

Patrice's smile was at its kindest, and for a moment she looked like a loving, benevolent grandmother ready with warm gingerbread and milk. And indeed, Niki might have been taken in but for a sudden commotion at the door.

Newton, one of the men who had been put on guard with Denley and the boys, opened the door without request and pushed a man into the room ahead of him. The shove was enough to send the stranger to the floor, where he caught himself on his hands and turned back to Newton to spit something out in angry French.

"This man crawled through the window of

the boys' room," Newton explained, not taking his irate eyes from the intruder.

In stunned silence the occupants of the room stared down at the man on the floor, his face bruised and bleeding. His intent needed no explanation.

Walker ordered him to be taken away and held. The words were no more out of his mouth when Niki came to her feet and faced her husband's mother.

"Get out, Patrice," she told her. "Get out and never come back."

Patrice came to her feet as well. All vestiges of kindness fell away. She glared at Niki before beginning her verbal attack.

"You'll never rest," Patrice hissed, her face growing red with agitation. "You'll be watching over your shoulder day and night, never knowing when one of my men will come for those boys. My grandsons!"

"What do you think my life has been like?" Niki asked, her own anger coming out. "You made the choice to rob me of my children, and now the loss is yours. Do you actually think you could win their affection now? I mean everything to them."

"They're young," Patrice insisted wildly. "Children adapt."

"Do you hear yourself?" Edward spoke for the first time, also using French. "Out of your own selfish need you would take those boys and turn their world upside down."

"How dare you speak to me! Shut your mouth!"

"I won't." Edward's voice was deadly calm. "You dare to come here, threaten our lives and our happiness, and then expect me to remain still, but I won't. There's one more thing you should know. The authorities in Collingbourne have been made aware of your arrival. My brother has even written to a friend at Scotland Yard, telling him Niki's story and the part you played. And don't ever forget this, Mrs Bettencourt: Niki is an Englishwoman and as such is protected by the laws of our land."

It was on Patrice's mind to tell them that her grandsons were French and belonged in her land, but another tactic was needed here. She let her shoulders slump, her face crumple.

"It's been so long," she spoke wretchedly. "My dear Louis is gone, and I long to see his children."

Upon these pitifully spoken words, she dropped into a chair, her face in her hands as she quietly wept. It took a few moments for her to realize that no one had spoken or come to comfort her. She looked up to find no pity in the faces watching her. The amazement she felt showed in her eyes. She studied the four faces before her and then spoke to her daughter-in-law.

"You're not going to let me see them, are you, Nicola?"

"No, not today and probably never."

The calm she heard in Nicola's voice chilled Patrice to the bone.

"Why?" was all she could think to say.

"You're not to be trusted. Your little counterplot today has more than proved that. No matter how many years pass, I'll never forget that my children were terrified of me. I can only imagine the horrible things you did or told them. You still feel you have rights here. You've stood before us and issued threats. You're no grandmother; you're a monster."

The hatred that blazed from her mother-in-law's eyes shook Niki. Patrice stood to her magnificent height, her chin high and her voice clear.

"I will have those boys before I die.

They're mine by birthright, and I will see the job done."

"Then someone will be hurt or killed, or imprisoned at the very least," Edward said quietly. "Not a one of us will stand back while you attempt this deed. If you send someone to do this task or come yourself, there will be bloodshed if that's what it takes to protect those boys."

Patrice's eyes swung to Niki. "And you agree with what this man has said?"

"Completely."

The hatred in the French woman's face made her ugly. Niki mentally flinched from what she saw there but held her ground.

Without a word to anyone in the room, Patrice Bettencourt swept toward the door and exited, slamming the portal behind her.

"I'll make sure she's gone," Walker said, moving to follow.

Niki sat down, all strength leaving her. "Please, Edward," she begged softly. "I must see the boys. Please make sure she doesn't take them."

With a hand to her cheek, Edward said, "I'll bring them to you right now."

Mary was at Niki's side in the next moment, her arms going around her.

"The worst is over now, Niki. You were wonderful."

"She'll be back."

"She might be, but you'll know what to do, and you'll teach the boys what to do if and when she ever confronts them."

Niki raised her head and looked into her aunt's eyes.

"Why didn't I think of that? Why have I not seen that I could tell them about her and teach them what to do?"

Mary smiled gently into Niki's eyes and fixed one of the little curls on her forehead, knowing there was no need to answer. And anyway, there wasn't time. Edward arrived a moment later, the boys on his back. Niki took them into her arms and held them tight. Edward joined her on the sofa, and Mary knew that right now she wasn't needed at all.

ഏ ഇ

"What happened?" Mary asked of Walker over the dinner table that evening. Walker had been gone a good deal of the afternoon. Niki had eaten early with the boys.

"Newton and I took Yvon into town," he

said, referring to the man who had broken in.

"That's his name?"

"Yes, he told us that much. He confessed to being hired by Patrice Bettencourt, and when I left, Yvon was locked up and Mrs Bettencourt was being questioned."

"Was she upset over that?"

Walker shook his head at the woman's temerity.

"She's only making herself look worse with the fits she throws. She refused to speak in English until I told the constable that she could."

"That must have gone down rather hard."

"Yes, it did, but as I said, she's only hurting herself. Where is Niki, by the way?"

"She dined early with the boys, and now they're upstairs."

Walker nodded. "I'll go up after the boys are asleep and tell her what happened."

"I can't think she'll be too pleased that Mrs Bettencourt is still here."

"The constable knows that I want to be kept abreast of the situation. I left Newton in town to keep an eye on things."

"That's a comfort."

Even as she said the words, Mary

thought about the uncertainties of this life. Was there a safe place for any of them? No, there wasn't. Not truly safe, not outside of God's hands.

Feeling more tired than she had in weeks, Mary was glad that Walker was finished talking. She finished her meal, kissed her husband and thanked him for all he'd done, and then retired to her room for the rest of the night.

❧ ☙

"Why does she want to take us?" Christopher asked his mother after the three of them had talked for nearly an hour.

"She thinks she needs to be your mother."

"But you're our mother."

"Yes, I am. And that's why you need to be careful not to go anywhere with or speak to anyone you don't know."

"And if someone should try to touch us, we get to yell."

Niki smiled into Richard's eyes. He had made it sound like a privilege, but if it worked, that was fine with her.

Walker poked his head in long enough to

tell Niki he needed to have a word with her, so she urged the boys under the covers and then bent to kiss them.

"Mama?" Richard said before she could blow out the lantern.

"Yes, Rich."

"Chris wants to go to heaven with us."

Niki stopped all movements. She looked over at Christopher, who was watching her, his face a little uncertain. Niki smiled at him and he smiled back.

"When did you decide this, Chris?"

"When that man came in the window. I thought he was going to kill us."

Niki reached for the little boy, gathered him close, and held him tightly in her arms. She knew Walker wanted to speak to her but also that he would understand. This was about eternity, and Niki was swiftly learning that there wasn't anything more important.

ℜ ℜ

"How are you?" Edward asked Niki the next morning while on a walk. The boys had run ahead toward the creek, and because they were still in view, Edward and Niki took their time.

"I'm doing very well."

Edward turned to look at her.

"I believe you are," he agreed with a smile.

"I never dreamed that something good could come of yesterday, Edward, but it has."

Edward stopped, not wanting to miss a word.

"Chris was so frightened that he wanted to talk about salvation. He prayed with Rich and me last night."

Edward's eyes closed as emotion filled him. He'd prayed for that little boy every day, and now, with only a few weeks gone by, Christopher Bettencourt believed. Christopher Bettencourt knew the Savior.

"I so wish I could take you in my arms," Edward said, remembering that they had to keep up with the boys.

"You can take Chris in your arms." Niki's voice sounded pleased. "But then he'll want to know why."

"Then I won't. I'll wait for him to tell me when he's ready."

Niki abruptly stopped walking, so Edward stopped with her. She looked into the eyes of the man she wanted to father her children. His tenderness and caring never ceased to amaze her. The boys felt it too.

"He'll want to tell you," she said confidently.

"How do you know?" Edward asked, but Niki didn't answer. She began to walk again, and Edward happily followed. She didn't have a lot more to say, but the smile on her face made Edward's heart turn over in his chest.

I think she's the one, Lord. Please help me to lead with my head, especially when my heart wants to gallop away with me.

ॐ ॐ

Newcomb Park

"It's big!" Richard said with wonder, his eyes on the large, dead insect Henry Steele presented in his study.

"It's from Africa," Henry told the boys. "Edward sent it to me, but then when I visited, I brought something home for myself."

This said, Henry brought out a snake skin—very long, wide, and colorful—that made the boys' eyes huge and their mouths gape. Edward, also in the group and quietly watching their faces, started to laugh, thinking this was fun.

The idea had originated with Henry. Niki had not been to Collingbourne to shop or have tea since she arrived. Much as Edward would have liked to go with her, he thought she might agree to the outing if he took the boys for the day.

Lizzy, Cassandra, and Marianne picked up Niki, the boys, and Mary Walker midmorning. In great spirits, they dropped the boys at Newcomb Park and headed toward Collingbourne. If the smiles and laughter coming from both groups were any indication, the day was sure to be a success.

❧ ❧

Blackburn Manor

"Mrs Bettencourt," Denley said to Niki when he interrupted the family at the breakfast table on Monday morning. "There's someone here who would like to see you."

Niki rose without question, telling the boys to stay put when they made to follow her, and exited the room. She followed Denley all the way to the foyer and found Gar and Juliana waiting. Their reunion was joyful and tearful all at the same time.

"I've missed you so much," Juliana said, holding onto Niki as though she would never let go.

Gar was next, but his hug was much swifter because he had a question.

"Niki, where are those boys?"

"Come this way," Niki invited, knowing she would be forgiven for the interruption.

And an interruption it was. The boys would not stop touching or talking to Gar, and Niki could barely make the introductions.

"Please join us for breakfast," Mary inserted when there was a slight lull, and when at last the guests joined the table, Walker asked Gar if they had moved successfully.

"As a matter of fact, we have not. We've been traveling around since we wrote to Niki."

"What of Kendal-in-the-Forest?" Niki asked.

"We hadn't the heart to give it up," Juliana said. "We left a small staff to look after things, but we couldn't bring ourselves to sell it."

"I can't tell you how relieved I am," Niki

said, a hand to her face. "My heart was broken when you said you had to leave."

"We're just gypsies right now," Juliana told her, clearly enjoying the fact.

"Well, I have a good bit of news to tell you," Niki said. "You won't have to be gypsies much longer. Unless, of course, you want to."

"I've rather enjoyed it," Gar stated, not surprising Niki in the least.

The men fell into conversation then, conversation that lasted the rest of the meal. Mary took the boys off to play for a time, and the women sneaked away to Niki's room so they could talk.

❧ ❧

"She was here," Niki told Juliana when that woman began to question her. "Patrice was here."

"What happened?"

"I confronted her and sent her away."

Juliana's mouth opened. "How did you have the courage to do this?"

Niki wanted to tell her about her belief in Christ but wasn't sure how to go about it. Edward came to mind instead.

"There's something I never wrote to you about," Niki confessed to her friend.

"What is it?"

"Edward Steele lives here in Collingbourne."

"Edward Steele? The Edward Steele from the ship? The one who made you smile?"

Niki had to laugh. "Yes, the same."

Niki laughed again when Juliana threw her arms around her and tried to hug the life from her.

"I knew he was the one! You must tell me everything. Do you see him often? Does he notice you? How about the boys? Does he love the boys? He must love the boys!"

Niki could only laugh at her.

"Come along," Juliana demanded. "Tell me all."

"Well, yes, I would say he's noticed me," Niki said quietly, her eyes a bit dreamy, "and, yes, he does love the boys."

Juliana stared at her.

"You're in love with him."

"I believe I am."

"And does he love you?"

"It would certainly seem that way."

Juliana sighed, her romantic heart touched.

"Anyway," Niki went on. "Edward was with me when she came, as were Aunt Mary and Walker. Patrice was as angry and awful as I expected her to be, but Edward and I stood up to her. If she comes back, she'll have to answer to the law."

"Are you afraid?"

"Not like I was."

"I'm so glad, Niki. What a horrible time it's been for you and the boys."

"Not much fun for you either."

Juliana put a hand on Niki's arm.

"Never worry after Gar and me, my dear. We love you and the boys. We would do it all over again in an instant."

Niki put her arms around her friend, so thankful she was there. Juliana hugged her back, completely unaware of the way Niki asked God to give her wisdom and courage to talk about Him.

❧ ❧

"Thank you, Walker and Mrs Walker," Edward said at the end of the evening. "I had a wonderful time."

"Tell Henry what he missed," Walker teased a little.

"I will," Edward smiled, turning next to the Lawtons. "It was very fine meeting you," he said, bowing to them both.

"We'll probably see you again," Gar said kindly, and Juliana smiled at him.

Niki slipped away to walk him to the door, smiling when their eyes met.

"I can see why you like them," Edward said at the door.

"They're wonderful. I'm so glad they came."

Edward took her hand.

"I'm going to keep my distance for a few days," he told her. "I think the boys need time with Gar and Juliana. It's not fair of me to be around and make them feel as though they have to choose."

"That's sweet of you."

"I don't think I've been called sweet before."

Niki only smiled, blushing a little.

"I'll miss you," he said quietly, bending to kiss her cheek before slipping out the door.

Niki stood in the same spot for a long time, her heart echoing his words. *I'll miss you too.*

❧ ❧

"What do we know about this man?" Gar demanded of his wife as soon as they were behind closed doors.

"Edward Steele?"

"Yes, Edward Steele! She clearly loves that man, and I would say he loves her in return."

"Well, what's wrong with that?"

"Nothing, as long as we know he's worthy of her and the boys. Does he know the situation? Will he protect them?"

"Gar," his wife said patiently. "He's the one she met on ship. He's the one who knew she was a woman dressed as a man."

Gar looked affronted.

"No one ever tells me anything," he said gruffly, ruthlessly pulling at the buttons on his shirt.

"I'm sorry." Juliana was very contrite, even though she wanted to laugh. She expected Gar to turn and smile at her in complete forgiveness, but that didn't happen. His agitated movements told her he was still upset.

"Gar." Juliana called his name and waited.

Gar didn't immediately turn to her. When he did, his face was not open and kind as it usually was. Juliana could not keep the concern from her voice.

"Edgar, what is it? What's really troubling you?"

Gar looked her in the eye, betrayal covering every feature.

"If she marries this man, she won't come back to us. I'll not have the boys anymore."

Juliana went and put her arms around him. She hugged him close and was hugged in return. After a moment, she stepped back to look at his face.

"This is going to happen. They're very much in love, and I'm sure it's only a matter of time before he asks her to marry him. But there are ways around this. We don't have to live all year at Kendal. We can find a place closer to Collingbourne and spend part of our year here."

The idea had not occurred to Gar. His features relaxed in comprehension, and he pulled his wife back into his arms. Juliana stood quietly and let him hold her for as long as he needed. She had known that he was missing the boys, but she'd not counted on the depth of Gar's loss. She missed them too, but it was somehow different for Gar.

She didn't know what the following days and weeks would look like, but knowing how her husband felt meant everything to her. She kissed him gently and told him not to worry anymore. Gar kissed her back and then held onto her almost fiercely. Juliana was certain that in his heart, he was really holding onto those two little boys.

Chapter Twenty-One

"You go to church?" Gar questioned Niki, not sure he'd heard her right.

"Yes, and because we're going tomorrow morning, I wanted to make sure you knew you could join us."

Her friends looked at her as she thought they might. She felt her courage draining and asked the Lord to remind her that eternity was at stake.

"You don't have to come," Niki felt she must add, "but I'd like it if you would."

"Do the boys go with you?" Gar asked.

"Yes."

"Why do you go, Niki?" Juliana spoke for the first time.

"Some time ago I made a decision to include God in my life. I believed in Him to save me, but I had not learned anything since. Then when I came here, my Aunt Mary and I began talking about spiritual issues. She's helped me to see how much

God has for me and how studying the Bible can change me."

"Are you talking about Christianity?" Gar asked.

"Yes."

"But I didn't think that Christians could do the things you do."

"Like what for instance?"

"Like going about dressed as a man and deceiving people."

"I don't have all the answers, Gar," Niki admitted, hoping she wasn't in over her head. "I'm not sure how I should have handled my situation. I know it's my job to take care of my sons, but I don't always know exactly what that looks like."

"Gar wasn't judging you, Niki," Juliana felt she must put in.

"Of course not," Gar said, wanting there to be no misunderstanding.

"I didn't think that, Gar. You may ask me anything you wish."

Gar looked at her and nodded. "I don't have any questions right now, Niki. I'm not even sure why I said what I did."

"Well, if you do, just ask me," Niki replied, waiting. But her friends didn't speak. "So will you come to church?" she prompted.

"No," Gar said kindly but with finality. "It would be hypocrisy if I did. Juliana might wish to, but I've never felt a need for God, and I'm not going to pretend I do."

Niki nodded, not at all surprised to hear this. He'd said, however, that Juliana could go.

"How about it, Juliana?" Niki asked. "Do you wish to join us?"

"I think I will," the lady responded. "You're certain you don't mind, Gar?"

"Not at all," he said, meaning it.

"All right then," Juliana offered with a smile. "I'll go with you in the morning, Niki."

"We leave after breakfast," Niki told her, glad that at least one of them was going.

"We've made a decision," Gar suddenly said.

"About what?" Niki queried.

"On Monday we'll be heading back to Kendal, but in the near future we'll be looking for a second home in or near Collingbourne."

Niki couldn't help herself. She jumped to her feet and threw her arms about Gar, giving him a great hug before turning to Juliana. The women hugged for a long time.

"Well, Gar," Juliana said, an arm still

around Niki, "I think she likes the idea. You worried for nothing."

Gar's laughter filled the room. Niki and Juliana laughed with him. Juliana was just happy that they would not have to be separated again, at least not for long. Niki was happy because she never dreamed that God would do this. She had prayed for her friends and believed that God could reach them, but this idea had never come to mind.

With a final laugh, this one at herself, Niki found herself thankful that she wasn't the one in charge.

❧ ❧

Newcomb Park

Edward ate his meal without comment, but it wasn't easy. Something was on Henry's mind, but he wasn't sharing. Edward could feel his gaze on him almost constantly, but when asked about it, Henry only shook his head and didn't speak.

Edward knew that if he gave Henry enough time, he would spout, but in truth he wanted to get to Blackburn as soon as he could.

"How are you feeling about Niki these days?" Henry suddenly asked.

"How do you think I feel?"

"I think you're in love with her."

"You're right, I am."

"Then why have you not asked her to marry you?"

"The Lawtons have only just left, Henry. When have I been able to see Niki alone?"

Henry did not look understanding. Clearly he wanted the matter settled, and that was the end of it. Edward wanted to laugh but didn't. Henry's face was too serious to risk mirth.

"How will you go about it?" Henry asked.

Edward looked astonished.

"I can't believe you asked me that."

"Go ahead," this new Henry demanded. "Tell me."

Edward stared at him, not able to keep the smile from his face.

"I think you should go for a walk," Henry went on. "Niki seems to like the out-of-doors."

Unable to believe his ears, Edward sat back, his meal forgotten.

"Although if you do that and can't find a

place for Niki to sit, you'll be far below her when you go down on one knee."

"You think I should go down on one knee?"

In another uncharacteristic move, Henry rolled his eyes.

"What else would you do?"

"I could just ask her."

Henry shook his head. "That won't work at all. Years from now the children, especially your daughters, will want to know how you asked their mother to marry you. It's got to be something memorable, something special."

"Henry," Edward said quietly, "I do believe you *are* a romantic."

"You doubted?"

Edward's head went back as he laughed. Henry had used his dry, almost sarcastic tone, and it never failed to be Edward's undoing. Henry was smiling a little himself, but he was also serious.

"Are you going to Blackburn this morning?"

"Yes."

"Do it today."

The two brothers stared at each other.

"Why, Henry? Why today?"

"Don't you want to?"

"Yes, but I want to know why you want it to be today."

"Because it's time. You've discussed every issue you can think of; your sisters adore her; you know you have my blessing; and on top of that, she needs you."

Edward told himself to breathe deeply. Henry's words had a strange effect on his heart. It was probably true that Niki did need him, but he also needed her—more than he could say.

"All right, Henry. I'll see if I can talk to her today."

"And you'll make it special?"

Edward hid a smile. "If I can."

Henry nodded in satisfaction and stood. He made his way down to Edward's end of the table and placed a hand on his shoulder. He didn't speak but looked down at his brother for several seconds, patted Edward's shoulder, and exited the room.

Edward thought he could become very emotional just then but fought off the temptation. He had a special lady to see and a special question to ask. And only a short time to figure out a way in which to do it.

❧ ❧

Blackburn Manor

Niki was in the small parlor when Edward arrived. Bertram took him directly there, and he slipped in quietly to find Niki sitting very still.

"Good morning," he said, sitting on the sofa with her. "How are you?"

"I'm very well. How are you?"

Just happy to be near you, he thought, but said, "I'm well, thank you. Did the Lawtons get on their way?"

"Yes. It was so good to see them."

"I certainly enjoyed meeting them. Gar is fascinating."

"Yes, he is," Niki said with a smile.

"Did Juliana say anything about the church service?"

"No, but they'll be back, and maybe I can ask her about it then."

Not until that moment did Edward see a letter in Niki's lap.

"Have you had news?" Edward asked, indicating the paper.

Niki's smile was wry as she said, "Patrice is trying a new tactic."

"How many letters does this make?"

"Well, let's see." Niki cocked her head a little. "The first letter threatened to get a lawyer, the second letter was contrite, so this would be the third."

"What does she want this time?"

Niki's eyes went back to the letter. She spoke as she scanned.

"I'm to contact the authorities and say it was all a mistake, that she would be no threat to anyone. She would then be free to move to England to be near the boys."

"That's quite a plan."

"But that's not the end of it. She would want me to live in London because she couldn't possibly be made comfortable in a small town like Collingbourne. She's sure I'll understand."

Edward had to laugh. The woman was remarkable. He'd never known such gall.

"What will you do?"

"Nothing right now. I hadn't even answered her second letter, and now this has come."

"You don't want her living close, do you?"

"Positively not. The woman is a threat and can't be trusted."

"You'll probably have to write that very thing to her."

"She won't like it," Niki said ruefully.

"She's made her choices."

Niki nodded, her eyes on some distant spot. Edward studied her profile, smiling at what he saw. Niki suddenly felt his eyes on her and turned.

"I love you," Edward said, not for the first time.

"I love you," Niki told him, gladly giving her hand when he reached for it.

"Will you go for a walk with me?"

"Certainly."

"Shall I tell the boys?"

Edward smiled.

"I think this time it might be nice to go on our own."

Niki smiled, liking the sound of that and letting Denley know as they slipped outside on this warm June morning.

For a time they walked in silence, Blackburn's flowers making the world smell like a garden. Edward tried to relax and enjoy it, but he felt almost tense, wishing that Henry had not been so vocal this morning. Suddenly Edward wanted to laugh. His brother was such a quiet, reserved man. Having him give instructions on how to propose had been nothing short of preposterous.

"What are you smiling about?" Niki asked.

Edward did not know that she had been watching.

"I'll have to tell you sometime."

"Not now?"

Edward stopped, and Niki naturally stopped with him. He had always been completely honest with her and was not going to be anything else now.

"Henry seems to think that I've been dragging my feet where you're concerned."

Niki looked surprised.

"I told him you had company, but he didn't seem to think that mattered."

Niki laughed a little. "That must have been a little odd, coming from Henry."

"I did a good deal of laughing, but he was serious."

Niki nodded. "Is that why you didn't want the boys along?"

"Yes."

"And would you have wanted the day to be today if Henry hadn't prompted you?"

"I wanted the day to be weeks ago, but I told myself to wait."

Niki looked up into his eyes. She couldn't remember a love this deep, not even for

Louis, whom she had cared about very much.

"How does a man say what's in his heart?" Edward asked, his eyes on hers as well. "How does a man explain the mix of joy and uncertainty, the euphoria and fear?"

"I think you just did."

"Henry said I must get down on one knee."

Niki started to laugh. "He didn't!"

"He did. He said it must be special, so when our daughters ask about it, we'll have the right answer."

"Henry is a dear," Niki said, sighing a little.

Edward suddenly cupped her face in his hands, his thumbs stroking the smooth skin on her cheekbones.

"Marry me, Niki. Please say you will. Please become my wife and my partner. Have children with me, and help me to be the man God wants me to be."

"I would love to marry you, Edward. I would love it more than I can say."

His hands still holding her gently, he tilted her face just enough to claim her lips with his own.

"I forgot the knee!" Edward suddenly

said, and Niki began to giggle. "Quickly," he took her hand. "We've got to find a rock or something for you to sit on. You know Henry will ask."

By the time Edward found a place for Niki to sit, they were both laughing uncontrollably. And it didn't help that the large rock Edward found was lumpy and not very comfortable, or that Edward had to kneel in the damp grass in a pair of new pants.

"All right now," he said, trying to be serious. "I've got to do this properly."

Niki schooled her features and waited, but before Edward could speak, she was lost in his eyes again.

"When did you start to love me, Edward?"

Edward smiled. "I'm not sure. I know it was after you came here, but my memories of you are very mixed. In my mind's eye, I can still see you dressed as Osborne."

Niki made a face.

"No, no, I'm serious." Edward's gaze warmed. "After I got used to the idea, you began to look a little too good in those pants."

Niki bit her lip, and for a moment the two looked at each other. Edward took her hand in his and spoke quietly.

"Mrs Bettencourt, will you consent to be my wife?"

"Yes, I will, Mr Steele."

"When, Niki?" Edward dropped the formality just that fast. "When can we be married?"

"I don't know, but soon I think."

"Soon would be nice."

"Shall we go and tell the boys?"

"Yes, and then the family."

Edward helped her off the rock and took her hand. They didn't move swiftly. It was all too wonderful to be rushed. They walked back toward the house to find the boys and tell them immediately, but not before they talked and made plans. It would be a lovely wedding. The boys could stand up with them. And Edward already had his eye on a house—a beautiful house that the four of them would love.

By the time they reached the back door, both felt as if they were floating on air.

ɷ ɷ

Newcomb Park

"Good morning, Henry," Cassandra greeted her brother in the foyer, going on tiptoe to give him a kiss. "Is Edward about? I have something to show him."

"He's at Blackburn Manor this morning."

Cassandra dimpled. "Do you suppose he's gained the courage to ask the question?"

"I don't know," Henry said with a smile, even though he felt quite confident about Edward's plans. "We'll have to wait and see."

"I guess we will. May I leave this for him?"

"Certainly." Henry took a folded slip of paper from her. "How are you feeling, by the way?"

"Very well. I'm headed into town to do a little shopping."

"Alone?"

"Yes, Tate had accounts spread out all about him, and Lizzy is entertaining."

"Would you like me to go with you?"

Cassandra's mouth opened in surprised pleasure.

"Why, Henry, that would be lovely."

Henry smiled. Shopping was not at all his idea of a fun morning, but being with his sister and seeing her delight appealed to him very much.

Leaving word where he was going, Henry

took a moment to get his hat and jacket and followed his sister to her coach.

He didn't think he'd actually shop, but getting out of the house was just what he needed. Maybe Edward would be there with good news by the time he arrived back home. Even as the coach lurched into motion, Henry found himself praying that Edward would have the courage to get the job done.

What if the lady doesn't accept?

Where this thought had come from Henry didn't know, but he dismissed it immediately. If there were two people more in love and suited for each other than Edward Steele and Niki Bettencourt, he'd like to meet them.

Cassandra took that moment to say something about stopping for tea, and Henry's attention was drawn to her.

Maybe I have met them, Henry said to himself, thinking about all three of his sisters and the fine men they'd married.

With a deep sigh of contentment, Henry made himself more comfortable in the seat and settled back to enjoy the ride and his sister's company, thinking that God's blessings never ceased to amaze him.

Epilogue

Billings Park

Niki Steele's breathing became labored. She thrashed against the images in her mind, panic and fear filling her. She was terrified and helpless, desperate to do something but unable to think or act.

"Niki." Edward's voice came to her, his hand coming to rest on her waist. "Wake up, Niki."

With a start, Niki came out of the dream. She panted in fear, even as Edward's arms came around her.

"It's all right. It was just a dream."

"The boys," she said, hugging her husband tightly. "I dreamed that she came. They cried for me. They were so little."

Edward held her until her breathing was normal again. Only then did he let go of her to light the lantern. They both squinted against the light as they tried to see each other.

"Do you want me to go and check on them?"

"No," Niki shook her head. "I know it was just a dream."

"It might be like this for a time, Niki, but I still think we did the right thing."

Niki nodded, remembering along with Edward the way they'd recently gone to Patrice Bettencourt's deathbed and taken the children with them.

Niki had been so certain Patrice would repent after years of letters and threats. Niki envisioned that when Patrice saw how big the boys were, she would see how much she'd given up and be sorry, but it hadn't happened that way.

With eyes and words only for Richard and Christopher, Patrice had told the boys how selfish their mother had been and how ashamed their father would have been of her. It had not gone well, but the boys held no bitterness toward their grandmother, and because she'd left her entire estate to them, they'd enjoyed the freedom of seeing portraits of their father and gaining a glimpse into his life.

"Maybe I should go check on them," Niki said, having second thoughts.

Edward chuckled.

"What's so funny?" she asked, still rather groggy.

"They're 17, Niki, and larger than I am. Even if Patrice were still alive, neither one of them would sit still for an abduction."

Niki was forced to agree, even as her mind went to their other five children. Michelle was almost ten; young Edward was nine; the younger twins, Jocelyn and Sunny, were six; and Emmaline was two. Patrice had never even asked about Richard and Christopher's half siblings. She had had eyes only for them, and selfish eyes they were, wanting things her way or not at all.

"Can you sleep now?" Edward interrupted her thoughts.

"I think so."

"It must be after midnight, which means the wedding is today, and a long day it will be."

Niki smiled as she remembered. Penny Jennings, Marianne's stepdaughter, was marrying Jeffrey Hurst, Pastor and Judith's oldest.

Jeffrey had been abroad for several years, being mentored by a friend of his father's. When he'd come home, he was surprised to find Penny Jennings quite grown up and as beautiful as she had been as a child. There were several years between them, but no one seemed to notice. Jeffrey found himself unable to think about much else, and Penny welcomed his interest.

They had courted for the better part of a year, nearly everyone waiting in anticipation for Jeffrey to ask for her hand, and finally the day had come. Penny didn't seem to have any problem with the wait, even as she watched both of her older brothers get married, as well as cousins Frank, Walt, and Emma Palmer. Two of Jeffrey's siblings, Jane and Margaret, were also wed. Some married young people from the church family, and others found their spouses from other districts.

This day, however, the pastor's son and a longtime member of the community were going to be married, and it was going to be something of a celebration. Family members had already started to gather, and knowing how full Thornton Hall and Blackburn Manor were, Niki fell asleep thinking about all who would come.

☙ ❧

Thornton Hall

"Are you just coming to bed?" Jennings asked of his wife when the moonlight from the window allowed him to watch her slip into their room.

"No, but I was restless and didn't want to wake you."

Marianne climbed into bed, but Jennings could tell she was not ready to go back to sleep.

"You're going to be exhausted in the morning."

"You're probably right, but I'm not sure I can help myself. I don't know why I'm so excited. The boys got married with little fuss, but with Penny I'm falling apart."

"It might be the difference between sons and daughters."

"Maybe so," Marianne said, a yawn accompanying these words.

Jennings remained quiet, thinking she might be headed back to sleep, and sure enough, her breathing evened out after a short time.

It was, however, too late for Jennings. His own little Penny, his oldest daughter, was getting married in a matter of hours. At the moment sleep was miles away.

❧ ❧

The Manse

"You're up early," Judith said to Frederick as he stood peering into his closet very early on Saturday morning.

"Do you think my suit is all right?"

"I think it's fine. Do you have a problem with it?"

Frederick turned to look at her.

"Our oldest child is getting married today. I want to look especially nice."

"Why do I think I'm the one who is supposed to be saying that?"

Frederick's eyes twinkled at having been caught out. Nevertheless, he inspected his suit a moment longer, flicked at a speck of lint, and rehung it in the closet. He then joined his wife on the bed, sitting so his back was against the footboard. Judith watched him, amazed to find tears in his eyes.

"Frederick," she said softly. "What is it?"

"I'm just so proud of him, Judith. He's a fine man, and although he's wanted to be married for years, he's waited for God's timing."

"And to our own little Penny," Judith said with a smile, wanting to cry as well.

Husband and wife looked at each other and shared a smile. The church family had grown over the years. There had been many marriages and new families started. Some couples had settled nearby, and others had moved away.

Their own Margaret had not stayed in the area but lived closer to London. Jeffrey and Penny had chosen a home here, something for which the Hursts and Jenningses were thankful.

A noise at the door suddenly made them turn. Ten-year-old Elizabeth, the youngest in the family, poked her head in, coming forward as soon as she saw they were awake. Her dress for the wedding was dangling from her hand.

"Eliza," her mother asked. "Why are you up so early?"

"It's my dress. I'm not sure it's all right for the wedding."

Frederick and Judith looked at each other, mouths open, before bursting into laughter. It was several minutes before they could even find breath to explain to their bemused daughter.

๙ ๗

Marianne Jennings, Anne Weston, Lizzy Morland, Cassandra Tate, and Niki Steele all found themselves standing outside of the church building after the wedding. The bride and groom had already left, but no one else seemed in much of a hurry to leave. Children came and went—they each had many—asking questions of their mothers and being told to stay clean, but as soon as they were able, the five women went back to talking each time.

"She looked beautiful," Lizzy said, thinking about the bride.

"I think Penny might have looked good in a flour sack," Anne said dryly.

Marianne only smiled, but she couldn't have agreed more. Penny's long, dark hair and huge, lovely eyes had been hard to miss, not to mention the love that shone on her face as she stood at the altar with Jeffrey, whose new suit fit him very well.

"It made me think of my wedding," Niki

admitted, and for a moment, all the women smiled.

Having been married on the same day, Cassandra and Lizzy exchanged glances, sharing a look as they remembered back to that occasion.

"Mother." Christopher was suddenly at Niki's side. Taller than his mother, his voice growing more masculine every day, Niki turned to him.

"What is it, Chris?"

"Edward says that Emma is wet through and starting to cry."

"I'll be right along."

Niki said her goodbyes to the women in the group and followed after her son. She kissed Christopher and Richard goodbye—they were spending the night with their Uncle Henry—before climbing into the coach. Emmaline wanted her mother's lap for the ride home, and by the time they arrived at Billings Park, they both needed a bath.

Emmaline was seen to first and then tucked into bed by her father. Edward went in search of his wife and found her in the bathtub, hair piled atop her head, water up to her neck. He sat on the edge of the tub to speak to her.

"This looks relaxing."

"It is. I can tell I didn't sleep very well."

Niki ran her washing cloth up one arm before she looked up to find Edward's eyes on her. She stared at him for a moment.

"I was thinking about our wedding day today," he said.

Niki looked as pleased as she felt. "I thought about it too."

"As pretty as Penny was, she couldn't compare with you in your wedding dress."

Niki smiled. Edward always had loving things to say, even after all these years.

Niki was opening her mouth to say something to him when someone knocked on the door. Edward went to answer it, finding Sunny outside the room, looking for her mother.

"She'll be out in a little while," her father told her, and shut the door again.

Edward looked back to find Niki out of the tub and wrapped in a thick robe. He returned to stand in front of her and took her in his arms. Not needing words, they hugged and kissed for a long time.

Edward decided, not for the first time, that God's timing and will were perfect. He wasn't looking for love when he went to

Africa. He wasn't looking for a wife when Niki Bettencourt came across his path, but God, in His imponderable way, had had a plan.

"Edward," Niki said, having caught a look on his face. "What are you thinking about?"

Edward knew he would never be able to explain and said only, "Just thanking God for you."

Niki smiled in her tender way and went up on tiptoe to kiss him again.

About the Author

LORI WICK is one of the most versatile Christian fiction writers in the market today. Her works include pioneer fiction, a series set in Victorian England, and contemporary novels. Lori's books (more than 3.5 million copies in print) continue to delight readers and top the Christian bestselling fiction list. Lori and her husband, Bob, live in Wisconsin with "the three coolest kids in the world."

Books by Lori Wick

A Place Called Home Series
A Place Called Home
A Song for Silas
The Long Road Home
A Gathering of Memories

The Californians
Whatever Tomorrow Brings
As Time Goes By
Sean Donovan
Donovan's Daughter

Kensington Chronicles
The Hawk and the Jewel
Wings of the Morning
Who Brings Forth the Wind
The Knight and the Dove

Rocky Mountain Memories
Where the Wild Rose Blooms
Whispers of Moonlight
To Know Her by Name
Promise Me Tomorrow

The Yellow Rose Trilogy
Every Little Thing About You
A Texas Sky
City Girl

English Garden Series
The Proposal
The Rescue
The Visitor
The Pursuit

Contemporary Fiction
Bamboo & Lace
Beyond the Picket Fence (Short Stories)
Pretense
The Princess
Sophie's Heart

Children's Books
Kirby, the Disgruntled Tree